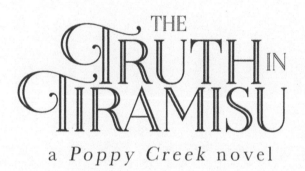

THE TRUTH IN TIRAMISU

a *Poppy Creek* novel

RACHAEL BLOOME

Cover Design: Ana Grigoriu-Voicu with Books-Design.

Editing: Beth Attwood

Proofing: Krista Dapkey with KD Proofreading

SERIES READING ORDER

THE CLAUSE IN CHRISTMAS

THE TRUTH IN TIRAMISU

THE SECRET IN SANDCASTLES

THE MEANING IN MISTLETOE

THE FAITH IN FLOWERS

Mom & Dad,
You made this possible.

LETTER FROM THE AUTHOR

*D*ear friends,

Welcome back to Poppy Creek! It's my sincerest hope that you enjoy this visit as much as the first.

When I started this novel, my life was business as usual. But part way through, everything changed. The global COVID-19 crisis tipped the world upside down. And, at first, I found it difficult to write. But the longer I stayed away from the keyboard, the more I missed my beloved town and characters. Poppy Creek became my sanctuary. And I hope it does the same for you.

If you're reading this after the pandemic has passed, may it still bring you joy and hope in your current season of life.

As always, I would love to hear from you. You can email me at hello@rachaelbloome.com or find me on my website. While you're there, don't forget to download your free gifts.

Blessings & Blooms,

Rachael Bloome

CHAPTER 1

*E*very time Eliza Carter closed her eyes, she saw his face.
And for the last few months, after glimpsing his shadowy figure engulfed in the commotion of New Year's Eve revelry, she'd been able to think of little else. Her tumultuous thoughts couldn't have come at a worse time, with her best friend's wedding and the grand opening of their joint business venture less than a month away.

In times like these, baking became her only solace. Something about blending the chaos of different ingredients to create a new, tantalizing dessert set Eliza's world at ease.

She cracked open the oven door, welcoming the blast of heat that lent her full cheeks a rosy tint. The warm steam carried notes of rich dark chocolate, tart raspberries, and a hint of mint, all of which teased a satisfied smile from her lips.

When the idea for the recipe first sprang to mind, Eliza wasn't sure how the concoction would turn out. But based on the mouthwatering aroma, the chocolate raspberry cupcakes would be a perfect addition to the bakery's menu. Donning two polka-dot oven mitts, Eliza carefully slid the cupcake pan from the middle rack so she didn't disturb the plump, delicate domes. She clamped her lips together, convinced a single breath would cause the cupcakes to collapse into themselves, destroying their coveted lighter-than-air texture.

Inching across the hardwood floor, she'd almost reached the cooling rack on the kitchen island when the front door slammed, causing Eliza to lurch forward. The pan sailed from her grasp and clattered against the white tile countertop.

"Hi, Mom! We're home!" Ben charged into the kitchen with all the boisterous energy befitting his seven years. "Whatcha makin'? Sure smells good!" He dumped his backpack on the island before clambering up the barstool.

Eliza watched the perfect peaks sink slowly. But before she could respond, her mother appeared in the doorway, her disapproving frown contrasting starkly with Ben's cheerful grin.

"Before you indulge him, he has something to tell you." Sylvia Carter raised a heavily penciled eyebrow at her grandson.

Ben's expression deflated along with the cupcakes as he reached inside his backpack. Without quite meeting his mother's gaze, he handed her a plain white envelope. "Miss Holden asked me to give you this."

A familiar tightness gripped Eliza's chest as she ripped open the seal and withdrew the letter. Daphne Holden's cutesy penmanship filled the page, belying the note's severity.

Eliza skimmed over the contents, picking out the inauspicious phrases.

Zero retention. Easily distracted. Disinterested. Worrisome lack of progress.

Heat crept up Eliza's neck, escalating to a full-on boil when she reached Daphne's recommendation to make Ben repeat second grade, citing the end of the school year in a few weeks as insufficient time to raise his test scores to a satisfactory level.

Anger, humiliation, and guilt wrapped around Eliza's heart, making it difficult to breathe. She crumpled the note into a ball before tossing it in the trash can beneath the sink.

"That bad?" Sylvia asked, her tone laced with sympathy.

"Certainly not appropriate subject matter for a note," Eliza mumbled crossly. "She could have at least asked for a parent-teacher meeting."

Sylvia snorted. "You realize she's been trying to arrange one for months. But you've been so busy with renovations and wedding planning, you kept putting it off."

Eliza's guilt wrestled her anger and humiliation to the mat, winning the match. And her trophy would read Worst Mother of the Year. Swallowing the lump in her throat, she turned to her son.

Ben sat motionless on the stool, staring at his hands clasped in his lap.

Her stomach twisted at the look of shame on his face.

No matter what Daphne Holden said, her son wasn't the problem. Eliza spent countless hours each night working with Ben on his homework. She'd never noticed any of the issues Daphne mentioned. Clearly, something else was going on. And she would get to the bottom of it.

But for now, Eliza simply wanted to restore Ben's carefree smile.

Softening her tone, she said, "Why don't we add some frosting to these cupcakes? Then we'll take a plate of them to your room and work on your homework together, okay?"

He tilted his chin, bringing his gaze to meet hers. His huge chocolate eyes were so like her own. And his butter-blond hair had the same golden highlights framing his face. To the casual observer, Ben could be Eliza's Mini-Me.

But try as she might, Eliza couldn't ignore the evidence of his father—the stubborn cowlick, dark, expressive eyebrows, and smattering of freckles across the bridge of his nose.

It was moments like this one that made her heart ache for what she couldn't have.

Ben's father never was, and never would be, a part of their lives.

Of that, she was certain.

---

*G*rant Parker knew he should be more excited. A contract with Morris Bio Tech would push his boutique web design business into the big leagues. Plus, he genuinely believed in Landon Morris's vision—high quality yet inexpensive biodegradable packaging products for mass production. It seemed like a niche market. Yet, in less than three years, Landon, the chief biochemical engineer and CEO, had turned a company manufacturing biodegradable straws that didn't turn soggy in a glass of soda to a multibillion-dollar business. And thanks to word of mouth, Landon wanted Grant and his small San Francisco-based team to handle all of his website needs.

Grant should be ecstatic.

Or at the very least, not so morose.

But seeing the woman who smashed his heart to smithereens could do that to a guy.

His decision to go home on New Year's Eve had turned out to be worse than the time he ate week-old sushi.

"Grant, are you listening?"

Adjusting his rectangular wire-rimmed glasses, Grant tore his gaze from a framed photograph on his desk to focus on the chiseled features of Landon Morris. It really wasn't fair that the guy had both a billion-dollar bank account and movie-star good looks.

"Am I boring you?" Landon asked with a lighthearted grin. "I want the website design to be sleek and simple, not put people to sleep." He chuckled, and Grant tried to join in, but it sounded forced.

Landon leaned forward, snatching the black photo frame that

had occupied Grant's attention. "Friends of yours?" He gestured to the five teenage boys with their arms draped across each other's shoulders.

"Friends from high school. The one in the middle is getting married in a few weeks."

"Nice. If you're into that kind of thing." Landon set the photograph back on the desk. "Personally, I don't see the appeal. Marriage is a time suck. Especially if you have kids."

Grant absentmindedly straightened the frame. "I have to agree with you there." Although, the time constraint wasn't his main reason for never wanting kids. Not that he'd share something so personal with a guy he barely knew. Heck, he wouldn't even tell a shrink the real reason.

"So, you're a groomsman?" Landon asked.

Grant hesitated. How had they gotten on this topic? "No, I'm not. We lost touch several years ago. The photo's simply a reminder of the good old days."

"That's too bad. But I hear ya." Landon nodded in solidarity. "When my business took off, I learned who my true friends were in a hurry. And I gotta say, there weren't that many."

Guilt lodged in Grant's throat, and he coughed a few times to clear it. "I'm sorry to hear that."

Grant only wished he could empathize. But, in his case, *he* was the terrible friend.

Landon shrugged. "Live and learn, right? But I'll tell ya... the friends I do have are gold. And if one of them ever decides to make the long death march to marriage, I won't miss it."

Grant let Landon's words sink in as he stared past his shoulder at the muted gray wall.

"Hey," Landon said casually, rising from the slick leather chair. "You clearly have a lot on your mind. Why don't I come back tomorrow to go over more of the details?"

Grant suppressed a groan. *Just great. Way to screw up the biggest deal of your career, knucklehead.* "Are you sure? We can go over them now."

"Nah!" Landon waved away his offer. "Don't worry about it. I have to get ready for a date tonight, anyway. I'm taking her on a chopper ride to Alcatraz."

"You're allowed to land on the island?" Grant asked in surprise.

"Depends on who you know." Landon winked before strolling out of Grant's office.

Grant shook his head with a bemused smile, watching his office door swing shut behind Landon before his gaze traveled back to the photograph.

Gently, he turned it over and rested it facedown on the desk. His heartbeat quickened as he twisted the metal tabs to remove the backboard and slowly slipped the photograph from between the glass and matting, revealing a second one hidden underneath.

Pain shot through his chest as a pair of dazzling dark eyes stared back at him.

The same ones he'd seen on New Year's Eve that had filled him with both agony and longing.

Did he have the strength to see them again?

Because one thing remained certain.

If he returned home to Poppy Creek for Luke Davis's wedding, it would be impossible to avoid Eliza Carter.

CHAPTER 2

*T*he smell of fresh paint and sawdust overwhelmed the lingering aroma of buttery cinnamon rolls—a hefty price to pay for the bakery's new and improved look. Ever on an emotional rollercoaster, Eliza vacillated between excited and pensive with each new change.

"I'm so glad Maggie promised to make her cinnamon rolls on opening day. Whenever that will be," Eliza added with a discouraged grimace. The remodel was already two weeks behind schedule.

She brushed her fingertip against the white brick wall, checking to see if the paint had dried. Eliza would have preferred the brick's original ruddy color, but it had long been painted over with Pepto-Bismol pink. Not a good look in any decade. A truth that became a frequent topic of good-natured teasing between Eliza and the previous owner, Maggie Davis.

"At least the paint is finally dry!" Waving her unmarked finger, Eliza turned toward Cassie and Luke.

The two lovebirds quickly broke apart, blushing as Eliza caught them mid-smooch. She seemed to catch them canoodling quite often these days. Which both amused and amazed her. Just a few months ago, Luke Davis was a confirmed bachelor, devoting all his time to helping others at the expense of his love life. But Eliza knew the instant Cassie Hayward waltzed into town that she'd be the one woman to win Luke's heart. And, eventually, the heart of everyone in Poppy Creek.

Chuckling, Eliza planted one hand on her hip, feigning disapproval. "No wonder we're behind schedule. This is the last time I hire a work crew that's getting married in a couple of weeks. Those shelves aren't going to hang themselves, you know."

"Sorry, Liza." Luke slid both arms around Cassie's waist and gazed adoringly into her affection-filled eyes. "I just can't believe she'll be mine in less than a month." He kissed the tip of Cassie's nose, and Eliza groaned.

"Honestly, if you two weren't my best friends, I wouldn't hang out with you anymore," she teased. "Your cheesiness is out of control."

Cassie laughed. "You mean best friend *and* business partner."

Eliza's gaze traveled the expansive space, mentally noting their ever-growing to-do list. "It's not much of a business yet. Unless customers want to buy a turn at the hardwood floor buffer instead of pastries and coffee."

"Not a bad idea," Luke chuckled. "We can sell tickets. The pressure washer is pretty fun, too."

"Did someone say pressure washer?" Jack Gardener, owner of the local diner and barbecue aficionado, strolled through the front door carrying two takeout bags. The tangy scent of his signature barbecue sauce instantly flooded the room. "I'll trade these pulled pork sandwiches for a go with it."

"You've got yourself a deal." Luke slapped his friend on the shoulder before nabbing one of the brown paper bags.

"Perfect." Jack grinned. He pulled out a chair and wiped off the inch of sawdust before lowering his burly frame. "By the way, did you guys know your sign is crooked?"

Eliza released a heavy sigh. "I'll take care of it."

"Can't we fix it after lunch?" Cassie asked, sitting so close to Luke they might as well have shared the same seat.

"It'll take me two seconds. Start without me." Eliza grabbed the ladder leaning against the wall by the front door and dragged it outside.

Blinking a few times, it took her dark eyes a minute to adjust to the brilliant afternoon sunlight.

Across the street, Mac Houston, owner of the mercantile, fussed with an unruly display of onions. More than one toppled to the ground as Mac waved at Bill Tucker and his pet pig, Peggy Sue, who strutted on her leash as proudly as a prized poodle, a trail of chubby, curly-tailed piglets waddling behind her.

The small town of Poppy Creek buzzed with life in late spring, but the real rush of activity wouldn't start for a few more weeks when school ended and droves of city folk flocked to the foothills for summer adventures like hiking, canoeing, and spelunking.

Eliza set the ladder on the sidewalk, struggling to find firm footing on the uneven cobblestone.

Finally satisfied she wouldn't fall and break her neck with the faintest gust of wind, she climbed a few rungs until she could reach the hand-carved sign Luke had made them.

The Calendar Café.

Eliza's stomach fluttered with nerves every time she glimpsed the new name.

Taking over the bakery after Maggie Davis retired was monumental. Luke's mother had worked tirelessly to turn the place into a town institution for locals and tourists alike. Plus, Eliza still felt indebted to the older woman. Not many people would have hired a pregnant teen with zero professional baking experience.

Swallowing the lump of gratitude lodged in her throat, Eliza tugged the metal chain securing the wooden sign to the eave.

The motion disturbed the ladder's precarious footing, and before Eliza could cry for help, it teetered toward the ground.

"Whoa, there!" Strong hands wrapped around the ladder's frame, instantly righting it, and Eliza found herself sandwiched between a hard chest and the cold metal rungs. "Are you okay?"

His warm breath tickled the back of her neck, sending shivers coursing down her spine. It had been years since she'd heard that voice. But she would have recognized it anywhere.

With her heartbeat pulsing faster than her industrial mixer, Eliza turned until her gaze met familiar turquoise-blue eyes. They'd always reminded her of a tropical ocean—alluring and exotic. And yet, if she wasn't careful, she could easily be lost at sea.

"Colt? What are you doing here?"

Surprise flickered across his handsome features. But only for a second, quickly replaced by a smoldering smile, including an adorable dimple in his left cheek. "Little Liza, is that you?"

Eliza bristled. She'd always hated his pet name for her. Partly because it poked fun at her petite five-foot-four frame. But mostly because it meant he viewed her as his kid sister.

She'd only stopped caring about Colt's colossal lack of interest when Grant Parker moved into town their freshman year of high school. Soon, it was no longer Colt's name doodled inside her notebook, encircled by large swirly hearts and wedding bells.

Colt's appreciative gaze traveled from Eliza's blushing face to the crooked sign. "Wow, it's weird not to see my mom's name above the door anymore." A crease appeared on his tanned forehead as he ran a hand through his sun-kissed hair, releasing a low whistle. "Man, so much has changed around here."

"It wouldn't be such a shock if you visited more than once every five years," Eliza pointed out.

Colt laughed. "I see you still have a big mouth for someone so small."

Eliza huffed indignantly, jabbing his arm. "And I see you left your manners in Los Angeles. Oh, wait. You never had any." She smirked as he let out another deep chuckle.

Colt always did have the nicest laugh. Like the soothing rumble of her KitchenAid's knead cycle.

"So, what brings you home?" She repeated her question, trying not to brush against him as she hopped off the ladder.

"I thought that was obvious. My only brother is getting married. Or did you forget?" His eyes twinkled playfully.

"No, I didn't forget. I just assumed you'd show up at the last possible minute to avoid helping with the prep work."

He laughed again, sending the butterflies in her stomach into a frenzy. "You know me well."

Not as well as I'd like...

Eliza's eyes widened at the sudden, and extremely unwelcome, thought. What had gotten into her? Her crush on Colt had ended eons ago. Not only that, but her heart belonged to someone else. Sure, someone who didn't want it anymore, but still. It wasn't hers to give away. Not that she'd give it to Colt, even if she could. The guy wore "unreliable" like a badge of honor.

"Are you okay?" Colt peered at her, his forehead crinkled. "Your face turned kind of pale."

Was she okay? She most certainly was *not* okay! She was flirting with Colt Davis. Which could only mean one thing...

Eliza Carter had completely lost her mind.

A heaviness settled across Grant's chest as he turned off the main road onto his parents' quiet lane. He barely noticed the crunch of the gravel beneath his tires or the vibrant array of colors greeting him from his mother's meticulously groomed flower beds.

Coming home after being absent for almost a decade should have been a joyous occasion. Yet Grant wrestled with conflicting emotions as pleasant childhood memories clashed with the most soul-crushing time in his life.

Grant swallowed against the tightness in his throat as the pristine Cape Cod–style home came into view. The crisp white siding and emerald-green shutters shimmered in the afternoon sunlight as though they'd recently been treated to a fresh coat of paint. Grant suspected his mother's rigorous spring cleaning routine had extended to outside the house this year, considering the white picket fence looked equally glossy.

Parking beside his father's pickup truck, Grant drew in a deep breath, gathering courage as well as oxygen. He should have called. But given the chance, his mother would have tried to talk him out of coming home. Which is why he hadn't told her about his spur-of-the-moment visit on New Year's Eve. He'd planned to, but when he'd arrived late to the festivities and caught sight of Eliza in the crowd, he'd skipped town before Harriet could shoo him away herself.

Not that she didn't love her only son. But no one had been happier than Harriet Parker the day Grant left home to attend the San Francisco Art Institute. Grant tried not to take it personally, knowing his mother wanted to see both of her children escape what she called "the doldrums of small-town life."

Even at fourteen years old, Grant noticed the undercurrent of resentment when his father moved them from New York City to the West Coast the summer before he entered high school. He would lie awake at night listening to his parents argue. Or rather, listening to his mother mourn the loss of her high society life. Apparently, becoming the head of every committee in Poppy Creek, from the knitting circle to the book club, didn't make up for what she'd left behind.

Stan Parker never uttered a word, as per usual. Apart from mandating their cross-country relocation—for reasons unknown

—Grant's father was the head of the household in title only. Harriet Parker not only wore the pants in the family, she wore the entire ensemble.

"Mom, I'm home." Grant wheeled his suitcase across the threshold, pausing in the foyer. The slick hardwood floor glistened and smelled of lemon oil and eucalyptus.

"Grant?" Harriet poked her head from the kitchen, peering down the hallway in surprise. "What are you doing here?"

"Nice to see you, too." Grant flashed a teasing grin as he bent to untie his shoelaces.

Harriet leaned the mop against the door frame before snapping off her rubber gloves. "Don't be cute with me. You didn't call."

"I didn't realize I needed to." Grant cringed as the soapy water seeped through his socks.

"It's not that you *need* to," Harriet huffed. "But you caught me right in the middle of spring cleaning."

"I'll be sure to stay out of the way," Grant promised. "Where'd you banish Dad?"

Harriet blinked, as though, for a moment, she'd forgotten all about her husband and his whereabouts. "He's... fishing, I think."

"Okay. Well, I'll head into town for a bit, then. Unless you'd like help?" Grant suppressed a smile, knowing full well his mother would refuse. They'd had chores growing up, but no one could meet Harriet's high standards. In the end, she'd inevitably wind up redoing whatever task they were assigned.

"No, no. I'm almost done." Harriet waved aside his offer, then hesitated. A solitary wrinkle appeared in her unnaturally smooth forehead. "But maybe going into town isn't such a good idea."

"Why not?"

"Because..." Harriet trailed off, the crease in her brow deepening. After a brief pause, she sighed, throwing up her hands. "Don't make me say it."

"Eliza?" Grant asked.

His mother winced at the mention of his ex-girlfriend's name, then nodded slowly.

"Mom, I'll be fine," Grant assured her, despite being riddled with self doubt. "It's been ages since we broke up. We have to move on at some point, right?"

Harriet pressed her lips into a thin line, a question burning behind her piercing blue eyes. Finally, she spoke barely above a whisper. "Why did you come back? Not to..." As though she couldn't bring herself to say the words out loud, she snapped her mouth shut.

A tiny jolt of defensiveness pricked Grant's heart. He knew his mother hated Eliza for dumping him the summer after their high school graduation, but there were times Grant felt her dislike bordered on irrational. She seemed terrified he'd come to make amends with his ex.

Or worse...

Get back together.

"Don't worry. Me coming home has nothing to do with Eliza."

But even as the words left his lips, Grant realized they weren't entirely true.

CHAPTER 3

*W*isps of steam curled from the flaky golden crusts of the mini rhubarb pies as Eliza sprinkled a handful of coarsely ground sugar over the buttery glaze.

"This is quite the lineup." Penny Heart's coppery eyes darted from the pies to the lemon squares with candied citrus peels artfully arranged on top to the half dozen other desserts spread out before them. "I should have worn my Thanksgiving pants."

Penny playfully rubbed her stomach, drawing Eliza's attention to her tall, slender figure draped in a gauzy peasant dress. Although Penny's wardrobe consisted entirely of vintage second-hand pieces from her thrift store, Thistle & Thorn, she could inspire even the most pretentious fashion photographers. And yet, Eliza had never met a kinder, more unassuming soul.

From the second the shy, skittish girl with auburn pigtails and delicate doll-like features moved into town, Eliza made it her personal mission to ensure she felt at home. And ever since then, they'd become fast and fierce friends.

"Please, you could eat your weight in pastries without gaining a single pound," Eliza teased.

Although she had to admit, the smorgasbord of decadent

treats *did* look a tad excessive engulfing her parents' modest kitchen island. But since the new equipment hadn't been installed at the bakery yet, Eliza worked with the space she had.

"They all look heavenly! I can't wait to try them." Cassie lifted her fork, ready to tackle the mountain of calories. "Although, Dolores will probably have to alter my wedding dress after this."

"Our grand opening is in a few weeks. We have to serve something special. Something with a 'wow' factor." Eliza brushed her hands together, scattering the remaining sugar granules across the white tile countertop. "Hopefully, one of these will be the winner."

"How did you come up with so many ideas?" Penny dug her spoon into a ramekin of perfectly caramelized crème brûlée.

Eliza shrugged. "I simply asked a few people to tell me their favorite desserts."

"Mm... who's responsible for this mouthwatering masterpiece?" Cassie mumbled between bites. "And what is it?"

"Tiramisu," Eliza said proudly. "Ben's favorite and my specialty."

"That's quite a sophisticated dessert for a seven-year-old," Penny laughed, sampling the cheesecake next.

"Is there coffee in it?" Cassie asked, unabashedly helping herself to thirds.

Eliza's heart swelled with affection for her sweet, coffee-inclined friend. No one had an affinity for the caffeinated beverage quite like Cassie. She could probably taste a teaspoon in a gallon of cream. "Yep. The sponge cake is soaked in it."

Cassie closed her eyes, releasing a soft moan of delight as she savored her fourth bite. "How have I never tried this before? I hope you realize you've ruined me for all other desserts. From now on, if it doesn't have coffee in it, it's not worth the calories."

Eliza chuckled, but her breath caught in her throat as an idea gripped her. "That's it!"

"What's it?" Cassie and Penny asked in unison.

"The something special I've been looking for!"

Eliza paced the hardwood floor, tapping a finger to her lips as she mulled it over. She stopped abruptly, her dark eyes flashing with excitement. "The Calendar Café will be Poppy Creek's first coffeehouse, right?"

Her friends exchanged a confused glance at her rhetorical question.

"Yes..." Cassie trailed off. "So?"

"*So...* what if I create an entire line of coffee-infused desserts? Tiramisu, of course. And a few original recipes, too. They can be our signature. What do you think?"

Cassie didn't hesitate. "I love it! It's a brilliant idea."

Eliza beamed, thrilled by Cassie's enthusiasm.

"Whatever you do, make sure you include this cheesecake on the menu," Penny added, licking a smear of caramel sauce from her bottom lip. "It's incredible."

"Maybe I'll combine it with the tiramisu." Eliza giggled, her joy bubbling over with the endless possibilities.

"Is it too late to serve this at the wedding?" Sliding the plate in front of her, Cassie gave up all pretense of sharing the Italian delicacy.

"I'll add it to the dessert bar," Eliza promised.

"Speaking of the wedding..." Penny arched both eyebrows as she reached for a coconut macaroon. "I heard a certain prodigal son has returned to Poppy Creek for the celebration."

Suddenly self-conscious, Eliza pulled at a loose thread on her pinstripe apron, avoiding Penny's gaze.

"You mean Colt?" Cassie asked. "I met him for the first time last night during dinner at Maggie's. I wasn't sure what to expect based on the few tidbits Luke has shared, but he seems quite sweet and charming, actually."

Penny groaned, rolling her eyes toward the ceiling. "Oh, Cass. Don't tell me he's fooled you, too."

"He's not that bad," Eliza blurted before refocusing her attention on the wayward thread, heat singeing her cheeks.

Penny narrowed her gaze. "You know as well as I do that the guy is bad news. He's immature, irresponsible, selfish—"

"It's been years, Pen. Maybe he's changed?" Eliza didn't dare look up for fear Penny would see right through her.

"Eliza has a point," Cassie offered. "People change. Look at Frank! Last year, he was a grumpy old hermit. Now he's dating the most darling woman in the world. And without the coffee he's graciously offered to roast for us, Eliza and I wouldn't have a business." Cassie paused, her pretty features scrunched in thought. "Actually, scratch that. Forget Frank. Look at *me!* I can't believe how much my life has changed in such a short amount of time. Some days, I hardly recognize myself."

Eliza smiled, grateful for her friend's bright outlook. She stole a glance at Penny, who seemed to soften slightly.

"Fine," Penny sighed. "I'll postpone my final judgment. And for the record, I hope I'm wrong about him."

Eliza did, too.

More than she wanted to admit.

✦

*A*s Grant strolled down Main Street, he marveled at how little the town had changed. The Buttercup Bistro, Hank's Hardware and Video Rental, Mac's Mercantile... all exactly where he'd left them.

But a few things were markedly different. And something in particular seemed especially *off*. He just couldn't put his finger on it...

Closing his eyes, Grant drew in a deep breath, welcoming the wave of nostalgia carried on the late afternoon breeze. The sweet floral scent of wisteria mixed with...

Grant hesitated, his eyes fluttering open. Did he smell

sawdust? And where was the delectable aroma of Maggie's freshly baked cinnamon rolls?

He picked up his pace, letting muscle memory lead him to his favorite childhood haunt. But when his feet paused in front of a white brick building with a rustic wooden door and hand-carved sign dangling above the entrance, his heart sank.

The Calendar Café? What happened to Maggie's Place? In high school, they would frequent the bakery nearly every Saturday afternoon to devour the plump, gooey pastries.

Grant's gaze darted across the town square to Luke's law office, confident Luke would have the answer.

If he agreed to talk to him, that is.

As Grant strode purposefully across the center lawn, blades of recently cut grass clung to the soles of his suede sneakers. He'd spent countless hours of his youth playing catch on the same field with Luke, Colt, and their dad. In many ways, Leonard Davis had filled the shoes his own father refused to wear. Which made it all the more painful to hear of his passing.

Grant had wanted to come home to pay his respects, but he'd fallen out of touch years ago. And, like the coward he was, he couldn't bring himself to face everyone he'd left behind. Instead, in true spineless fashion, he'd sent a card and flowers he couldn't afford.

Standing in front of the Western-style shiplap building, Grant hesitated. The bronze plaque on the front door still read L. Davis Law Office, and the aged patina and myriad of dents and scratches indicated Luke hadn't replaced it when he took over his father's law practice. A fact Grant found oddly comforting.

But as his gaze drifted upward, his brow furrowed in confusion. A huge wooden sign that read Davis Designs hung over the entrance. The subtitle was even more mystifying. Bespoke Furniture? It didn't make any sense. Unless Luke had simply kept his father's plaque as an homage when he'd switched to a new line of work.

Grant removed his glasses and wiped the lenses on the hem of his polo shirt before reading the sign again. His mother kept him fairly informed on the town gossip, but she hadn't mentioned anything about Luke leaving the family business in favor of woodworking.

But then, Grant had long suspected his mother of only divulging select information, with fewer and fewer details as the years passed. In fact, during their visit at Christmas, her insights into Luke's impending engagement seemed intentionally vague, spurring Grant's impulsive trip back home a few days later.

Determined to finally reconnect with long-missed friends, Grant could only hope he wouldn't chicken out this time around.

Steeling himself against the uncertainty, he squared his shoulders before pushing through the front door, immediately noting that the inside had changed even more drastically than the outside. Several walls had been knocked down, creating an expansive open space to showcase exquisitely crafted furniture. Grant's artistic eye led him toward a particularly impressive rocking chair with sleek lines and intricate engravings along the headboard.

As he reached out a hand to graze the smooth mahogany, a faint click-clacking sound drew his attention toward the large brick fireplace. An elderly woman slouched in a rocking chair by the hearth, her short-cropped silver curls bent over a pair of large knitting needles.

"Oh, excuse me! I..." Grant realized the woman hadn't budged an inch. Then he noticed the pair of headphones draped over her ears.

Grant took a step toward her, stumbling over something lying on the carpet. A loud hiss accompanied a bright orange blur as a rotund tabby cat dashed toward the fireplace and clawed its way up the mantel with surprising agility. The broad, pudgy face glowered at Grant from its perch.

"Whoops! Sorry about that," Grant apologized to the offended feline, realizing he'd accidentally stepped on its tail.

"Banjo has a soft spot for sardines, if you want to make it up to him." The woman pressed a button on her ancient cassette player and slipped off her headphones. "Canned in olive oil, not water. He's a bit particular, I'm afraid."

"Good to know." Grant offered a tentative smile, his pulse slowly returning to normal. "I'll be sure to bring some by."

The woman returned his smile, her kind blue eyes sparkling behind her thick glasses.

Grant squinted as he took in her round, plump features and rosy cheeks. She looked vaguely familiar...

Her face brightened as she recognized him first. "Why, Grant Parker! It's really you, isn't it?"

She rose to her feet and shuffled toward him, enveloping Grant in a warm, affectionate hug. The subtle aroma of rose oil and peppermint tea sparked his memory. Dolores Whittaker! The wife of his old high school principal! What was she doing in Luke's office? Or whatever this place was...

"Hi, Mrs. Whittaker. It's really nice to see you again." He'd always liked the sweet, spunky woman. She was famous for supplying every school function with her rich, homemade desserts.

To his surprise, she licked her thumb before smoothing down an unruly patch of his hair. "You haven't changed a bit. Same head of molasses-colored curls. You're a little taller, though. I didn't used to have to stand on my tiptoes to combat your ornery mane."

Once he recovered from his shock, Grant released a low rumble of laughter. Although he wasn't considered extraordinarily tall at five eleven, he *had* grown an inch or two since high school. "Thanks for looking out for me, Mrs. Whittaker."

"Goodness gracious! No one's called me that in years. Call me Dolores. Or DeeDee, if you like. Does Luke know you're back?"

Grant ran a nervous hand through his hair, undoing all of Dolores's efforts. "No. I, uh, thought I'd surprise him."

Dolores clicked her tongue. "Well, good thing I caught you first. Make sure he's not operating the handsaw when you spring yourself on him. A surprise of this magnitude could cause someone to lose a finger." She embraced Grant again, squeezing him even tighter this time. "Good to have you home, son. We've all missed you like the dickens."

As Grant inhaled her scent once more, noting the faintest whiff of Banjo's favorite salty treat, he couldn't help thinking how different her reception was to his own mother's.

He also couldn't help thinking not everyone in town would be as welcoming as Dolores Whittaker.

If only making amends with Luke would be as easy as offering him a can of sardines.

CHAPTER 4

*A*s Grant maneuvered around the furniture toward the back of the showroom, his heart hammered in his throat. Once he crossed the threshold into the courtyard, he'd have to face a decade of regret.

Maybe even a fist to his jaw.

One hand on the brass doorknob, Grant raised his chin a smidge higher. If Luke took a swing, he wouldn't even try to dodge it. He deserved whatever came his way. Who ditched town and didn't keep in touch with their best friends? A callous jerk, that's who.

Stepping into the courtyard, Grant flinched, shielding his eyes from a momentary glare as sunlight reflected off a metal paint can.

Luke dipped a brush into a can of ebony stain, whistling to himself as he dragged the bristles along the arm of an oversize Adirondack chair.

Grant cleared his throat.

As Luke glanced up from his kneeling position on the drop cloth, his smile faded, replaced by surprise, then confusion.

Setting down his brush, he slowly rose to his full six two of solid muscle.

Grant tensed but stood his ground as Luke approached.

Pausing a foot away, Luke surveyed Grant as though making sure he was really standing in front of him. Then his hazel eyes softened, and in one long stride, he pulled Grant into a bone-crushing hug.

Not exactly the way Grant had expected to receive bodily harm during the encounter.

"Welcome home, you oaf." Luke's deep, rich voice carried a teasing quality, and Grant immediately relaxed.

"Thanks."

The men stepped apart, but Luke kept one hand on Grant's shoulder. "I gotta admit. For a minute, I thought I'd seen a ghost."

Grant smiled sheepishly. "For a minute, I thought that paint can would wind up over my head."

Luke laughed, slapping Grant on the back. "Not gonna lie. You have a lot of explaining to do. But I never did see the point in holding a grudge. I'm just glad you're back."

Grant drew in a grateful breath, releasing it in one long, steady exhale. He should've known Luke would greet him with nothing but kindness. Even as kids, Luke was the guy who always put others first. "I appreciate that. But I owe you an apology." Grant paused. What should he say? For leaving home and losing touch? For missing every birthday? Your graduation from law school? Your father's funeral? He cringed. The list of grievances was endless, to be sure. But that one? Unforgivable.

"Consider yourself forgiven." Luke's compassion-filled eyes held his gaze a moment, as if wiping away Grant's transgressions in a single glance. "So, what brings you home after all these years?"

Grant swallowed, his throat suddenly tight. He fought the urge to hug Luke a second time. "Your wedding, truthfully. Not that I'm inviting myself. But I at least wanted to congratulate you in person and give you my best. I've missed too much already. I didn't want to add this to the list, too."

"Not invited? Heck! Now that you're back, I want you in the wedding!"

"Oh, no. Luke, you don't have to—"

"It's not a matter of *have* to," Luke assured him. "I want you to be a groomsman. Along with Colt, Jack, and Reed. We'll bring the gang back together. Just like old times."

Grant wavered. He loved the idea they could pick up where they'd left off. But could it really be that simple? "I don't know… Are you sure?"

"If you ask me one more time, I *will* shellac your face with that stain," Luke teased.

Grant managed a small smile, still a little dazed. "Okay. I guess I'll be sticking around town for a while, then."

"Perfect!" Luke strode back to where he'd left the paintbrush and plopped it in a rinse bucket. "We have some catching up to do. Starting with a plate of ribs at Jack's."

Grant chuckled. "I still can't believe Jack owns a diner."

"A lot has changed since you left." After securing the lid on the paint can, Luke glanced over his shoulder. "By the way, have you…"

Based on his hesitant expression, Grant could guess what Luke was about to ask. "No, I haven't seen Eliza yet. I know I'll have to eventually. But I'm not in a rush, if you know what I mean."

Luke's brow furrowed, and after a moment, he shook his head. "No, I'm afraid I don't know what you mean. What happened between you two? One minute you were inseparable. The next, it's like you never existed."

Grant winced. He'd always hoped Eliza had explained everything to Luke. At least then, Luke might have understood why he left. "It's a long story."

"We'll have plenty of time over lunch."

"Maybe at some point. But not today." Grant hoped his tone conveyed a note of finality.

Luke didn't look satisfied with Grant's response, but he pressed his lips in a firm line and set to work rinsing the brush.

Grant hated to blow him off, but if Luke wanted the truth about what happened between them, he'd have to ask Eliza.

*s Eliza rounded the bend in Walnut Tree Lane, her tense grip on the steering wheel relaxed, and she breathed a little easier as the picturesque Victorian cottage came into view.

Eliza had always thought Edith Hayward's home was stunning, with its bright white siding and gingerbread trim that was more elaborate than her finest piped icing. Including the enormous, ornate cake she'd recently baked for the Flannigans' fiftieth anniversary party.

But Eliza's favorite feature was the grand, sweeping walnut tree in the front yard, which would be the perfect spot for a bench swing. More than once, she'd allowed herself to daydream about sipping sweet tea from the rocking chair on the front porch, the loyal family dog lounging by her feet while Ben played on the swing. And during these momentary lapses in sanity, she'd envision loving, steady hands deftly swinging Ben high into the air, her son's gleeful giggles mingling with the songbirds perched on the branches overhead. Without fail, the strong, dependable hands belonged to one man, and one man only. Her first love and New Year's Eve phantom, Grant Parker.

Whenever the delusional thought squeezed past her defenses, Eliza quickly squelched the unwelcome intrusion. It wouldn't do her any good to hold out hope for the impossible. Besides, the cottage belonged to Cassie now, ever since she'd inherited it from her late grandmother last Christmas.

Eliza couldn't help but smile as the memories of last year's festivities bounded to the forefront of her mind. In less than six months, so many things had changed. And once again, her world seemed to be balancing on the edge of another precipice.

Colt Davis had asked her out! On a *date*.

And Eliza had no idea what to do about it.

As she parked her dilapidated Honda Accord next to Cassie's blueberry-colored Prius, her stomach twisted tighter than a garlic knot. Her life would be so much simpler if she turned Colt down. But seeing how happy Luke and Cassie were together stirred a painfully suppressed longing in Eliza's heart for a partner—someone to share her life with, both the good and the bad.

Pushing through the cheery red door, Eliza called out, "Cass, I'm here!"

"In the kitchen," Cassie hollered back.

But even if Cassie hadn't announced her whereabouts, Eliza would have followed the enticing aroma of freshly brewed coffee to the snug, homey kitchen.

"Whatever you're brewing smells amazing!" Leaning over the French press, Eliza closed her eyes and inhaled deeply, savoring the delicate tendrils of steam curling from the spout.

Oddly, Eliza had never cared for coffee until she met Cassie. She'd only ever tasted generic ground coffee from a can that had already lost all its flavor by the time it was brewed.

Now Eliza drank only the best blends—roasted by Cassie herself or Frank Barrie. Eliza's heart warmed at the thought of the kind yet cantankerous old man. Frank had lived nearly his entire adult life secluded from the outside world, penning best-selling books on coffee roasting under a pseudonym. Until Cassie's sweet spirit and shared love of the rich, full-bodied beverage drew him out of hiding. Cassie had an uncanny knack for bringing people together in ways even she couldn't foresee.

"Oh, I'm so glad you think so!" Cassie beamed, pressing the plunger on the French press, forcing the grounds to the bottom of the glass carafe. "It's a new blend Frank and I created. We thought its fruity undertones would pair well with your dessert idea." Cassie selected two floral mugs from the cupboard and set them on the counter. "Is that why you're here? Because if you make me taste any more of your experiments, I won't fit into my wedding dress." Cassie laughed as she filled both mugs with the dark, velvety liquid.

"Not this time." Eliza gratefully accepted the mug adorned with a single yellow daffodil, while Cassie kept the one covered in bright red poppies. That was another quirk of Cassie's—each person had a special mug. But she never told the recipient the meaning behind why theirs was chosen.

"What's wrong?" Cassie leaned against the kitchen island, both forearms resting on the smooth butcher block.

"I... need some advice."

"I'm all ears." Cassie's phone buzzed, but she immediately silenced the call.

"It's fine. You can answer." Eliza reached for it, suddenly uncomfortable with the prospect of discussing her love life.

Or lack thereof.

But Cassie beat her to it, snatching the cell and turning it off altogether. "Nope! You can't get out of the conversation now."

As if on cue, Eliza's upbeat ringtone reverberated from inside her purse. Eliza lunged for it, but Cassie was quicker.

Retrieving the phone, Cassie read the caller ID out loud. "It's Penny. We'll call her back after we discuss your problem." Raising an eyebrow as if daring Eliza to protest, Cassie stuffed it inside the cupboard between a stack of canned corn and chicken broth. "Now," she said, settling herself on the barstool. "Spill it."

Eliza sighed, running her fingertip along the rim of the mug. "Okay. I don't know how to say this, so I'm just going to lay it out there." She drew in a deep breath before blurting, "Colt asked me out. On a *real* date. And I don't know what to say. If I say no, things will stay the same. Which may or may not be a bad thing.

If I say yes, everything could change. Which, again, may or may not be a bad thing. I'm so confused!" The words left her lips in a rush. When she finally stopped for air, she flopped onto the counter, covering her face with both hands and mumbled between her interlaced fingers, "Help me."

Cassie laughed softly. "Is that all? I should think the answer is obvious. Say yes, of course."

"It's not that simple." Eliza pushed herself onto her elbows, meeting Cassie's gaze. "He invited me to the Secret Picnic. It's a huge event. Everyone in town will see us together."

"So?"

"*So...*" Eliza dragged out the vowel sound for emphasis. "Everyone will talk. And..." She hesitated before murmuring, "I'm tired of being the most scandalous story in Poppy Creek."

Her features softening with sympathy, Cassie draped her arm around Eliza's shoulders, offering a comforting squeeze. "How about this? Why don't we all go together? You, Ben, Colt, and me and Luke. No one will think twice about that. But you and Colt can still have the time together to get reacquainted. What do you think?"

The corner of Eliza's lips quirked up slightly. "That's not a terrible idea. As long as it's not officially a date. Just friends. Hanging out."

"It's a deal!" Cassie grinned, then scrunched her face in thought. "What exactly is a secret picnic, anyway?"

Eliza's smile broadened. "It's one of my favorite traditions. Mac Houston started it several years ago to raise awareness for the local food bank. In addition to bringing canned food and other donations, everyone packs a picnic lunch and meets in the town square. The baskets go into a huge pile, and then everyone picks a different one than the one they brought. It's a secret because you're not supposed to know who packed the basket you chose."

Cassie shook her head as she chuckled. "This town never ceases to amaze me. But it sounds complicated."

"Not really." Eliza shrugged. "There are certain guidelines to make it easier. Like, you have to pack enough food to feed at least four people. And you get to peek inside the baskets, in case you have certain food allergies or aversions. But everyone tries to outdo each other, so you wind up with the most incredible meal!"

"Oh, no!" Cassie laughed. "I hope you're packing the basket for our group, because I can barely make a peanut butter and jelly sandwich."

"I've got you covered," Eliza assured her. "Every spring, I plan my menu well in advance. This year, I'm making—" The sound of car tires skidding to a halt in the gravel drive interrupted Eliza's train of thought.

"What in the world?" Cassie's green eyes widened in surprise. "Who could that be?"

The front door creaked on its hinges before slamming shut.

"Cassie? Eliza?" Penny shouted as her kitten heels clacked across the parquet floor.

"In here," Cassie called out, concern etched across her forehead.

"Finally! I've been looking all over town for you two," Penny panted. "Neither of you answered your phones."

Cassie and Eliza exchanged a guilty glance.

"Sorry," Cassie said sheepishly. "We were in the middle of a pretty serious conversation."

"Oh, then you already know?" Penny looked relieved.

"Know what?" Eliza asked.

"That Grant Parker is back in town."

All the color drained from Eliza's face. And if she'd been balancing on the edge of a precipice before...

She'd just fallen off.

CHAPTER 5

*N*ormally, walking into the kitchen and immediately being enveloped by the inviting aroma of garlic and rosemary would have eased Eliza's troubled spirit. But tonight, the overpowering scent of her mother's famous garlic potatoes made her stomach turn.

Why had Grant Parker come back to Poppy Creek? When Eliza glimpsed Grant in the crowd on New Year's Eve, she'd thought it was a fluke. Or a figment of her imagination. Now, faced with the uncertainty of his unexpected arrival, her mind reeled with the possibilities.

"Hi, honey. Dinner's almost ready." Sylvia kept her back to Eliza as she chopped scallions for the Caesar salad.

"Thanks. Is Ben upstairs working on his homework?"

At the dejected lilt in Eliza's voice, Sylvia spun around, wielding a large chef's knife. "What's wrong?" She pointed the sharp blade, her cocoa-colored eyes narrowed in concern.

Eliza threw up her hands in mock defense. "Whoa. These are some questionable interrogation tactics, don't you think?"

"Don't deflect." Sylvia set down the knife and wiped both

hands on her paisley apron. "Sit." She gestured toward the high back barstool, taking the one beside it.

"Am I this bossy?" Eliza groaned.

"You're worse," Sylvia snorted. "Now, out with it. What's bothering you?"

For a moment, Eliza didn't speak, wondering which problem she should tackle first. Mentioning Grant would only open wounds she wasn't ready to face. Colt, on the other hand, was a marginally safer topic.

"I'm waiting." Sylvia pursed her heavily outlined lips. Even on a quiet weeknight at home, Sylvia Carter wouldn't be caught dead without a full face of makeup. Not to mention the flamboyant updo.

"I... have a date. Sort of."

"You have a date?" Sylvia squealed, clasping her hands together. "Thank goodness! I was beginning to think you'd die alone. You don't even have a cat."

"Gee, thanks." Eliza should be offended, except she'd heard the same lament a thousand times before.

"Hank!" Sylvia shouted. "We can finally book that Mediterranean cruise!"

Eliza rolled her eyes, ignoring the slight sting of her mother's words. "Dad's still in the garage working on Frida Connelly's sewing machine. The one she insists is broken all because her sister, Francine, can sew a straighter line." Eliza snickered, but Sylvia wasn't listening. The mention of Eliza's potential love life negated all other matters.

"Fine, I'll tell him later." Sylvia turned her hopeful gaze back on her daughter. "So, I want to hear all about him."

"There isn't much to tell. It's one date. Barely even a date, really. And I haven't decided if I want it to become more than that."

"Why not? Is there something wrong with him?"

"No. I'm just not sure I should be dating anyone right now."

Sylvia opened her mouth to protest, and Eliza held up her hand. "At this moment, I need to focus on my son. Especially with the trouble he's having in school. Speaking of which, I should go check on his homework."

Eliza slid off the stool and headed for the staircase, bracing herself for her mother's inevitable—and always theatrical—outcry. But when she'd reached the bottom step and the performance still hadn't come, Eliza stole a quick glance over her shoulder.

Sylvia met her gaze, her dark eyes soft, yet troubled.

"What?" Eliza asked against her better judgment.

"Nothing," Sylvia said quietly.

A mixture of unease and curiosity settled in Eliza's stomach. And despite the warning voice telling her to drop the subject, she persisted. "There's obviously something on your mind. What is it?"

Sylvia shifted her weight, her expression strained. She took a deep breath and released it slowly, speaking in a low, gentle voice. "Sweetheart, whatever you're holding on to, you have to let it go. You can't use Ben as an excuse forever."

At her mother's words, all the air rushed from Eliza's lungs, and she gripped the banister for support. How could her mother say that to her? A defensive retort rose in her throat, but Eliza chose to swallow the bitter irony, no matter how painfully it went down.

Holding back tears, she reminded herself that her mother didn't know the whole story.

And if she did, Sylvia, of all people, would beg Eliza to keep her secret safe, and never, *ever* let it go.

*S*eated in the booth next to Luke, and across from Colt Davis and Reed Hollis, Grant couldn't help but smile. It felt good to be home, surrounded by friends again. He could kick himself for waiting so long to reconnect.

"I still can't believe you both decided to show your ugly mugs around town again." A huge grin plastered across his face, Jack glanced from Grant to Colt as he set a steaming rack of ribs on the table. He lowered his lumbering frame into the tan leather booth, shoving Grant against Luke.

"Speaking of ugly mugs," Colt lobbed back, nabbing a curly fry. "Did a wild animal attach itself to your face?"

Chuckling, Jack ran a hand over his scruffy beard. "Watch it, Davis. It's not too late for me to tamper with your food. We're still waiting on the onion rings."

"Yeah." Reed jabbed Colt in the shoulder. "Respect your elders, man. In Jack's time, they learned to shave with the fang of a saber-toothed tiger."

Grant joined in their laughter, realizing it had been ages since he'd laughed so hard. Even though he hadn't seen the guys in years, some things never changed. Jack and Luke only had two years on them, but the old men jokes, ironically, never got old.

Gazing around the table, Grant marveled at how the four men had maintained such a strong friendship, yet couldn't be more different.

Jack, with his large, hulking build and penchant for flannel, could have been a lumberjack if he didn't already own the best restaurant in town. And although he doled out sarcasm as easily as barbecue sauce, he had the biggest heart and would do anything for a friend or stranger alike.

Out of the four, Grant had the most in common with Reed. Within the group, Reed could dish out the jokes with the best of them, but overall, he possessed a quieter spirit. Grant wasn't surprised to learn he'd opened his own nursery, cultivating plants with an artistic flare Grant found instantly relatable.

Luke was… well, *Luke*. Similarly, as in their childhood, he had a calm, grounding effect on those around him. And seemed to be the linchpin holding everyone together.

Then there was Luke's younger brother, Colt—Luke's opposite in every way. And to be honest, Grant wasn't sure how he felt about the guy.

Colt had been the quintessential high school heartthrob—quarterback of the football team, blond haired and blue eyed, with charm that oozed out of his pores. But besides being a romantic comedy cliché—right down to his ridiculous dimple—there was something about Colt that Grant didn't trust.

"So," Luke cut into Grant's thoughts. "How long are you guys sticking around town? Are you leaving right after the wedding?"

Colt shrugged, reaching across the table to grab a rib dripping with Jack's special barbecue sauce. "It depends."

"On what?" Reed asked, helping himself after Colt.

Colt didn't respond, merely wiggling his eyebrows as he tore into the meat like a caveman.

"It's a woman." Jack slapped his huge bear paw on the tabletop. "I knew it. You've been back less than twenty-four hours and you've already marked your prey."

Colt chuckled, wiping a smear of sauce with the back of his hand.

Grant shifted as much as he could manage while sandwiched between the broad shoulders of Jack and Luke. He didn't care for the turn the conversation had taken, although he couldn't pinpoint the reason why.

"Who's the unlucky victim?" Reed grinned, dunking a fry into a glob of ketchup before cramming the entire thing into his mouth.

"Eliza."

The table went deathly silent, all eyes on Grant.

Grant blinked. What did Colt say? It sounded like he'd said "Eliza," but that couldn't be right. Grant tugged on his collar, uncomfortably warm all of a sudden.

Someone cleared their throat.

"Colt," Luke interjected gently. "Do you really think that's a good idea?"

"Why not? Have you guys seen her? I can't believe she's still single."

Heat crept up Grant's neck, all the way to the tips of his ears. Their pitying stares seemed to bore straight through his forehead. And for a second, he considered slinking beneath the table.

"Oh…" Realization seemed to dawn on Colt, and he snapped his fingers. "That's right. You two used to date in high school. I'm an idiot. I'll back off. Unless you don't mind…."

Another throat cleared.

This time, everyone seemed to be trying their hardest *not* to look at Grant.

Grant forced himself to meet Colt's gaze.

How did the guy manage to look so innocent? Colt had to know his question gutted Grant to his core. But what could he say? It wasn't like he had any claim on Eliza. She was her own person. He didn't have any right to interfere in her dating life. Of course, that knowledge didn't stop him from wanting to reach across the table to flick the smug smile off Colt's face.

"I don't mind," Grant lied between clenched teeth.

"Great!" Colt nabbed another rib, satisfied the topic had been resolved.

But Luke didn't look as convinced. "There are other things to consider, Colt."

"Like what?"

"Like, she has a son."

"And you're an infant in a grown man's body," Jack added for good measure.

"Says the man wearing a bib." Colt gestured toward the

napkin tucked inside Jack's collar. Turning back to his brother, Colt said, "Look, I get that you're concerned. Sure, I don't have a stable job at the moment. Or a house with a white picket fence and a porch swing. Or whatever else girls fantasize about. But I'm not asking her to marry me. I just want to take her on a few dates and see where things go."

"See, that's exactly my point," Luke told him. "You can't be your usual carefree, no-strings-attached self with a girl like Eliza. You have to be intentional. She's not just another beautiful woman. She's a mom. Which means you're not only dating her. You're dating her kid, too."

When Colt pulled a face, Luke rolled his eyes. "You know what I mean."

Colt may not have understood, but Grant heard Luke loud and clear.

Like Colt, Grant had no business being anyone's dad—surrogate or otherwise.

And that meant, no matter what, Eliza was off-limits.

CHAPTER 6

*E*liza gazed mournfully at the heap of picnic baskets collected in the center of the town square, one hand on her churning stomach. In years past, she'd already be scouring the selection, zeroing in on the most scrumptious offering. Today, even the mere thought of a chicken pesto panini or grilled Reuben sandwich made her nauseous.

Rather than assess the plethora of lunch possibilities, Eliza scanned the throng of picnic-goers, flashing back to New Year's Eve. The last person she'd expected to see that night was Grant Parker. And now that he'd returned…

The normally sweet, lilac-scented air felt stifling.

"Nervous about your date?" Cassie's teasing tone pulled Eliza from her thoughts.

"No. Because it's not really a date. So, there's no reason to be nervous."

"Then, why do you look so pale?"

As if on cue, Grant appeared in the crowd, joined by Jack, Reed, and Penny.

With his head thrown back, Grant laughed at something Jack said, a winsome smile illuminating his handsome features.

The sight left Eliza winded and a little light-headed.

Cassie followed her gaze. "Is that Grant?"

Unable to find her voice, Eliza nodded.

Grant looked even more attractive than she remembered. While he'd been teased in high school for his glasses, lanky build, and artsy interests, Eliza had always found him irresistible. His lavender-hued, brooding eyes paired with impossibly thick and glossy ink-black hair made for a heart-pounding combination.

To Eliza's dismay, Grant still possessed every ounce of his youthful appeal, plus he'd filled out in the all the right places. She couldn't help noticing the way his light blue polo stretched across his broad chest and defined shoulders.

Dizziness swept over her, and Eliza suddenly found herself in desperate need of an ice-cold glass of water.

"Oh, Liza." Cassie wrapped an arm around her shoulders, giving them a sympathetic squeeze. "Are you okay? Do you want to leave?"

"No. I'm fine. Really."

"You don't look fine."

"I skipped breakfast in anticipation of the picnic. I'm just hungry."

Although Cassie didn't look convinced, she didn't press further.

Eliza released a grateful sigh, wondering how much longer until they could head for Larkspur Meadow. She needed to put some distance between her and Grant—*fast.*

"Hope you ladies don't mind, but I picked the basket for our group." Colt tapped a soft-sided cooler bag slung over his shoulder. "I heard rumblings about roast beef sandwiches, potato salad, and mini chocolate lava cakes, and couldn't resist."

"Works for me!" Cassie said brightly. "Did you ask Luke?"

"His exact response was, and I quote, 'Whatever Cassie wants.'" Colt chuckled. "You've trained him better than a Pomeranian."

"Very funny." Cassie rolled her eyes, but her soft smile and dreamy gaze gave away her delight.

"What'd you guys get?" Jack's deep, thunderous voice carried above the general hubbub in the town square as he crossed the field toward them. Reed, Penny, and Grant trailed behind his considerable stride.

Eliza sucked in a breath as they drew nearer, her pulse escalating with each step Grant took in her direction. How could he be so calm and relaxed? Especially when Eliza's heart had leapt into her throat.

"Like I'd tell you," Colt snorted. "I had to wrestle Bill Tucker for this cooler. Keep your mangy paws off it."

"Relax, princess." Jack grinned good-naturedly. "I'm not interested in stealing your lunch. Grant picked ours. And I have to say, I think he got the best one."

Curious, Eliza stole a glance at the wicker basket in Grant's hand, nearly losing her balance when she spotted the familiar gingham napkin peeking out of the top.

What were the odds that Grant had chosen *her* basket?

"Oh, yeah?" Colt inched closer, his thick eyebrows raised in curiosity. "What'd you get?"

"Oh, now you want to trade information?" Jack crossed his arms, his blue eyes glinting with humor.

Colt shrugged. "If I were you, I wouldn't tell me, either. We both know it won't compare." Patting the cooler bag, Colt twisted his lips into a challenging smirk.

"Okay, I'll call your bluff. But you tell first," Jack countered.

Eliza wrapped both arms around her stomach, watching the exchange with increasing discomfort. If they didn't stop arguing soon, she'd head off toward the meadow by herself. She couldn't spend two more seconds in Grant's company. And somehow, knowing he'd inadvertently chosen her picnic basket added to her unease. It felt too... intimate.

Penny groaned, apparently as fed up with their juvenile antics as Eliza. "You two are worse than toddlers." Grabbing the basket from Grant, she read the handmade note card tied to the handle. "It's stuffed focaccia sandwiches, antipasto salad, seasonal fruit, pomegranate lemonade, and espresso chip brownies."

"Huh. That does sound pretty good," Colt admitted.

"Why don't we all sit together and share?" Reed offered. "The sandwiches are cut in halves. We can easily divvy them up."

No, no, no! Eliza scrambled to come up with a reasonable objection, but nothing came to mind. Other than spending the afternoon with Grant being akin to cruel and unusual punishment. But it wasn't as if she could say *that* out loud.

"Um… are you guys sure? Sharing isn't against Secret Picnic rules, is it?" Cassie met Eliza's gaze, as if sensing her unease.

Eliza flashed an appreciative smile, wishing she could hug her on the spot.

"Nah." Reed waved away her concern. "It's not that rigid. What do you guys say? Can you agree to play nice?"

"I'm game if you are," Colt told Jack.

"It's a deal." Jack extended his hand, and the two men shook on it.

"Honestly, you're both unbelievable." Penny gathered her thick auburn hair into a low ponytail, securing the tie with an agitated snap.

"I'll take that as a compliment." Colt gifted her his most irresistible grin.

"Don't," Penny mumbled under her breath. Although Colt didn't seem to notice.

Eliza tried to suppress the wailing alarm reverberating inside her head that screamed, *Run away! Run away, now!*

The short walk to Larkspur Meadow would only take ten to fifteen minutes, but they'd be out there most of the afternoon eating lunch, then participating in the traditional picnic games. Heaven forbid they got paired for the three-legged race! She had to find a way out of this nightmare before things got any worse.

"Mom, Uncle Luke said I could carry the picnic blanket." Ben proudly hoisted a rolled-up quilt more than twice his size over his slender shoulder, unaware that Luke walked behind him supporting most of the weight.

Dismayed, Eliza's gaze darted to Grant, then back to her son. Too late.

The day had now become much, *much* worse.

❦

*G*rant wasn't sure what he expected when he showed up for the Secret Picnic, but it sure wasn't to get roped into spending the day with Eliza.

Or her son.

Eliza seemed to be equally uncomfortable with the prospect. Without so much as a fleeting introduction, she relegated her son to eating lunch with his grandparents. The little guy looked mildly disappointed until Eliza told him he could invite a friend to go along.

As Grant watched him skip toward Hank and Sylvia Carter, a strange weight settled in his stomach. But he wasn't sure if the heaviness stemmed from relief or regret.

Or maybe a mixture of the two.

Grant never hid the fact that children were outside his comfort zone. But something about meeting Eliza's son intrigued him. Grant wondered how much he took after his mother. He clearly resembled her in appearance. But would he have the same infectious laugh? Or a similar kindhearted propensity to befriend every new kid in town? For some reason, it made Grant supremely happy to imagine Ben as the spitting image of Eliza. But whenever Grant's mind wandered to Ben's father, his brain shut off, as if guarding him from the inevitable pain such thoughts would cause.

Suddenly somber, Grant hung back as Colt took command of

the group, leading them to the trailhead just past Main Street. No one else seemed to mind Colt's assertiveness, but it irked Grant whenever he assumed control. Mostly because, when push came to shove, Colt shirked any ounce of responsibility. Even as a teen, he'd relished being in charge as long as it didn't cost him anything.

Which is why Colt's interest in Eliza baffled Grant to no end. Sure, she was as gorgeous and effervescent as ever. But the single mother angle didn't fit Colt's MO, not even a little bit.

"Are you glad to be home?" Penny fell into step beside him, disrupting his thoughts.

"Yeah, mostly." Grant smiled, grateful for the distraction. He'd always liked Penny Heart. She'd been quiet in school, perpetually glued to a book. An introvert himself, Grant could relate. Plus, she never fell for Colt's affable charm like the other girls. A fact Grant admired.

"How's business?" she asked. "You were pretty big news around town when your company was featured in that fancy San Francisco magazine. What was the headline again? 'Super' something."

"'Superstar Startup,'" Grant chuckled. "Believe me, I didn't pick the headline. Business is doing well, though. I landed my biggest client to date last week. Landon Morris with—"

"Morris Bio Tech!" Penny's eyes lit up in excitement. "I love what he's doing in the sustainability field. Plus, he's not bad on the eyes, either."

"Trust me, I work with the guy. I don't need the reminder." Grant grinned, holding up a protruding branch so she could step underneath.

"Hey, you didn't turn out so bad yourself." Laughing, she nudged him playfully.

Out of the corner of his eye, Grant caught Eliza stealing a glance over her shoulder. Did he detect a jealous glint in her eyes? Or was that his imagination? Grant wasn't sure. But a moment later, she stumbled, lurching forward.

Colt's hand shot out, slithering around her waist as though he'd been waiting all day for that precise scenario to present itself.

Grant's fists clenched at his sides.

Frowning, Penny followed his gaze. "Don't worry, I don't see that going anywhere. Eliza's too smart for that."

"It's none of my business." Grant uncurled his fingers, trying to appear calm and unconcerned.

"Sure. Of course. And not that you care, but I have a feeling it wouldn't take much effort for someone else to swoop in and steal her away."

Grant couldn't help notice the slight twitch in Penny's lips as she hid a smile. "Right. Well, I'll be sure to pass along the information if I run into someone who's interested."

"Great. You do that." She grinned broadly now, and Grant found himself smiling, too. But as he glanced up ahead, his optimism instantly faded.

Framed by vibrant dogwood branches, Eliza and Colt walked a little too close for comfort.

And given the enraptured way Eliza gazed up at her captivating walking companion, Grant wasn't so sure Penny was right.

CHAPTER 7

The tension in Eliza's shoulders subsided the second she flipped on the light switch and the warm glow flooded the bakery kitchen, reflecting off the brand-new equipment installed the day before.

She'd barely survived the Secret Picnic, and after a long, grueling day avoiding emotions she'd kept suppressed for years, she craved some serious baking time. Caring, compassionate Cassie had begged to come along to keep her company, but Eliza graciously turned down her offer.

This time, cupcakes and girl talk wouldn't be enough.

It was time for the *Playlist*.

After cinching her pink-and-white-pinstripe apron around her waist, Eliza pressed play on her iPhone. It took a moment to connect to the portable Wi-Fi speakers, but once the boisterous, peppy notes of "I've Got You Under My Skin" filled the room, the pressure drained from Eliza's throbbing temples.

Big band music had a knack for bolstering her spirits. Even though each trill of a trumpet invariably made her think of Grant.

They'd taken a swing dancing class their freshman year of

high school and fallen in love over the Lindy Hop and Charleston. At first, Grant worried he'd be mercilessly teased by the other boys. But, in the end, the kick ball change and triple step won out over his fears. In fact, Grant had excelled far beyond anyone else in the class. Even more than Eliza, who'd practically pirouetted out of the womb, thanks to her mother's obsession with the performing arts.

Humming along with Sammy Davis Jr., Eliza assembled the ingredients she'd brought from home, arranging them in order of use on the stainless steel countertop. In times like these, she never followed a recipe, preferring to let her instincts take over.

Tonight, she'd make a concoction she called Mochaccino Truffle Cookies, an idea that had floated around in the back of her mind for days. The main ingredients consisted of dark brown sugar, organic cacao powder, and finely ground espresso, courtesy of Frank Barrie.

By the time the rich, caffeine-packed cookies were in the oven, Sammy had crooned the first few notes of "Can't We Be Friends."

Closing her eyes, she swayed to the melody, escaping to her happy place. Before long, Eliza found herself spinning and twirling across the porcelain tile floor, grateful Luke hadn't finished the huge butcher block prep-island, leaving the wide-open space for her impromptu performance. To her surprise, all the steps came rushing back to her, as well-known and welcome as long-lost friends.

In all her life, Eliza had never felt as free as she had when she'd danced with Grant. The rush of being lifted into the air, twirled over his shoulder, or flipped upside down transcended words. It even transcended baking.

Caught up in the music and memories, it took Eliza a moment to register the sensation of someone's arm sliding around her waist.

As her eyes flew open, Eliza gasped. "Grant? What are you

doing here?" He was the last person Eliza expected to see. And the sight of him, standing in her sacred space, left her tongue-tied and completely off-kilter.

"Do you remember the Lindy Flip?" Grant gripped her hand with assurance, his indigo eyes glinting with hopeful expectation.

Her heart pounding inside her throat, Eliza couldn't speak. Grant's touch felt at once foreign and familiar, safe yet scintillating. She should run away, be anywhere in the world but in Grant's arms. But she didn't move. She *couldn't* move.

Without waiting for a response, Grant drew her against his hip, flung her into the air, and spun her around his back before returning her to solid ground as effortlessly as breathing.

"I guess you remember," he chuckled, pulling her back into a basic box step.

Eliza melted against him as they moved in perfect rhythm. Somehow, after what felt like a lifetime apart, they hadn't missed a single beat. How was it that her body could still anticipate his every movement? How was it that her mind told her to flee, but every fiber in her being told her to stay?

"Are you ready?" Grant held her gaze, a playful smile curling the edges of his mouth.

"For what?"

"The Charleston Flip."

Eliza's breath caught in her throat. They'd only successfully managed the flip once—after several weeks of practice. Grant had to be crazy to attempt it after all these years. And yet, Eliza's body eagerly fell into step, her feet kicking off the ground as Grant flipped her backward over his arm.

For a moment, time slowed down, and a gleeful laugh escaped Eliza's lips as she flew in the air, suddenly free from every burden weighing her down.

As she prepared to land, a crucial part of the maneuver flickered through her mind. But it was too late. Failing to remove her arm from around his shoulders, Eliza's limbs tangled with Grant's, sending them both crashing to the cold, hard tile.

Grant's chest broke her fall, and he released a winded groan.

"I'm so sorry! Are you okay?" she breathed, scanning his body for signs of injury.

"Minus the cracked ribs, I'm completely fine." Grant flashed a lopsided grin. "Guess we need a little more practice."

"Guess so." Smiling, she poked him in the ribs. "Are they really broken?"

"No, just my pride. And maybe my glasses…." Grant reached for his wire frames lying a few feet away.

As he slipped them on his face, Eliza giggled. "They're a little crooked."

"Remind me to wear contacts next time."

"We did pretty well, considering we haven't danced together since…" Eliza's words hung in the small space between them, disrupting the delicate bubble that had momentarily separated them from their painful past.

Grant cleared his throat, and Eliza scrambled to her feet. "So, um, why are you here?" She smoothed down her blouse, unsure if she meant here at the bakery or back in Poppy Creek.

"Cassie told me where I could find you." Grant pushed off the ground, wincing slightly as he stood. "I wanted to apologize."

"For what?" Eliza turned away, tucking wayward strands of hair behind her ears.

"For showing up at the Secret Picnic without telling you first. I honestly didn't think we'd wind up eating lunch together. But, in hindsight, I should have known it would be a possibility."

"You don't owe me an apology. It's your hometown, too. You can visit whenever you'd like."

"Oh. Well, I thought…" Grant hesitated, clearly not receiving the reaction he'd expected. "It doesn't bother you that I'm back?"

"Why would it?" Eliza managed to keep her voice steady even though her pulse ran rampant.

"I guess, because of our history…"

"That was a long time ago, Grant."

"Was it, Lizzy?"

Eliza's breath hitched as he evoked her nickname, and Grant seemed to notice the effect he had on her.

Taking a step toward her, he closed the gap between them.

Eliza backed away, pressing herself against the counter.

"So, being near me doesn't bother you at all?" Grant moved closer, until he stood mere inches from her face.

"No," she lied. "Does it bother you?" Why did her voice sound strained and breathy all of a sudden?

"Nope." Grant leaned in, his gaze flickering to her lips.

"Good." Eliza tried to create distance between them, digging the edge of the metal counter into her lower back.

"So, we can be friends?" Grant asked, his husky tone sending shivers skittering up her spine.

"Uh-huh," she murmured, although she'd stopped listening. His lips were so close, she felt his warm breath on her skin.

Instinctively, she tilted her head back, her eyelids drifting shut.

Then the kitchen timer wailed.

*

Startled, Grant took a step back, readjusting his glasses as Eliza slipped on a pair of oven mitts.

As he watched her yank open the oven door, thick clouds of steam wafting toward her flushed face, Grant tried to get a grip on his emotions. He wasn't sure what had come over him. When he'd arrived at the bakery, he had every intention of clearing the air between them. Possibly rekindling a friendship. Or at the very least, he'd hoped to get back on speaking terms.

But after they'd danced…

Grant's heartbeat quickened simply thinking about it. She fit so perfectly in his arms. And her scent! She smelled faintly of brown sugar, sweet and completely intoxicating. Grant couldn't think straight, wondering if her lips would taste the same.

Eliza slid the baking sheet on top of the stove and removed her oven mitts, gently grazing one of the pillowy mounds with her fingertip. "Perfect timing."

Grant would have dwelled on the double entendre, except the tempting aroma of dark chocolate flooded his senses. He noticed the faintest whiff of something else, too. But he couldn't quite put his finger on it. "Those smell incredible."

"Thanks. I hope they taste okay. It's a new recipe."

"You always were an artist in the kitchen." Grant smiled as memories of afternoons spent baking together filled his mind. "Do you need a taste tester? I'm happy to oblige."

"How generous of you," Eliza laughed.

"You know me. Always willing to help in the kitchen."

Eliza blushed, as if she recalled a few memories of her own. "They might need a little more time to set."

"Remember, the soft melt-in-your-mouth cookies are my favorite."

"I remember." Eliza averted her gaze, the pink tint to her cheeks deepening.

Yeesh. Being friends would be harder than he'd thought. Grant couldn't seem to manage going two seconds without referencing their shared history.

Grabbing a slotted spatula, Eliza slid a cookie onto a plate, handing it to Grant.

As he tore off a bite-size morsel, aromatic steam escaped from the center, making his mouth water. As soon as the rich, gooey chocolate collided with his taste buds, Grant released a groan.

"Is it good?" Eliza bounced on her tiptoes, her eyes shimmering expectantly.

"It's amazing," Grant mumbled, going in for a second bite.

"Hooray! I was really hoping it would be. I need plenty of

fresh, original desserts to add to the menu." Sidling up next to him, she pinched a bite-sized piece, plopping it in her mouth.

For a moment, Grant forgot all about the sugary perfection melting on his tongue, completely enamored with Eliza stealing food off his plate, just like old times.

"Oh, wow. They really *are* good." Eliza closed her eyes, a smile playing about her lips.

Grant chuckled. Only Eliza could praise her own work while still being endearingly humble and genuine. "Have you decided on a name?"

"I'm thinking of calling them Mochaccino Truffle Cookies."

"So *that's* what it is!" Grant snapped his fingers. "I couldn't figure out the extra kick. You added coffee to the batter?"

"Yep. It's kind of a special project I'm working on. An entire line of coffee-infused desserts for the bakery. What do you think?"

"I think it's genius." Grant polished off the rest of the cookie while Eliza scooped another one onto his plate.

Swiveling back to the counter, she set to work transferring the rest of the cookies to a cooling rack.

While he nibbled, Grant cast his gaze around the kitchen, noting how different everything looked from when it was Maggie's Place. The brick walls were now painted a soft, antique white, which contrasted pleasantly with the dark, ebony-stained shelves lined with baking tools and supplies. To honor the bakery's original color, Eliza and Cassie had added pops of retro pink with accent pieces like the KitchenAid mixer and vintage storage canisters.

"It's really amazing what you've done with the place, Lizzy. I mean it. All the improvements you've made look fantastic. Maggie must be really proud." Grant wanted to tell her that he was proud, but thought it might be awkward.

"Thanks. I hope so. Cassie and I have big plans for this place."

"Do you have a website?"

"No, not yet. Neither one of us is very tech savvy. And I'm not sure what advantage a website would have. No offense," she added sheepishly.

"None taken. Although, a website could be a great way to direct tourist traffic your way. Plus, you could add helpful features like a tab for customers to place custom or bulk orders."

"Huh. I never thought of that." Eliza's eyebrows rose in interest. But she quickly shook her head. "It's a nice idea, but I don't think Cassie or I should be taking on a project like that right now. Not with the renovations and the wedding. Maybe sometime down the road we can—"

"I'll do it," Grant blurted before thinking it through.

"That's very kind of you to offer, but—"

"I should have added that I'll do it for free. Consider it a favor from a friend. You did say you were fine being friends, right?" He grinned, hoping she couldn't hear the heavy thundering of his heartbeat.

"Yes..." Her brow furrowed as though considering it.

"There isn't any reason we can't work together, is there?" Even as he asked the question, Grant could think of a thousand reasons. His rekindled feelings being reason number one.

"None that I can think of."

Grant noticed Eliza wouldn't quite meet his gaze. "Great. Then it's a deal." He held out his hand to shake on it.

But as soon as her fingers slipped through his, sending shocks of electricity coursing up his arm, Grant realized he'd made a monumental mistake.

CHAPTER 8

*T*he gentle creaking of the porch swing acted like a soothing balm on Eliza's troubled heart. Ever since she'd agreed to let Grant build them a website, she'd been plagued with regrets. She needed to keep him far, far away. Not have an excuse to be in regular contact. And she *definitely* needed to make sure she never danced with him again.

Eliza tucked her feet beneath her on the swing while Cassie used her heels to gently rock them back and forth. Only a few months ago, Frank Barrie's front porch had been a desolate wasteland of cracked, splintered boards and layers of dust and grime. A single rocking chair teetered in the wind as if to say, *There's no room for you here.* Not that many people ever ventured past his uninviting entrance overgrown with wild blackberry brambles.

Now Frank's porch not only boasted two rocking chairs, but a wicker porch swing adorned with cushions hand-stitched by Beverly Lawrence. The sweet, soft-spoken librarian had breathed new life into Frank, slowly chipping away at his gruff exterior. Seeing the two lovebirds find each other so late in life gave Eliza hope, even if only fleeting.

"What's on your mind?" Cassie gently nudged Eliza's shoulder.

Stirred from her thoughts, Eliza sighed. "Grant came by the bakery last night. But then, you already know that."

"Sorry. He caught me off guard when he asked about you." Cassie scrunched up her nose, offering an apologetic grimace. "But I thought it wouldn't be the worst idea in the world for you two to talk."

Eliza picked at a loose thread on her ripped jeans, worn in by years of chasing after Ben. She still hadn't untangled her thoughts on last night's encounter. On one hand, she no longer lived with the guilt of believing Grant hated her for breaking up with him. On the other hand, the flutter in her stomach when he'd held her in his arms didn't bode well for protecting her heart.

"So," Cassie pressed. "What did he want to talk about?"

"He... wanted to apologize. For showing up at the picnic unannounced."

"That's thoughtful of him. Especially since you were the one who dumped him, right?"

Eliza winced. She hated the expression *dumped*, as if ending their four-year relationship equated to tossing a used cupcake liner in the trash. "It was very thoughtful. He also..." She hesitated to share the news, knowing once she said it out loud, there was no going back. "He also offered to build us a website. For free."

Cassie's eyes widened, and the swing came to an abrupt halt as she planted her feet on the ground. "Really?"

"Yep."

"Liza, that's amazing!" Cassie squealed.

"What's amazing?" Frank pushed through the screen door, followed by Beverly. He set a tray of coffee mugs on the small wicker table, steam curling from their rims.

Beverly placed a plate of tea sandwiches beside the tray before settling in one of the rocking chairs with a worn copy of *Northanger Abbey.*

"Grant Parker is going to build us a website for the café," Cassie announced. "Isn't that fantastic?"

"Oh, how exciting!" Beverly beamed, removing a delicately embroidered bookmark.

"A website?" Frank grunted, handing Cassie one of the stoneware mugs. "What do you need one of those for?"

Cassie smiled as she eagerly accepted the cup of coffee, drawing it close to her face to inhale the aroma. "For exposure, mostly. Plus, websites can offer a lot of nice features. Like making it easier for people to place custom orders for weddings, birthdays, and anniversaries. What if you wanted to request a heart-shaped cookie with Beverly's name on it? With a website, you could do it in two clicks."

Frank flushed as he handed the second mug to Eliza. "Or I could pick up the phone and call you."

Eliza giggled. "Give up, Cass. Frank isn't your target market."

"I think you're right," Cassie chuckled, bringing the rim to her lips. "What are we tasting today?"

"This is the new blend we roasted yesterday."

Cassie's eyes brightened. "The blend of Central American coffees?"

Frank nodded, passing a delicate floral teacup to Beverly. Eliza didn't miss the small smile on Frank's lips as their fingers grazed.

"Oh, my goodness," Cassie gushed after swallowing her first sip. "Frank, you're a genius. You've really brought out the rich cocoa undertones. It'll go beautifully in Eliza's coffee-infused recipes."

"Careful, Cassie," Beverly chided with a teasing lilt. "He already has a big head. Don't go giving him too much praise."

Frank turned to Beverly with an affectionate gaze. "How can I have a big head when you won't touch a drop of my coffee?"

Glancing at Cassie and Eliza, he added, "But she'll drink her weight in fancy teas. You'd think a head librarian would've heard of a little something called the Boston Tea Party."

Beverly tipped her head back, her twinkling laugh lighting her pale-blue eyes. "My, you're ornery today."

"When isn't he?" Cassie smirked.

"I'll keep that comment in mind when you ask for seconds," Frank grumbled playfully, easing himself into the other rocking chair.

"Eliza, how's Ben doing in school?" Beverly asked, switching topics. "Your mother mentioned he's been having some trouble lately."

"He has," Eliza sighed. "Which is strange, because he does so well when we're studying at home. But Daphne says when she calls on him in class, he just stares blankly at the board and refuses to answer. It's not like Ben to be stubborn or uncooperative."

"Hmm... that is curious. I checked out some books for him at the library that might help. Let me go get them for you." Beverly rose and set the teacup back on the tray.

"I'll come with you," Cassie offered, popping up from the porch swing. "I'm ready for my refill and I don't dare ask *you know who.*"

Eliza suppressed another giggle as Frank dragged himself out of the rocking chair, his steel-gray eyes twinkling. "Sit down. I'll get it. The last thing I need is you rummaging around the house without supervision."

"Yes, because who knows what I'd find," Cassie teased. "Another best-selling book you wrote and didn't tell me about?"

Frank's robust laughter followed him and Beverly through the screen door.

Eliza waited until it swung shut behind them before asking, "How *is* the book coming along?"

"Really well, actually. Frank can be stubborn, but we make a pretty good team."

Eliza's heart swelled with happiness for her friend. When Frank had offered Cassie the opportunity to cowrite the revised edition of his coffee roasting manifesto, *The Mariposa Method*, he had inadvertently given Cassie the financial freedom to pursue her lifelong dream of opening a coffeehouse. Not to mention helping Eliza achieve her own entrepreneurial aspirations. But more than that, Frank had become like a surrogate grandfather to Cassie, and watching the two of them together made Eliza want to weep with joy.

"Speaking of Frank..." Eliza started, her throat constricting with emotion. "Have you asked him yet?"

Cassie shook her head. "No, the timing hasn't been right. We've been so busy with the book and creating blends for the café that the wedding has barely come up."

"What about your mom? Has she responded to any of your messages?"

"No." Cassie bit her bottom lip, an anxious crease etched across her forehead. "And I'm starting to worry. She's fallen off the map plenty of times before, but this time feels different. When I dropped her off at the rehab center right before Christmas, I honestly thought she wanted to turn her life around. There was this intense look in her eyes like..." With a heavy sigh, Cassie ran her fingers through her hair. "Oh, I don't know how to explain it. But it felt... *real.* Like she wasn't pretending this time. Then... well, you know the rest."

Sadly, Eliza did know. After getting Cassie's hopes up, Donna bailed on the program in less than forty-eight hours. The only silver lining in the ugly ordeal was that Cassie had received the huge $15,000 fee back, minus the thousand dollar deposit.

"I've thought about hiring a private investigator to find her," Cassie admitted softly. "But then I wonder if that's too extreme.

What do you think? Have you ever thought about hiring someone to find Ben's dad?"

Startled, Eliza flinched before quickly shaking her head. "No. Never."

But then, Eliza didn't need anyone to locate Ben's father.

She already knew exactly where to find him.

G rant inhaled the stifling scent of out-of-date encyclopedias and lingering Old Spice, releasing the breath in a single, sharp exhale as he mentally prepared for the conversation ahead. In hindsight, he shouldn't have arranged to have the video call with Landon Morris in his father's office. The formidable walls lined with heavy oak bookcases closed in around him, and the pervasive ticking of the grandfather clock pounded in his ears. Grant hated everything about the imposing space, especially the massive mahogany desk and all the broken promises it represented.

"Hey, man. Long time no see." Landon's jovial grin filled Grant's laptop screen.

Grant tried not to wince at Landon's offhand comment. He realized skipping town at the beginning of the Morris Bio Tech project didn't make the best impression. While he could pass off some of the more menial tasks to his team members, Landon expected Grant to work on the design personally. Grant couldn't very well admit he'd barely even started.

"Yeah, I'm sorry about that. I had to make a last-minute trip back home."

"No worries. You can do your job anywhere, right? I trust you to get it done."

Tugging on his collar, Grant forced a smile. "Great. I'll have a preliminary design ready by the end of the week. I'll send you a Google invite with the date and time of our next call."

"Looking forward to it."

They discussed a few more project details, followed by casual chitchat before saying goodbye.

Closing his laptop, Grant struggled to breathe, guilt pressing on his chest. He should be prioritizing this account. By now, his portfolio should be filled with dozens of sketches and watercolor paintings, ready to dazzle Landon with his creative, outside-the-box ideas. After all, that's why Landon hired him. No one else combined classical art with high-tech design, cultivating a unique look that set his clients apart from the rest of their industry. Days ago, Grant couldn't stop thinking about the project, dreaming up concepts that had even surprised himself. Now his thoughts were consumed by something else.

Or rather, *someone* else.

"Oh, you're still here." Stan paused in the doorway, hesitating as though unsure if he should enter or retreat.

"I just finished. I'll get out of your way." Grant stood, collecting his things.

"Wait." Stan cleared his throat, a look of discomfort shadowing his features.

Grant raised an eyebrow, waiting for his father to continue.

Shifting his feet, Stan scanned the room as if looking for a topic of conversation tucked between the stacks of accounting textbooks. His gaze settled on an antique chess set resting on an accent table near the bay window. "Care for a game?"

"Of chess?" Grant couldn't remember his dad ever asking him to play chess. In fact, as a child, he'd been forbidden to touch the heavy marble pieces.

"I have backgammon, too," Stan offered. "If you'd prefer that."

Grant scratched his jawline. What exactly was happening?

For a brief moment, he considered saying yes. But instantly thought better of it. He'd waited his whole life for his dad to show interest in him. Grant wouldn't get his hopes up now. "Maybe some other time."

"Sure. Of course." Stan stared at the floor, coughing into his hand. "I'll, uh, just get my book. I think I left it... Ah, yes. There it is." Crossing the room, Stan plucked an autobiography of George Washington off the side table by his armchair. "Don't rush on my account. I'll read in the den. I'm glad to see this place getting some use again." Tipping his head, he shuffled out of the room, leaving Grant slightly winded.

The entire exchange baffled him, but Grant didn't want to linger in the stuffy room any longer than necessary. He gathered his laptop and sketchbook before tucking his cell phone into his back pocket.

Taking one last glance around the space, Grant noticed the bookcases looked a little dustier than he remembered. He supposed now that his father was mostly retired, he didn't have much use for them. Strange, considering Grant could hardly recall a time when his father wasn't locked inside his office. True, it was much worse in New York when he handled the accounting for several prominent hedge fund managers. But even after relocating to Poppy Creek, Stan kept busy, splitting his time between tax preparation for locals and working remotely for a few of his previous clients.

Bitterness wriggled around Grant's heart, and he shook his head, dismissing the toxic thoughts before they took hold.

Grant needed to start Landon's project, but he would never be able to harness his creativity surrounded by so many painful memories.

Moving to the back porch, Grant arranged his laptop and sketchbook on the bistro table overlooking his mother's magazine-worthy garden that abutted a thick grove of white pines and mountain hemlock. Grant relished the seclusion, but Harriet constantly complained about her battle with poison oak, a rash-inducing shrub that pervaded the area. Another way in which his mother had never learned to embrace their move.

Serenaded by two cardinals perched on the patio umbrella

overhead, Grant opened his laptop and clicked the file for Morris Bio Tech. But after staring blankly at the screen for several minutes, Grant closed the lid and flipped open his sketchbook.

Over the next two hours, the ideas poured from his fingertips, creating magic on the page. Albeit for a completely different project. The desire to show Eliza his designs for her website and get her input consumed Grant, filling him with pure, unbridled excitement.

Her face flashed into his mind—the uncertain yet burning glint in her eyes from last night. For a moment, Grant thought he could put their troubled past behind him. Maybe he could forgive the way she'd broken his heart more than once. First, when she'd abruptly ended things, without so much as an explanation. Then, when he'd found out she was having someone else's child. How had his mother put it? *Some tourist passing through town.*

The words had dripped from his mother's lips like acid, eating away at his soul. At first, Grant hadn't believed her. It didn't sound like Eliza. She didn't have flings. And she'd never wanted kids. Neither of them had. But if they'd ever changed their minds, Grant had assumed they would take that leap together.

But maybe he didn't know Eliza as well as he thought he did.

CHAPTER 9

*B*right streaks of light streamed through the bakery windows, reflecting off Grant's laptop screen, making it difficult for Eliza to concentrate.

"What do you think?" Grant glanced in her direction, his intense blue eyes bright and expectant.

Eliza blinked, momentarily distracted by the wisp of hair draped across his forehead. To her dismay, she had an irresistible urge to brush it aside and run her fingers through his thick, unruly waves.

Biting her lip, Eliza forced her attention to the table where Grant had set up his laptop and laid out several sketches and watercolors of various logo designs and branding ideas.

"I think..." she began, then hesitated. His work was exquisite. But spending time together was starting to get... complicated.

Filling Eliza's pause, Cassie gushed, "They're stunning! Truly gorgeous. In fact, I want to frame this one on the wall." Cassie lifted a watercolor depicting a matching mug and saucer with a vibrant red poppy resting on the edge of the plate next to a French-style macaron. Based on the coloring, Eliza suspected the flavor might be café au lait—a tiny yet telling detail that made her emotions even more conflicted.

"I'm glad you like them." Pushing his glasses up the bridge of his nose, Grant stole a glance at Eliza. "What do you think?"

I think... I think... Eliza furrowed her brow, trying to focus. What cologne was he wearing? It smelled spicy and faintly sweet, like gingerbread dipped in dark chocolate.

"Liza?" Cassie prompted, tugging Eliza from her scent-induced trance.

"Oh, um..." Flustered, she forced her attention to the design Cassie held in her hand. The striking red of the poppy paired beautifully with the soft, robin's-egg blue of the mug and saucer. And as Eliza peered closer at the petals, she noticed brushstrokes of cerise and magenta, melding her favorite color with Cassie's. "It's perfect," she murmured, a slight catch in her throat.

Her gaze met Grant's, and a current of awareness rippled between them.

Grant removed his glasses, wiping them on the hem of his T-shirt. "Great. So, I was thinking the website layout could—"

"Mom! Mom! Guess what?" Ben barged through the front door, waving a piece of paper as though he'd found a treasure map.

Luke strolled into the bakery behind him, an affectionate grin on his face. "Someone has great news."

Eliza cast a furtive glance in Grant's direction before returning her focus to her son. "Oh, yeah? Let's hear it." She smiled, although her pulse skittered anxiously.

"Look! I got an A!" Ben shoved the paper into her hands, beaming from ear to ear.

Eliza's heart swelled at the look of pure joy on his face. After months of poor grades and concerned letters from his teacher, this one A had brought the light back into his eyes. And it came as no surprise to Eliza that it was the result of an art project.

She gazed fondly at the forest of trees surrounding a large body of water in the center. "Willow Lake?"

Ben nodded, his cheeks flushed with pride.

"It's beautiful, Bug." Eliza used his special nickname, and his grin grew even wider.

"Great composition." Grant stood, peering at the painting over Eliza's shoulder.

His nearness made the back of her neck tingle.

"You have an artistic eye," Grant told Ben with a smile.

"Wow, Ben. That's quite the compliment coming from Grant." Luke nudged Ben on the shoulder. "Grant went to school for art. He knows his stuff."

"Really?" Ben's dark eyes doubled in size as he gazed at Grant with newfound interest.

"I majored in graphic design with a minor in fine art."

Ben pointed at the artwork on the table. "Did you make these?"

"Yep. It's some stuff I'm working on for your mom and Cassie. Want to see?"

"Yeah!" Ben dumped his backpack on the floor and scrambled onto the chair eagerly.

Luke slid an arm around Cassie's waist, planting a kiss on her forehead. "Think I can get a licorice latte in exchange for hanging that mug rack?"

Cassie giggled. "Eliza might even throw in a couple cookies if you hang the menu board, too."

"Is that so?" Luke chuckled. "You ladies drive a hard bargain."

Eliza attempted a faint smile, but she couldn't focus on their banter.

Not when Grant had all of his attention focused on her son.

A permanent smile adorned Grant's face as he showed Ben how he diluted the red paint to make pink, then added a touch of blue to alter the hue. Seeing the way Ben's eyes illuminated with excitement stirred something inside Grant.... A desire to pass on everything he knew to someone who shared the same passion for art. In some ways, Ben's eagerness to learn reminded Grant of himself when he was that age.

As Grant hung out with Ben while Luke, Cassie, and Eliza worked on various projects around the bakery, he had no concept of the passage of time. Completely immersed in showing Ben various techniques, Grant rarely diverted his attention. And when he did, it was purely to sneak glimpses of Eliza.

Standing barefoot on the back counter draped with a drop cloth, Eliza stretched on her tiptoes to reach the chalkboard overhead, hand-printing the bakery's new menu. With her silky blond hair gathered in a messy bun, Grant admired the slender curve of her neck as she tilted her head to the side, surveying her work. "How does it look?"

"Perfect!" Cassie nodded her approval, then frowned. "Wait... something is missing." Turning to Grant, she asked, "Do you think you could add some artwork? A cup of coffee, a cupcake, stuff like that? Oh, and can you draw a big square, like on a calendar? We can list a different daily special inside."

"Great idea. I'd be happy to." Leaving Ben with a color wheel assignment, Grant kicked off his flip-flops and hoisted himself onto the counter.

He took the piece of chalk from Eliza, his heart undulating as their fingers grazed. Even after all this time, her touch left him woozy.

Trying to steady his pulse, Grant studied the menu, looking for inspiration. The coffee side of the chalkboard would be easy. A few coffee beans sprinkled here and there, a cappuccino topped with foam.... But when it came to the desserts, Grant could be more creative.

He scanned the options, deciding he'd draw one of Maggie's enormous cinnamon rolls. A mulberry pie with a lattice crust would also make for an appealing design. What else? His gaze traveling the list of desserts, Grant froze as he landed on the second to last item—tiramisu cheesecake. One half of that combo was Grant's all-time favorite indulgence.

His pulse quickened, although the reaction seemed foolish. It wasn't as if Eliza had included it simply for his sake. Still, he stole a glance in her direction.

She stared intently at the chalk dust covering her hands, a faint blush tinting her cheeks.

Grant fought the urge to point out the tiramisu cheesecake and gauge her reaction, but before he even had the chance, Eliza hopped off the counter.

"Hey, Cass," she called out, a nervous trill to her voice. "Is the espresso machine still on? I could really use a latte."

"Of course." Cassie set down one end of a shelf she was holding for Luke, telling him, "I'll be right back."

As Grant refocused his attention on the chalkboard, he couldn't help wondering if he still had an effect on Eliza. Did he make her breath catch in her throat? Did he send goosebumps tingling across her skin? Not a day had gone by when he hadn't thought of her at least once. Sometimes, he recalled a certain phrase or mannerism, like the way her nose crinkled when she laughed. Other times, a faint memory would push its way to the forefront of his mind, making his arms ache to hold her. She'd never stopped being a part of his life, no matter how hard he'd tried to block her out.

A few minutes later, Grant had completed a detailed sketch of a layered cheesecake, complete with a raspberry and mint leaf perched on top. He'd decided to make one slice missing, set on its own plate nearby.

"Grant, that's perfect!" Cassie clasped her hands together, clutching them against her heart. "Don't you think so, Liza?"

Eliza gazed over the top of a tall glass mug piled high with thick, white froth.

Their eyes locked, and Grant nearly lost his footing at the intense look that passed between them.

Eliza parted her lips, but before a single word escaped, Luke said, "It looks great, but I think you might have smudged something. Is that supposed to say goose pie?"

Cassie giggled. "I think it's supposed to say goose*berry* pie. Although goose pie doesn't sound any more ridiculous than mincemeat pie, and we're both fond of that."

Cassie and Luke exchanged a dreamy, doe-eyed gaze, and Grant suspected there was a story behind her comment. A pang of envy shot through him. He missed stolen glances and the intimacy of inside jokes he and Eliza used to share.

He cleared his thoughts with a cough. "Sorry, I'll fix it."

"It's okay, I'll do it." Eliza set down her latte. "So the lettering is consistent."

Grant reached out his hand to help her up, and Eliza hesitated a moment before accepting it.

As he lifted her onto the counter, Grant tugged with a little more force than necessary, nearly pulling her into his arms.

Eliza braced herself with one palm against his chest, and Grant felt the heat from her touch all the way through his T-shirt.

Briskly stepping aside, he silently scolded himself. He needed to get a grip. He couldn't go weak in the knees every time she glanced his way or made the slightest contact. They were friends, nothing more. Which meant he needed to get a handle on his attraction before he made a complete fool out of himself.

"Looking good, guys." Colt breezed into the bakery, instantly setting Grant on edge. Ever since Colt announced his interest in

Eliza, he couldn't look at the guy without his fingers curling into fists.

Colt zeroed in on Grant's drawing. "Cake?"

"Tiramisu cheesecake," Grant corrected, as if it mattered.

"Creative. But give me regular old New York style any day."

"I suppose vanilla is your favorite ice cream flavor?" Eliza smirked, staring down at him from her perch on the counter.

"Maybe. What's yours? Chocolate?"

"Tied with strawberry."

"Perfect. Then we can share a scoop of Neapolitan ice cream on our date tomorrow night."

Grant's blood chilled, and his gaze darted to Eliza.

She looked equally shocked. "Our what?"

"Our date. The Secret Picnic didn't count. I'd like to take you on a proper date. Just the two of us. Are you free tomorrow night?"

Grant held his breath, waiting for Eliza's response. It took every ounce of self-control not to shout *Not a chance* on her behalf.

"Yes…" she said slowly.

"Great. I'll pick you up at seven."

And in a matter of seconds, the day went from being one of the best in Grant's life…

To one of the worst.

CHAPTER 10

*D*aylight filtered through tall stained glass windows, diffusing muted colors throughout the cluttered room. Squinting, Eliza did her best to focus on the dusty shelves overflowing with a random assortment of trinkets and collectibles. While she rarely ventured into the back storage room of Thistle & Thorn for fear she'd never come out, today the chaos served as a welcome distraction from the horror plastered across Penny's face.

"Why on earth did you agree to a date with Colt?" Penny gaped at her from behind a stack of multicolored depression-era glassware.

"He caught me off guard." Eliza squirmed, deciding not to mention her state of panic over the surge of unwanted chemistry between her and Grant.

"Can you tell him you've changed your mind?"

"I don't know...." Eliza caressed a delicate rose-colored vase, drawn to the subtle pink hue. "Wouldn't that seem kind of mean on such short notice? Besides, it's only one date. What's the worst that could happen?"

"We could be picking out centerpieces for your wedding with Colt," Penny said with a derisive snort.

Eliza laughed. "Not likely. He's not the marrying type." She set down the vase and lifted an amber apothecary jar. "Speaking of centerpieces, let's go with the amber-colored glass. It's more Cassie. And I think it'll look beautiful with the flowers Reed picked out for the floral arrangements."

"Good point," Penny agreed. "I can't wait until Cassie sees the surprise he's been working on!"

"Me, too! Did you notice the way he guarded his greenhouse the last time we stopped by? I thought for sure she'd be suspicious."

"She's in love. Love makes you oblivious. Or so I'm told," Penny added with a shrug.

Eliza studied her friend over the rim of a crystal candy dish. To her knowledge, Penny had never been in love. Although she'd had her fair share of interested suitors, no one seemed to tempt her away from her collection of treasured novels. But maybe Penny had the right idea. Book boyfriends were far less likely to break your heart than real ones.

"Okay," Eliza sighed. "I'll call Colt and tell him the date is off."

"I think you're dodging a bullet."

Digging her phone out of her back pocket, Eliza pulled up Colt's number. As it rang, she sidestepped a leather steamer trunk and ducked behind a Tudor-style armoire, out of Penny's earshot.

"Hey!" Colt's delight reverberated through the speakers.

"Hi." Eliza sucked in a breath, nervously fidgeting with the fringed tassel of a vintage lampshade that still carried the faint aroma of moth balls and pipe tobacco. "Listen. About tonight…"

"Don't tell me you can't make it," Colt groaned.

"It's just that Ben has this project due tomorrow and—"

"Then we'll postpone."

Gathering her courage, Eliza inhaled the musty scent permeating the room, then slowly released it. "The truth is, I'm not sure going on a date is such a good idea."

A long pause filled the silence, and Eliza's stomach tumbled with nerves.

"Okay, I can respect that," Colt said at last, surprising Eliza with his sincerity. "Let's not think of it as a date, then. Just two friends hanging out. We'll get a bite to eat. Maybe some ice cream afterward."

A small smile tugged at her lips. "Sounds an awful lot like a date to me."

"I'll only let you get one scoop. Plain cone, not waffle. And definitely no sprinkles."

Eliza giggled. "Gee, you're a stingy friend, aren't you?"

Colt's deep, rich laugh rumbled through the phone, causing her heart to flutter. "I'll pick you up tomorrow night. Same time."

"See you then."

After exchanging goodbyes, Eliza ended the call slightly breathless.

What had just happened?

And even more importantly, how would she explain it to Penny?

***

The time span between the moment Colt asked out Eliza to the evening after their date had almost killed Grant. He'd contemplated tying himself to a chair to keep from skulking about town with the intent of sabotaging their date. Instead, he'd focused his pent-up energy working on Eliza's website. Fortunately, it also happened to be the perfect excuse to stop by her house. And if he received an update on her date, so be it. He wasn't one to pry.

Yeah, right....

Who was he kidding? He'd definitely pry.

A surge of fond memories washed over Grant as he mounted the broad porch steps leading up to the periwinkle-blue farmhouse.

The Carter residence had always been like a second home to Grant. After school, they would often split their time between homework around the kitchen island—devouring whatever baked good Eliza had concocted for them—and helping Hank at his hardware store.

To his surprise, Grant noticed most of the landscaping had remained the same. A brick pathway Sylvia had dubbed The Red Carpet cut through a lush English garden, ushering visitors to the house. Long strands of bistro lights canopied the lawn, casting an ethereal glow Sylvia fondly referred to as "stage lighting."

Grant smiled at the memory, grateful Eliza had inherited her mother's warm, vivacious personality, without all of her other idiosyncrasies.

However, the more Grant surveyed the familiar surroundings, the more the similarities bothered him. As if the unaltered details hid the fact that everything inside the house—at least, everything that mattered—had completely changed.

Adjusting the strap of his leather portfolio strung over his shoulder, Grant rapped on the front door.

Seconds later, Sylvia greeted him on the other side, her broad smile momentarily distracting Grant from her frilly feather-trimmed house coat.

"Did I... come at a bad time?" Grant faltered, trying not to gawk at the ostentatious plumes of her matching slippers. "Why, Grant Parker! Aren't you a sight for sore eyes?" Sylvia pulled him into a hug so tight, Grant's glasses nearly popped off his face. "Don't be silly. Come in! Come in! To what do we owe the pleasure?"

"I was hoping to show Eliza some new ideas I had for her

website." As Grant crossed the threshold, familiar sights and scents bombarded his senses. The plush, whimsical furnishings befitting the dressing room of a headlining actress, complete with framed movie posters. And the mouthwatering aroma of vanilla bean and warm chocolate chip cookies.

Sylvia's smile faded. "Oh, honey. Didn't you hear? She's on a date with Colt tonight."

"I thought that was last night?" Grant's gaze flickered around the entryway, as though Eliza would appear any second.

"Well, it was. Except Ben had a big project due this morning so they postponed it to tonight. That child runs her life, you know."

Sylvia laughed but Grant didn't know what to say. Feeling foolish, he took a step toward the door. "Sorry to bother you. I'll—"

"Grant!" Ben's bright, exuberant greeting carried down the hallway as he skipped toward them. "You're here!"

Something about the boy's excitement in seeing him tugged at Grant's heartstrings. "Hey, Ben. I stopped by to show your mom something, but I'm on my way out."

"Do you have to go?" Ben's dark eyes pleaded with him to stay. "I have something to show you."

"Oh, um…" Grant hesitated, caught off guard by the invitation.

"Yes, please stay," Sylvia encouraged. "In fact, you should join us for dinner. Hank would love to see you."

"Thank you, but I couldn't impose."

"Don't be silly!" Sylvia waved her hand with a dramatic flourish. "I always make plenty. And goodness knows there's enough dessert around here to feed the entire cast of *Les Mis*."

Grant chuckled as Sylvia's affable banter put him at ease. "Okay, then. I'd be happy to stay for dinner. Thank you."

"Hooray!" Ben cheered, grabbing his hand. "Come see what I made. I used the color wheel, just like you showed me."

As Ben tugged him down the hallway, Grant marveled at the sensation of Ben's small hand in his, as though one simple gesture carried an unspoken pact of trust and confidence.

One Grant realized he would do almost anything not to break.

CHAPTER 11

*E*liza ended the night thankful Colt had insisted on their "non-date." If only because it confirmed, once and for all, that they had no future together.

Not only had she spent the entire evening at the Buttercup Bistro wishing she'd shared the plate of chili lime sweet potato fries with Grant, Colt seemed every bit as impulsive and irresponsible as Penny claimed.

In the years since high school, he'd lived in five different cities and had dozens of jobs ranging from skydiving instructor to exotic car salesman. He had a pilot's license, but rarely flew. Learned French, but never spoke a word. Spent a year in culinary school, but didn't cook.

The man was an enigma. And one Eliza had zero interest in figuring out.

Ben needed stability. For his sake, she couldn't fall for anyone who didn't have plans to stay in Poppy Creek. A rule that extended to San Francisco–based web designers, too....

Colt rolled to a stop beside Eliza's Honda in the driveway and killed the engine.

Eliza suppressed a groan, dreading the awkward goodbye.

Colt reached for the door handle.

"You don't have to walk me inside." Eliza hastily unbuckled her seat belt.

"This may not be a date, but I'm not a monster," Colt laughed, striding around the car to open the passenger door for her.

Her heart thrumming nervously, Eliza trudged beside him to the front porch.

The bistro lights shimmering overhead lit their path, a strong breeze swinging the strands back and forth creating curious shadows across the brick walkway. Eliza shivered, wishing she'd thought to bring a lightweight sweater. *Oh, well.* The evening would be over soon enough. Gnawing on her pink-tinted bubblegum lip balm, she pondered what she'd say if Colt asked for a second date.

"Here's fine." Eliza paused before the bottom step, turning to face him. "Thanks for a fun evening."

"My pleasure." His mouth quirked in an adorably crooked grin, Colt took a step toward her. "We should do it again sometime."

Eliza parted her lips, ready to let him down gently.

But Colt must have misread the signal.

Taking another step closer, he dipped his chin, lowering his lips to hers.

⁂

*A*s Sylvia walked him to the door, Grant clutched Ben's painting in his hand as though he were holding a price-less Monet, lightly grazing his thumb over the smears of red paint in the upper-right hand corner that spelled out his name.

"Thank you for dinner. I had a great time."

"No, thank *you!*" Sylvia gushed, pressing a hand to her heart. "Seeing the way Ben lit up when you showed him that watercolor trick where you wet the paper first..." She released a dramatic sigh. "Well, that made my heart so happy. The poor boy's had a rough time at school lately, so I know tonight meant a lot to him."

"He's a great kid." The words slipped from Grant's lips before he realized it. And he was surprised by how adamantly he meant them.

"He is. All thanks to that incredible mom of his. And no thanks to his delinquent father," Sylvia scowled.

"He doesn't have any contact with Ben?" The thought sent a jolt of fury blazing through Grant's chest.

"No. And he completely fell off the face of the earth, far as I can tell. Liza doesn't like to talk about it. She loves Ben, don't get me wrong. But I know that moment in her life fills her with regret. She still beats herself up about it. But heartache makes people do stupid things. And she was never more heartbroken than when she broke up..." Sylvia's eyes grew wide, as though she'd only recently been made aware of Grant's presence. Her mouth snapped shut and her face turned a shocking shade of puce. "You know what... I almost forgot to box up some desserts for you to take home. I'll be right back."

Before Grant could respond, Sylvia turned on her heel and scurried toward the kitchen.

Grant lingered in the entryway, his stomach wrenching as he mulled over Sylvia's admission. He knew all about regret. A single haunting memory from one weak moment frequented his thoughts daily.

Fidgeting with his keys, Grant paced the Persian-style runner, pausing when movement outside the window caught his eye. As the two figures came into focus, illuminated by the porch light, Grant's keys clattered to the floor.

He watched, his heartbeat raging against his rib cage as Colt leaned toward Eliza, lowering his mouth to hers.

"Don't eat too many of these tonight." Sylvia's warning tore Grant's gaze from the window. "They're full of caffeine and will keep you awake for hours."

When she noticed Grant's blanched features, Sylvia squinted in concern. "Are you all right? You look like Jimmy Stewart in *Rear Window* when he witnesses the murder."

"I... I'm fine," Grant stammered, stooping to grab his keys. "Thank you for the dessert." With shaky hands, he accepted the Tupperware, careful not to smudge Ben's painting, and turned toward the door. But how could he go outside after what he'd seen?

"Good night, dear." Sylvia shot him one last quizzical glance before retreating to the kitchen.

Grant stood facing the solid oak door, unable to open it, knowing what awaited him on the other side. Any minute now, Eliza would come bounding up the front steps, her cheeks flushed, and an *I've just been kissed* glaze in her dazzling eyes. Grant couldn't bear to see it. But what choice did he have?

Gripping the nickel-plated doorknob, Grant forced his wrist to turn, and his feet to step out into the brisk night air. But he moved slowly, with an apprehensive gait.

The low hum of a car engine and crunch of tires on the gravel drive drew his attention to the one spot he'd been too afraid to look.

Eliza stood at the bottom of the steps, completely alone.

Turning toward the house, she blinked in surprise. "Grant?"

"Hey." Grant hoped the waver in his voice didn't betray his heartache.

"What are you doing here?" She climbed the steps to meet him on the porch.

"I, uh, came to show you a few more ideas for the website but... you weren't home." *Obviously. Dummy. Get it together.*

"Right." Eliza glanced at the ground, tucking a strand of hair behind her ear.

Attempting to fill the uncomfortable silence, Grant blurted, "Look what Ben made me."

Eliza's gaze flickered to her son's painting, then to Grant's face. She wore an unreadable expression, but her dark eyes shone with a wistful, almost pensive glint. "It's you," she murmured in a voice so soft, Grant barely heard her.

"What did you say?"

"It's you," she repeated, reaching out to graze the edge of the paper with her fingertips, before jerking her hand back to her side.

Grant glanced at the painting, focusing on the blurry figure with black curly hair and rectangular framed glasses. He attempted a rueful smile. "My first portrait. What do you think? Do I have what it takes to be an art model?"

A small smirk tugged at the corner of Eliza's mouth. "Maybe for Picasso."

"Ouch." Grant chuckled, feeling a weight release around his heart. Why couldn't it always be like this? The two of them together, comfortable and uncomplicated?

"Well, it's late...." Eliza shuffled closer to the door, and taking the hint, Grant sidestepped out of the way.

Ask her about the date.... The thought pushed its way to the forefront of Grant's mind, but he quickly dismissed it. He didn't need to ask. He'd seen Colt lean in for the kiss. Why would he torture himself with the details?

"Good night," Eliza called over her shoulder, one hand on the doorknob.

"Good night, Lizzy."

Grant stood on the porch and watched her duck inside, closing the door behind her.

The click of the latch, though barely more than a whisper, sounded deafening in his ears.

If he'd ever had a chance to win Eliza back, it was long gone now.

CHAPTER 12

*T*he warm late spring air buzzed with excitement as half the town converged at the Poppy Creek trailhead, clothed in swimsuits and water shoes.

"Can you explain the Creek Walk to me?" Cassie asked, her features scrunched in confusion. "Luke's been talking about it all week, but I have to say… the way he describes it doesn't make any sense. And it doesn't sound anything like a walk."

Eliza and Penny laughed.

"That's because it isn't." Eliza grinned, fastening her hair into a messy bun on top of her head. "At least, not anymore."

"The Poppy Creek Historical Society started it decades ago as a way to commemorate the town founders who had to cross the creek when they first settled here," Penny explained. "According to folklore, the creek was several feet wide in those days, and crossing with all of their supplies was no easy feat. Now, since the creek is so narrow, we walk downstream instead of across."

Cassie frowned. "If it's just a walk, why have Luke and Colt been warming up all morning? From their competitive banter, you'd think they were about to run a marathon."

Eliza leaned into a deep lunge, stretching her arms over her head. "Because traditions in Poppy Creek have a way of escalating. Several years ago, a few of the guys decided to turn it into a race. Now it's a free-for-all. Some of us still walk it. But some compete to be the Creek Walk king."

"Or queen," Penny added. "Sadie won three years ago."

"That's true. The look on Jack's face when she sprinted past him at the finish line was priceless," Eliza giggled.

"You don't compete?" Cassie took in Penny's white capris and peplum blouse.

"I stay behind and help set up the celebratory barbecue in the town square for after the race."

"You ladies ready?" Sadie Hamilton approached wearing a Nike one-piece topped with knee-length board shorts.

Eliza smiled at the goggles draped around her neck. Although sweet as saltwater taffy, Sadie, the owner of the local candy store, was as competitive as they came. And her tall, muscular frame gave her an edge on the competition.

"Ready!" Eliza cinched the double knot on her hot-pink swim shorts before slipping on her water shoes.

Cassie twisted the end of her long braid, casting a nervous glance at the creek. "I don't know... the water looks cold."

"It's freezing," Penny told her, before Eliza shot her a warning glance.

"Don't scare her," Eliza chided. "You get used to the temperature after a few minutes. Besides, once you start running, it'll feel nice."

"I'm not sure I'm coordinated enough for this." Cassie gazed at her knees, which bore a couple of small scars. "I've been known to trip walking off escalators."

"I'll hang back with you." Eliza slung her arm around Cassie's shoulders.

"Me, too!" Sadie offered.

"Oh, no you don't," Penny chided. "You give those boys a run for their money. Colt's back this year. You don't want to listen to his smug bragging all week, do you?"

"Good point," Sadie chuckled, securing her nose clip.

"Remember, no foul play," Eliza added, still feeling guilty about last night. He'd looked so hurt when she'd rebuffed his kiss, she almost hoped Colt would win, if only to bolster his wounded pride. "The rules clearly state no physical contact."

"Okay, but I'm not above splashing a little water in his eyes." Sadie laughed as she positioned the goggles on top of her head. "Let's move to the starting line, shall we?"

"Good luck!" Penny called out as they joined the rest of the runners on the bank of the creek.

Eliza scanned the mass of brightly colored bathing suits and tanned skin, her heart stopping when she laid eyes on Colt and Grant stretching a few feet ahead.

Both men wore nothing but their board shorts, their broad, toned backs on full display. Though Colt's physique boasted more rippling muscles, Eliza couldn't tear her gaze from Grant's lean lines, preferring the svelte form of a dancer over a bulky, athletic build.

Her throat went dry as she noticed the palpable tension surging between them. Was it purely the competitive spirit of the race?

Or was there more behind their adversarial glances?

*

Normally, Grant wasn't the competitive type. As kids, he'd participated in the Creek Walk with an *all in good fun* mentality, never minding that he always finished several minutes behind the rest of the guys. But today, adrenaline coursed through his body, providing energy and agility he didn't know he possessed. Keeping Colt in his sights, he managed to pass Luke, Jack, and Reed. Sadie came next. He had to hand it to her; she made the exertion seem effortless, while he panted like he might pass out any second.

Finally, it was Grant and Colt in the lead.

A few feet up ahead, the creek emptied into a large swimming hole, too deep to stand. Grant expected Colt to dive in headfirst, then kick off with a skilled breaststroke. Much like he'd done in high school.

Instead, Colt veered to the right, making a beeline for a massive fallen tree stump that acted like a bridge across the swimming hole.

Grant followed, curious as to what move Colt would make next.

To Grant's surprise, Colt hoisted himself onto the log and took off running, his footsteps echoing against the hollow trunk.

Grant's chest expanded in irritation. It was so like Colt to look for the shortcut.

An image of Colt leaning in to kiss Eliza flashed before Grant's eyes, and suddenly, his focus shifted from winning the race to making sure Colt *didn't* win. At any cost.

Pulling himself onto the log, Grant pursued his rival with a dogged intensity, never once taking his eyes off his mark.

Colt must have heard Grant's footsteps close in behind him because he turned and flashed a devilish grin.

"Give up, Parker. I've as good as won!"

The image of Colt and Eliza flickered in his mind again, but this time, his imagination filled in the gaps. Envisioning Colt's lips on Eliza sent a surge of outrage coursing through Grant's body. And before he knew what had happened, he'd tackled Colt, plunging them into the icy water.

Grant resurfaced first, followed by Colt, who gasped for air.

"What the heck, man?" Colt sputtered. "What was that for?"

The reality of what he'd done slowly dawned on Grant, and he glanced around to see if anyone had witnessed his impulsive outburst.

His gaze landed on Eliza, who stood at the juncture where the creek spilled into the swimming hole. The shocked look on her face told Grant that she'd seen everything.

Colt followed his sight line. "Oh… I get it."

Grant snapped his focus back to Colt. "Get what?"

"Look," Colt said with a sigh. "You don't have to worry."

"What are you talking about?" As the adrenaline left his body, Grant struggled to tread water. His entire body felt weighed down, either by exhaustion or embarrassment at acting like a jealous idiot.

"She shot me down," Colt confessed. "And if I had to guess, I'd say she's hung up on someone else."

Grant didn't know what to say, but he instantly felt lighter, as though the anchor tied to his ankles had been cut loose. He opened his mouth to respond, then got a face full of water.

"Hey!" Jack called out, splashing them again as he swam by. "Do you want to practice water aerobics all day? Or win a race?" Chuckling, he flipped to a backstroke, kicking more water in their direction.

Colt raised an eyebrow at Grant. "We're not going to let Geriatric Jack beat us, are we?"

Grant grinned. "Nope."

"Then let's go. Although, he'll probably get a cramp before he reaches the other side." Colt laughed, taking off after Jack.

Grant followed behind, but his heart wasn't in the race anymore.

He couldn't stop thinking about Colt's words.

If I had to guess, I'd say she's hung up on someone else....

Could it be him? Or was it Ben's father?

CHAPTER 13

*G*rant couldn't stop smiling even though his calves ached and his left ear contained a creek's worth of water.

Eliza had called things off with Colt!

And the kiss he'd imagined never actually happened.

The day couldn't possibly get any better.

After the exertion of the Creek Walk and hardly eating anything during the last forty-eight hours, Grant suddenly felt ravenous. It had been years since he'd been around for one of Poppy Creek's town-wide barbecues, and his mouth watered just thinking about the monstrous hamburgers and surplus of inventive side dishes.

As he finished toweling off, Grant scanned the town square, searching for Eliza, wondering if he could somehow finagle sitting together. His breath strangled when he caught sight of her across the lawn. As she stepped out of her pink swim shorts, his gaze traveled the length of her long, lean legs to her sleek black one-piece. How was it possible she could look so alluring in such a simple, modest outfit? He tried to swallow, but his throat had gone completely dry.

"You're making a big mistake."

Startled, Grant whirled around to find his mother standing behind him. She wore a scowl like an accessory, complementing her Gucci sunglasses.

"Geez, Mom. You scared me. Practicing your ninja skills?" Grant teased. Even her pinched features couldn't dampen his good mood.

"This isn't a laughing matter," Harriet scolded through clenched teeth.

"Right. It's a very serious matter, indeed." Grant tossed the towel on the back of a folding chair and slipped on his T-shirt. "What monumental mistake am I making this time? Am I supposed to wait thirty minutes to eat after I swim? Or is it the other way around? I can never remember." He chuckled at his own lame joke, but the laughter died in the breeze as Harriet's glower intensified.

"Do you think you're funny? Because I don't. Especially not after the stunt you pulled today."

"You mean tackling Colt?" Grant asked sheepishly. Okay, he did feel a little bad about that. But it hardly seemed deserving of a tongue-lashing from his mother as if they were sixteen again.

"We all know who that was about," Harriet hissed, sidling in closer so no one would overhear their conversation.

"Who?" Grant asked innocently. Had he been that obvious? Did Eliza know? And, ultimately, did he even care if she did?

Seeing Colt with Eliza had solidified Grant's feelings. And not simply because of his jealousy. Colt had forced him to confront the truth. He wasn't over her. Not even close. And while he may not have wanted to admit it at first, he'd come back to Poppy Creek to see if there was still something between them. It took almost losing her again to get his answer. Now, if only he knew what to do about it....

"Stay away from her, Grant. I mean it."

Grant flinched at her frigid tone. "You make Eliza sound like some... I don't know. Like a felon or something."

"There are things about her you don't know."

"Like what?" Grant felt the frustration build in his chest, stifling the joy he'd hoped to savor for as long as possible. "What is this all about?"

Harriet lowered her voice another octave. "I'm not at liberty to say. But you have to trust me. She's not who you think she is."

A chill ran up Grant's spine despite the late afternoon sun beating down on them. "What are you talking about?"

"Just stay away from her. Or I'll have to take matters into my own hands."

"Mom, you're starting to sound a little crazy. This is some kind of joke, right?" Grant attempted a laugh, but the fierce look in Harriet's eyes as she raised her sunglasses silenced him. Running his fingers through his hair, Grant sighed. "Look. I appreciate your… concern, I guess. But I'm telling you, you have the wrong idea about Eliza."

Harriet crossed her arms in front of her chest, parting her lips, ready to challenge him.

"But…" Grant interjected quickly, hoping to end the conversation, "if it makes you feel better, I won't go rushing into anything. Okay?"

Grant leaned in to kiss her cheek, and Harriet stiffened. "Try to relax, Mom. It's a beautiful day. Have something to eat."

He squeezed her shoulder before heading across the lawn to join the guys around the grill with Jack. But as he put distance between them, the odd exchange echoed in his mind, stirring an unsettled feeling in the pit of his stomach.

What exactly did his mother know that he didn't?

⚜

As Eliza loaded up her plate with five different pasta salads, she hummed softly to herself.

The moment she saw Grant tackle Colt into the swimming

hole, she knew he still had feelings for her. She could see it written across his face when their eyes locked across the water.

"Someone seems happy." Penny squeezed in beside Eliza and scooped a huge spoonful of seven-layer dip onto her plate, followed by a handful of tortilla chips.

"Why wouldn't I be?" Sensing a telltale heat creep up her neck, Eliza shifted her attention to the plethora of potato salads, trying to decide between classic and Cajun-style. "It's a lovely day. The weather is perfect. The food is delicious…."

Penny leaned in, lowering her voice. "Are you sure it doesn't have more to do with the fact that Grant dunked Colt in the swimming hole?"

"How'd you hear about that?"

"Honey, everyone knew about it five seconds after it happened. I'm only sorry I missed it," Penny giggled.

"Don't you think you're a little hard on Colt?" Eliza asked, trying to detour the topic away from Grant.

Penny shrugged, crunching on another chip. "He can handle it. Now, stop changing the subject." She glanced left and right as if to make sure no one was in earshot before whispering, "I think Grant still has a thing for you."

By now, the heat had traveled up Eliza's neck and blazed across her cheeks. "I think you're imagining things."

"Deny it all you want, but you two are definitely getting back together." Penny plopped another chip in her mouth before sauntering off, tossing a wink over her shoulder.

Eliza's lips twitched, fighting a smile. Oh, how she wanted to believe Penny was right. But under the circumstances, a second chance for her and Grant simply didn't seem possible.

Moving to the refreshment stand, Eliza slid her plate onto the table and grabbed a tall mason jar. Turning the spout of the beverage dispenser, she searched the crowd for Ben while her glass filled. She'd told her parents not to let him run wild with his friends until after lunch, but once Sylvia got to chatting, she easily lost track.

"Looking for someone?"

The hairs on the back of Eliza's neck prickled as she met Harriet's icy gaze.

"Yes, my son."

Harriet raised one sharply penciled eyebrow. "Really? Are you sure you weren't looking for someone else?"

Eliza's heartbeat stilled, every muscle in her body tense. What exactly was Harriet insinuating?

Suddenly, Eliza's cup overflowed. Ice-cold lemonade drenched her hands and the hem of the sundress she'd thrown over her bathing suit after the race. Frantic, she scrambled to switch off the spout.

"Here, let me help you." Harriet grabbed a handful of napkins and stepped in front of Eliza, keeping her head lowered as she dabbed the sticky, sopping-wet stain. "You should really be more careful."

Harriet's venomous tone made Eliza's blood run cold. And Eliza instantly knew she wasn't talking about the lemonade.

Taking a step back, Eliza yanked the hem of her dress from Harriet's grasp. "I'm fine, thank you."

"Glad to hear it. And how are your parents?" Harriet asked pointedly, a small, almost imperceptible sneer playing about her lips.

Eliza's breath hitched in her throat, and she glanced around for a quick path of escape.

Harriet took a step toward her, her eyes narrowing. "You remember our agreement, don't you, Eliza?"

Swallowing past the lump of fear in her throat, Eliza whispered, "Yes."

"Good. Then it would serve you well not to forget it." Harriet crumpled the soiled napkins into a ball in her fist before tossing them in the nearby trash can. "Have a nice day." With a sharp wave of her hand, she disappeared into the throng of merriment, leaving Eliza breathless and trembling.

"Mom! Mom!" Ben appeared by her side, tugging on her arm. "Grant asked us to sit with him at lunch. Can we? Can we?"

"Um…" Eliza blinked several times, trying to reorient to her surroundings, shaking away the tremors in her hands with a flick of her wrists. Concentrating on Ben, she forced a wobbly smile. "Not today, Bug. Let's sit with Grandma and Grandpa, okay?"

Ben's lower lip protruded in a pout. "Okay." Within a millisecond, his face brightened, as if he'd forgotten all about his previous disappointment. "Can I have some lemonade?"

"Sure. Second time's the charm."

Ben tilted his head, gazing at her with a quizzical expression.

"Never mind." Eliza smiled. "Help yourself."

As Ben filled his mason jar, he asked, "Can we have Grant over for dinner tomorrow?"

Eliza winced internally. "I don't think so. We need to focus on homework tomorrow night. And Grant's a busy guy. He can't spend all of his time painting with you."

Ben's face instantly fell, and Eliza regretted being so dismissive.

But how could she possibly explain to him that they needed to steer clear of Grant from now on?

If not for their sakes, then for her parents'.

CHAPTER 14

*H*er heartbeat thrumming wildly, Eliza screeched into the school parking lot and slammed on the brakes. Agitated, she lunged for her purse on the passenger seat, dropping her keys in the footwell. After bending to retrieve them, she whacked the back of her head on the steering wheel as she straightened. Pain shot through her temples, and Eliza released a low moan.

She'd been a wreck ever since her run-in with Harriet at the barbecue yesterday. Even Cassie mentioned she seemed jittery and absentminded after she'd charred an entire tray of White Chocolate Cappuccino cookies. But the worst offense was forgetting Career Day at Ben's school. As if she needed another reason to be on Daphne's bad side. Fortunately, her mother had reminded her with a few minutes to spare.

She raced up the front steps of the old brick schoolhouse and froze when she spotted Grant at the top of the staircase. "What are you doing here?"

"Hi!" His smile faded as he took in her ashen appearance. "Are you okay?"

"What are you doing here?" Eliza repeated, pressing a hand to her forehead. The intense throbbing seemed to match the staccato tempo of her pulse.

Grant's eyes widened in surprise. "I... I'm speaking in Ben's class for Career Day. He asked me yesterday at the barbecue. Didn't he tell you?"

Suddenly nauseous, Eliza gripped the wooden railing to keep from collapsing on the stone steps.

"Are you okay? You look like you might throw up." Grant set his portfolio and laptop bag on the bench and moved to her side, offering his arm for support.

Eliza waved him aside. "I'm fine." She needed to collect herself and salvage the situation as quickly as possible. If Harriet found out that Grant—Eliza shook her head sharply. No, Harriet wouldn't find out. She couldn't. "You shouldn't be here."

"What do you mean?" Grant took a step back, his eyebrows raised in confusion. "Ben asked me to—"

"It doesn't matter," Eliza snapped, squinting as another sharp pain pierced the back of her eyes. "Career Day is for parents. Not acquaintances."

Grant flinched, his features crumbling. "Okay... point taken." For a moment, he stared at her as though he'd never seen her before, and Eliza's nausea returned tenfold.

She had no reason to be so unkind to Grant, but panic had completely taken over.

Steeling herself against another wave of anxiety, Eliza squared her shoulders, meeting his gaze with an apology poised on the tip of her tongue. "Grant, I—"

He held up his hand. "Say no more. I think you've been perfectly clear." Looking away, he gathered his belongings from the bench and slung his laptop bag over his shoulder. "Please explain my absence to Ben."

Guilt constricting her throat, Eliza nodded.

Grant passed by her on the steps without another word, but

she felt the frustration radiating from his body like steam curling from a pie crust.

She didn't blame him. Her harsh words were inexcusable. What was happening to her? The lines between right and wrong, the truth and lies... Everything seemed blurry, painted in shades of gray. She hated gray.

Her eyes burned and Eliza squeezed them shut, fighting back tears. Slowly breathing in and out, she concentrated on the rhythm of her pulse, the warmth of the sun on her bare arms, the *tap, tap, tap* of a woodpecker in the distance. Finally, she thought about Ben. Focusing her attention on her son usually centered her.

But in her mind's eye, Ben became a part of the gray landscape, disappearing into the drab, faded background.

Fear gripped Eliza's heart and her eyelids flew open.

She needed to find a way out of this mess before she lost everything that mattered to her.

Especially her son.

C onfused and humiliated, Grant kicked the car door shut with the heel of his suede loafer.

What had just happened? Ever since the race yesterday, Eliza had been avoiding him. It was almost as if...

Grant paused halfway down the slate walkway, a weight settling in the pit of his stomach.

Oh, no...

The bitter realization fell over him like a dark shadow.

Eliza had discovered he still had feelings for her! And this was her way of rejecting him.

Pain stabbed his heart, and Grant ran his fingers through his hair, trying to collect himself.

Could it really be over between them? Less than twenty-four

hours ago, it seemed like their lives were just beginning. He'd been almost certain he'd felt a spark, a strong electrical current that ran both ways. What had snuffed it out so swiftly?

Dragging himself up the porch steps, Grant didn't even notice his father reading on the wicker bench overlooking the front garden. Lost in his thoughts, Grant skulked past him into the house, still agonizing over every syllable he'd exchanged with Eliza.

Could he be misreading things? Even if Eliza didn't want to get back together, why did she have to push him away from Ben so fiercely? While only a friend, Luke seemed to fill the role of father figure in the boy's life. And, in some ways, so did Jack and Reed. Why couldn't Grant be another one of Ben's role models? Unless...

Suddenly queasy, Grant yanked open the refrigerator and grabbed a bottle of sarsaparilla, popping off the cap on the edge of the counter. Leaning against the sink, he threw his head back and chugged, waiting for the subtle licorice flavor of the soft drink to work its calming magic on his churning stomach.

Who was he kidding? Grant couldn't blame Eliza for not wanting him around her son. His rapport with his own father was fraught with tension and bitterness, dysfunction Eliza had witnessed with her own eyes on numerous occasions. That type of toxicity was bound to worm its way into other relationships—the exact reason Grant never wanted kids. He didn't trust himself to do things differently.

So why did being around Ben make him want to try? Before coming back to Poppy Creek, he'd been content to remain child-free for the rest of his life. But over the last several days, something had shifted. He couldn't explain it. But deep in his gut, something about the possibility of being cut out of Ben's life felt... personal.

"Everything all right?" Stan appeared in the doorway.

"Just peachy," Grant muttered dryly, taking another swig of

sarsaparilla. Realizing it was empty, he tossed the glass bottle into the recycling bin and grabbed another one from the fridge.

Propping the cap against the counter, Grant attempted to pop it off like the first, but it wouldn't budge. Frustration building in his chest, Grant yanked open kitchen drawers, rummaging through them in search of a bottle opener. "Where's Mom?" he growled, feeling angry with the world.

"Knitting club." Stan removed the keychain clipped to his belt loop and tossed it to Grant. "There's a bottle opener in the Swiss army knife."

"Thanks," Grant mumbled, snapping off the bottle cap before tossing the keys back to his dad.

"Rough day?"

"You could say that." Grant downed another gulp, the carbonation burning the back of his throat.

"Want to talk about it?"

"Not really." Grant stared at the tile floor, realizing he'd forgotten to remove his shoes when he'd entered the house. *Fantastic.* As if he wasn't already on his mother's bad side lately. Although, she'd be happy to hear about the day's altercation. It seemed that his mother and Eliza were finally on the same side.

The thought fueled Grant's irritation, causing the words to tumble from his lips before he could stop them. "I showed up at Ben's school today. For Career Day. He *asked* me to speak in front of his class, by the way." Grant placed extra emphasis on the invitation, a dull ache settling around his heart as he recalled Ben's hopeful expression when he'd made his request. "So, there I was, giving up a few hours out of my day for a kid that's not even mine, and guess what?"

Pacing back and forth across the kitchen, Grant didn't wait for Stan to respond before blurting, "Eliza tells me to get lost."

"She actually said that?" Stan's eyebrows rose in surprise.

"Well, not in so many words, but basically. She told me I had no reason to be there because Career Day is for parents."

"I see," Stan said softly.

Something in the cautious edge to his father's tone irked Grant, feeding into his agitated state of mind. "What?"

"Nothing."

"Clearly, it's something. I take it you agree with her?" A not-so-subtle voice inside Grant's head told him to stop now and walk away. He needed to cool off and think before he spoke. But an even louder voice—the reckless one—wanted his father to say it out loud.

"Well…" Stan started slowly. "You're not the boy's father—"

"And if anyone knows about *not* being a father…" Grant trailed off, short of the final blow. But it didn't matter. He'd made his point. It was stamped across Stan's pallid features.

Regret pierced Grant's heart, and he set down the soda bottle, ready to apologize. "Dad, I—"

Stan cleared his throat. "Your mother said she won't be back in time for dinner, so she left a casserole in the fridge. The heating instructions are on the notepad on the counter. I'll be at a card game at Mac's tonight."

Without another word, Stan strode out of the kitchen.

Leaving Grant to stew in his remorse.

CHAPTER 15

Wincing, Grant dropped the square of sandpaper, flicking his wrist to dull the pain as it fluttered to the floor. He deserved the splinter. And then some.

Grant thought helping Luke with the wedding arch would clear his head, surrounded by the restorative scent of cedar and pine sap. Not to mention the repetitive motion of sanding. But he couldn't stop thinking about the harsh words he'd said to his father earlier that day. True or not, they never should have left his lips.

"Careful," Luke told him. "The wood's pretty rough. I've received my fair share of splinters on this project."

"Then I have some catching up to do." Grant attempted a smile as he stooped to pluck the sandpaper from the pile of sawdust covering the hardpan floor.

As he straightened, he took a moment to soak up the surroundings. Grant had to hand it to Luke. The man had built an impressive workshop. When he'd first reconnected with Luke behind his store in town, Grant had assumed Luke did most of his woodworking in the courtyard. But now, seeing the enormity of Luke's converted garage, Grant realized how off-base his assumption had been. "I have to say, this is quite the setup."

"Thanks." Luke gazed around his workspace with a satisfied smile. "It's taken me several years to build it up to this point, but I'm pretty proud of it."

"I take it Cassie is moving in to your place after the wedding, then?" The answer seemed obvious to Grant, considering Luke's home and workshop sat on an enormous piece of land flanked by a lush pine forest and tranquil stream, a slice of heaven in an already idyllic setting.

Plus, Luke's house wasn't your typical bachelor pad. The striking two-story log cabin could easily grace the cover of *Architectural Digest*.

To Grant's surprise, Luke's smile faltered. "We're still discussing it."

"Really? I might be dense, but who *wouldn't* want to live here?"

Luke's smile reappeared, albeit more subtle this time. "I appreciate that. But a lot of factors go into the decision. While my whole life is here, the cottage means a lot to Cassie. And she hasn't lived there very long." Luke sighed, casting a wistful gaze around the room. "It would be hard to leave this place. But I want to be wherever Cassie is, as sappy as that sounds."

A familiar ache gripped Grant's heart. And while he wouldn't admit it, he knew exactly how Luke felt. He'd gladly give up his life in San Francisco to be with Eliza. A dream that had never seemed more out of reach. "I'm sure you guys will figure it out." Grant offered a smile he hoped communicated both sympathy and optimism.

"Yeah, I'm sure we will."

The two men went back to work, settling into a comfortable silence.

Lulled by the rhythmic *swish, swish, swish* of the sandpaper, Grant's thoughts returned to the conversation with his father.

Being back home had forced him to face emotions he'd

artfully repressed. Or *thought* he'd repressed. But considering he'd never quite settled into a rich, full life in San Francisco, preferring to keep to himself rather than make meaningful connections…. Grant had to acknowledge the facts. If he didn't resolve his issues—both with his father and Eliza—he'd be destined to live a life secluded in bitter isolation whether he remained in Poppy Creek or not. Because the walls he'd built had nothing to do with his apartment in the city. And everything to do with the walls around his heart.

"What about you?" Luke asked, disrupting his moment of introspection.

"What about me?"

"Something's clearly on your mind. Is it Eliza?"

"Not this time." Although, Grant couldn't deny it was a good guess. Eliza seemed to consume his thoughts on an increasingly more frequent basis these days.

"Then it must be serious." Luke pulled a stool from beneath his drafting table. "Wanna sit?"

"No, thanks." Grant kept his gaze fixed on a knot in the wood, pressing firmer than necessary with the sandpaper. Something about smoothing out the rough edges of the beam felt like progress, even if he'd barely grazed the surface of his own issues.

"Come on," Luke cajoled. "Cassie tells me I'm a good listener." He used the steel toe of his boot to nudge the stool toward Grant.

"Is it because you're a good listener? Or because you hang on her every word?" Grant teased.

"Maybe a bit of both," Luke chuckled. "But there's a good way to test the theory."

"Touché." Grant flashed a rueful grin. "Fine, you win. I'll spill. But only if we keep working."

"Deal." Luke flipped open his red pocket knife, ready to continue his engraving.

Grant returned his attention to the gnarled wood, grateful for the distraction. "I got in a fight with my dad this morning. And it was... pretty ugly."

Luke's hand stilled a moment, but he quickly resumed carving, not uttering a word.

"I might have called him a bad father." Grant cringed with the admission, reliving the awful moment all over again.

"And..." Luke prompted.

"And what? I called my dad a bad father. It doesn't get much worse than that, does it?"

"I mean, did you apologize?"

"He didn't give me the chance. At the first sign of conflict, he skulked out of the room. Like he usually does." Grant flinched. There he went again.... It was like a mean-spirited reflex. And he hated it about himself. He never used to be so caustic. But after years of carrying around the pain in his pocket, like a trinket commemorating his unhappy childhood, certain trains of thought had become an unwelcome habit.

Luke didn't respond right away, and feeling self-conscious, Grant filled the gap. "You and Colt were lucky. You could buy one of those World's Greatest Dad mugs and it wouldn't be ironic."

Deep in thought, Luke kept his gaze glued on his task, digging the blade into the wood, flecks of sawdust flitting to the ground as he removed the excess to expose the beauty underneath.

Swish, swish, swish.

Grant raked the sandpaper over the coarse beam, the muscles in his fingers clenched, waiting for Luke to end his deafening silence.

"Yeah, we were lucky," Luke said at last, a slight catch in his throat. "I'd give anything to have one more day with him. Even if it was our worst day."

At Luke's words, the sandpaper slipped from Grant's fingertips and drifted to the floor. This time, he didn't bother to pick it up. "I never got a chance to say this in person. And I should have."

Grant paused, realizing whatever he said next would never be enough. "I am so unbelievably sorry about your dad." His apology escaped in a hoarse whisper, barely making it past the emotion constricting his throat.

Luke met his gaze from the opposite end of the arch, the spark of pain in his hazel eyes evident in the glow of the overhead light. "Do me a favor, Parker."

"Anything."

"Try to patch things up with your dad. You never know how much time you have left."

Sitting on Maggie's kitchen counter with a mixing bowl poised on her lap, Eliza felt like she was five years old again. Which was fitting, considering her immature outburst that morning at Ben's school. The devastated look on Grant's face still haunted her. How could she have been so cruel?

Tears pricking her eyes, Eliza watched Maggie crush walnuts for the top of her world-famous cinnamon rolls, taking a mental picture of each subtle movement. The way Maggie's strong yet graceful hands moved with the rolling pin as though they were molded together. And the streaks of silver peppering her dark curls, coupled with how she brushed them from her forehead using the back of her wrist. Eliza even wanted to remember the soft crunch of the walnuts and the sharp scent of yeast and buttermilk. She wasn't sure how many more times she'd have the opportunity to bake with Maggie in her bright, sunny kitchen. And she didn't want to forget a single detail.

Maggie had been offering to teach Eliza her special recipe for months, but Eliza kept putting it off. The cinnamon rolls were Maggie's final link to the bakery—a coveted connection Eliza wasn't ready to sever.

Although grateful for the opportunity to run her own business, Eliza had practically raised Ben in the bakery. It was a part of her—of *them*. And it wasn't lost on Eliza that she still called it the bakery, and not the café, despite its new name and menu.

Eliza gripped the wooden spoon until her knuckles turned white, wrestling with a lifetime of regrets. Nothing had gone the way she'd planned. And she only had herself to blame.

"Maggie," Eliza said softly. "Why did you hire me?"

"What do you mean, dear?"

"Over seven years ago, when I asked you for a job at the bakery, why did you hire me? I had zero job experience. No formal baking skills. And at the very least, being an unwed, teenage mother showed I had terrible judgment."

"Show me a person without sin, and I'll show you a catfish that barks like a dog." Maggie recited the strange words as though they were a common expression.

"What?" Eliza frowned, uncertain she'd heard correctly.

A smile hid behind Maggie's hazel eyes as she explained. "It's something my father said when he caught my sister, Sandy, and I gossiping about a girl in our school."

"A girl who was pregnant?" The cinnamon rolls forgotten, Eliza let the wooden spoon rest against the side of the mixing bowl.

"Yes." Maggie gave a short, remorseful shake of her head. "And I'm sorry to say my sister and I weren't very kind to her. After overhearing our hurtful gossip, our father sat us down and asked us an important question: 'When we bring our sin to the Lord, does He remove it as far as the east is from the west?' Of course, Sandy and I agreed that He did. 'So,' he asked us. 'Why do you two insist on looking for it?'" Maggie's eyes misted over at the memory.

Dropping her gaze, Eliza stared intently at the flour dusting her hands, a tightness in her throat.

Gently taking the bowl from her grasp, Maggie set it on the

counter. "Do you want to know what I saw the day you showed up at the bakery and asked me for a job?"

Blinking back tears, Eliza nodded.

Maggie took Eliza's hands in hers, her eyes glistening with motherly warmth and affection. "I saw a young girl who'd taken the wrong path. But rather than continue down that road, she made a difficult choice. She changed her entire life for a child she hadn't even named yet. To me, that made you incredibly brave. And exactly the kind of woman I wanted to hire. Not a day goes by that I'm not reminded I made the right decision."

Sliding off the counter, Eliza wrapped her arms around Maggie's neck, her silent tears dampening the ruffled collar of her apron.

With a soothing hand, Maggie stroked Eliza's hair, cooing softly. "Oh, sweet girl. Living with shame is a lot like baking with arsenic. The cupcake may look beautiful on the outside, but inside…"

Maggie's unfinished thought touched Eliza's heart where it had never been reached before. And Eliza gave herself permission to cry without reproach for the first time in years.

"There, there, sweetheart. It'll be okay," Maggie purred.

Sniffling, Eliza lifted her tearful gaze to meet Maggie's. "Thank you," she whispered, hoping those two simple words could carry the weight of her gratitude.

Wiping her damp cheeks with the hem of her apron, Eliza asked, "Do you mind if we come back to the cinnamon rolls later? There's something important I need to do."

"Of course, dear. I'm not going anywhere."

A smile broke through Eliza's tears as she realized Maggie was referring to far more than the cinnamon rolls.

CHAPTER 16

*W*ith a purposeful stride, Grant headed for his father's office. After finding the rest of the house empty, he figured it was worth a shot, and crossed his fingers his dad hadn't left for Mac's already.

Grant had gone over his apology a thousand times on the drive home from Luke's, even reciting a few phrases out loud. While he'd expected some resistance, or a bitter taste in his mouth, the words rolled off his tongue easily, as though they'd been waiting for Grant to summon the necessary courage. He only hoped the same would hold true when he looked his father in the eye.

The late afternoon sun filtered through heavy wooden blinds, casting strange shadows across the vacant room. Discouraged, Grant turned to go, when a flickering ray of light reflected off one of the marble chess pieces.

Grant hesitated only a moment before spanning the short distance.

While the idea seemed ludicrous, or foolish at best, Grant couldn't keep his fingers from curling around the smooth marble pawn, moving it forward one space.

Then he scribbled a note on a Post-it and secured it to the chess board.

Grant's lips spread into a slow smile as he read the two simple words that spoke volumes.

Your move.

&

*B*acking out of the driveway, Grant decided to head to Jack's for dinner. After an emotionally exhausting day, he could use the light banter and good-natured ribbing.

Prepared to pull onto the main road, Grant slammed on the brakes when a Honda Accord cut him off, turning down his parents' driveway.

Coming to an abrupt stop, Eliza leaned out of the window and shouted, "Get out!"

Grant blinked in confusion. "What?"

"Get out of the car," she repeated, gesturing for Grant to pull off to the side and park.

Grant obliged, his heart hammering as he climbed out of his Tesla. What in the world was she doing here? "Is this a carjacking? Because you should know, this car is a pain up here. I have to stop in Primrose Valley to charge it." He attempted a joke, but his voice fell flat thanks to the nervous jitter in his stomach.

Reaching over the console, Eliza popped open the passenger door. "Get in."

The magic effects of her infectious grin set Grant's erratic pulse at ease. "So, it's a kidnapping?" he teased, hopping inside.

"I prefer to call it luring you to an undisclosed location with the promise of your favorite foods."

"Well, why didn't you say so?" Grant chuckled as he secured his seat belt, marveling at the magnetic charge between them.

How was it that no matter how much time had passed, or

what transpired between them, they so easily fell into a place of comfort, like coming home after a long journey.

"Are you a better driver than you were in high school?" he asked with a grin.

"What do you mean?" Eliza shot him look as she lurched onto the main road. "I was a great driver."

"Sure you were." Still smiling, Grant leaned against the head-rest, relishing the crisp, cool breeze whipping through his hair. "Didn't you put Mrs. Locan in the hospital during your final road test?"

"No! She got stung by a bee and went into anaphylactic shock. If anything, I'm a hero. I got her to the hospital in record time."

"And who opened the window that let in the bee?" Grant raised one eyebrow, suppressing a laugh.

"Fine." Eliza smirked. "I see how it is. Better be careful, then." She eyed Grant's open window with a mischievous glint.

"Good thing I'm not allergic." Grant sank deeper into the frayed upholstery, at once relaxed and uncertain. Would they talk about their argument that morning? Or pretend like it never happened?

As if reading his mind, Eliza murmured, "I'm so sorry, Grant."

She kept her eyes on the road, but Grant noticed the way her fingers clenched around the steering wheel and the slight tremor in her jaw.

"I shouldn't have said those things to you earlier."

"It's okay." He shrugged. "You were right, anyway. Ben's not my son. I shouldn't have taken it so personally when you asked me not to speak in front of his class." Grant wasn't sure if his words were meant to console Eliza or himself.

She stole a quick glance in his direction before refocusing on the road, her grip tightening until her knuckles blanched.

For the rest of the drive, they rode in silence, save for the radio turned on low to an oldies station. Grant didn't mind the absence of chitchat and was reminded of countless drives in the countryside when they'd play all their favorite songs, seeing where the road led them.

When Eliza turned into the entrance of Willow Lake, Grant smiled, recalling fond memories of their childhood spent around summer bonfires, racing on paddle boards, and holding rock-skipping competitions.

"We're here," Eliza announced with a dramatic flourish.

"What exactly does this kidnapping entail?" Grant's stomach flipped as his mind jumbled with possibilities. Although, simply being in Eliza's company already made this the best evening he'd had in years.

"A picnic dinner comprised of your favorite foods and a chance to win back your title of rock-skipping champion." Eliza slid out of the driver's seat, turning back with a heart-stopping smile. "I hope you've been practicing."

*A*s the sun dipped behind Lupine Ridge, the golden sky mirrored across the still water, drenching everything in soft sepia tones.

Eliza released a contented sigh, digging her toes into the cool blades of grass. While she'd had no idea what to expect when she picked up Grant earlier that evening, the night couldn't have turned out more perfectly.

She'd managed to keep her rock-skipping crown, with an even dozen skips on her fourth try.

Grant had peaked at six. Eliza giggled at the thought.

"Are you still laughing at me?" Grant pushed the picnic basket aside, making more room on the faded plaid blanket.

"Six? Really?" Eliza giggled again, the giddiness bubbling out of her uncontrollably. She couldn't remember the last time she'd felt so... happy.

"Hey! That's not bad considering I don't skip a lot of rocks in

San Francisco." Even in his protest, Grant's words carried a teasing, playful lilt that sent Eliza's heart soaring higher than the flock of sparrows overhead.

Grant sprawled out on the blanket, tucking his arms behind his head for support. But not before tugging Eliza's elbow to join him.

Her breath came in short, fast spurts as she settled beside him, being careful not to lie too close. Already the heat between them made her cardigan unnecessary. Skin-on-skin contact would put her over the edge, for sure.

Silently, they stared up at the sky as gold diffused to pink, followed by indigo; wispy clouds trailed past them, led by a gentle breeze.

Eliza closed her eyes, reveling in how the wind still carried the same scent of evening primrose and pine like the last time they'd visited this very spot. Or was the air sweeter?

The soothing chirp of crickets celebrating the onset of dusk threatened to lull Eliza to sleep. But even her most vivid dream couldn't compare to the sensations surrounding her. And she didn't want to miss a single whisper of wind or croak of a bullfrog.

"Lizzy," Grant murmured, his voice low and gravelly. "Can I ask you something?"

"Mm-hmm...."

"Why do you call Ben 'Bug'?"

Eliza's eyes fluttered open, the coveted moment shattered by her complicated reality. Eliza loved Ben more than anything in the world. But he'd forever be a reminder of the life she longed for, forever out of reach.

Shifting on the soft cotton blanket, she kept her gaze fixed on the sky. With the sun now hidden, a chill rippled through her.

"When I saw my first ultrasound," Eliza started, picking at a blade of grass, "I told the technician that Ben looked like a tiny bug on the screen. It sounds silly now, but I was nervous, desperate for something to say. I'd never been more terrified in all my life. And strangely, I'd never felt more alone."

Grant stirred, his hand finding hers.

Eliza didn't pull away, relishing the comforting connection of their entwined fingers. "At that point, I still hadn't decided on a name, so I wound up calling him Bug for nine whole months. I guess it stuck."

"How'd you finally decide on Ben?"

"Benjamin. My grandfather's name and my dad's middle name. I ultimately settled on family tradition. Go figure," Eliza laughed softly.

"So, what's Ben's middle name, then?"

Shifting position, Eliza slipped her hand from Grant's, wariness worming its way around her heart. "Why all the questions?" She stole a sideways glance in his direction, grateful for the concealing shadows of twilight.

"You have a child, Lizzy. He's a part of you. Is it so weird that I'd like to get to know him?"

Eliza's heartbeat fluttered at the earnestness in Grant's tone. Oh, how she'd longed for and feared this moment.

"Okay, one last question...." Grant rolled onto his side, propping himself up on his elbow.

Her pulse quickening, Eliza shut her eyes again, squeezing them tightly as though she could block out the world.

"Did you love him?"

Eliza's breath slowed, stalling in her throat.

When she didn't answer, Grant added, "Ben's father, I mean. Did you love him?"

Even with her eyes closed, Eliza felt Grant watching her, waiting for her response.

But what could she say?

He'd asked for an answer she simply couldn't give him.

No matter how badly she wanted to.

CHAPTER 17

No matter how hard he tried, Grant couldn't stop dwelling on the events of last night. The look on Eliza's face when he'd asked her about Ben's father still gave him chills. She'd turned ashen, the change visible even in the twilight. He hadn't been able to breathe, waiting in agony for her response.

But none came.

Only a single tear trailing softly down her cheek. Which could only mean one thing....

Eliza was still in love with Ben's father.

The realization gutted Grant, causing his chest to compress around his heart, as though she'd rolled one of the nearby boulders on top of him, leaving him gasping for air. What kind of man would abandon Eliza? And his own son? Did he even know what an incredible kid Ben was?

Anger ripped through him, and he tore the page from his sketchbook, crumpling it in his fist. He'd come out to the garden to concentrate and make some progress on Landon's project. But he struggled to think about anything other than Eliza. And the promising future that had slipped through his fingertips.

For a moment, Grant had dared to hope, encouraged by the perfect evening they'd spent together. But what chance did he have if Eliza's heart belonged to someone else?

Besides, even wishing for another outcome left him conflicted. If Eliza had a shot of making it work with Ben's father, shouldn't he be rooting for them?

The garden gate creaked, startling Grant from his thoughts.

Stan rested his fishing rod against the white picket fence before carrying the Coleman ice chest toward the back porch.

"Is that dinner?" Grant nodded to the cooler, and Stan flashed a wry grin.

"Are you kidding?" he chuckled, the corners of his eyes revealing laugh lines Grant hadn't noticed before. "Your mom won't cook anything that doesn't come prepackaged from Mac's Mercantile. I use the cooler to keep my sarsaparilla chilled. I'm strictly a catch and release fisherman these days."

Grant watched his father stop and set the cooler on the lawn, baffled by his cheery demeanor.

After peeking into his office earlier that morning, Grant noticed Stan had moved a chess piece, leaving behind the same note. Did his father's chipper mood have anything to do with their unconventional chess game? And Grant's even more unconventional apology?

"What are you working on?" Stan leaned over Grant's shoulder to get a closer look at his laptop. "Morris Bio Tech, huh? That's quite an account."

Grant sat a smidge straighter at the twinge of pride in his father's tone. "It's my biggest one to date."

"They're a manufacturing company, right?"

"Yes. Their focus is on sustainable packaging materials."

"So, how does the cupcake with a coffee bean on top tie in?"

Grant followed his father's gaze to a drawing he'd done for Eliza's website. He quickly covered it with loose papers. "Oh, that's nothing."

A small knowing smile tugged at the corner of Stan's mouth. "I'm sure it is."

Stan hovered over Grant's shoulder a few more minutes, the air between them thick with awkward tension despite the cool breeze rustling through the dogwood trees.

Grant waited for Stan to retreat inside, only to balk when he pulled out a chair and sat down. His mouth hanging open, Grant stared, dumbfounded, as Stan shuffled through the papers, unearthing a few of his other sketches.

"These are quite good."

Grant suppressed a sarcastic retort, making some progress on his vow to think before he spoke. But his father had never cared about his artistic talent before. And Grant had often wondered what direction his life would have taken if his dad hadn't wrenched them from New York. His mom had him on track to attend the Pratt Institute, claiming that one of the most prestigious art colleges in the world could land him any job he wanted. When she'd lost most of her social connections after their cross-country move, they'd switched their focus to a more *attainable* goal, as she'd put it.

"Thanks. It's a small side project. I'm helping Eliza and Cassie with a website for The Calendar Café." Grant hesitated before adding, "But maybe don't mention that to Mom."

Stan nodded with a look that said, *Say no more.* "I'm partial to this one." He selected a watercolor showcasing an old-fashioned coffeepot filled with cheerful daisies.

"Oh, yeah?" Grant tilted his head, studying it from the sideways angle. He'd liked that design, but not as much as the others.

"Daisies always seem so… optimistic."

Grant chuckled. "Dad, they're a flower."

"Make fun all you want, but it's true. Plus, they remind me of something…."

Not Mom… Grant almost mumbled. She was the furthest thing

from a daisy. Maybe a bird-of-paradise or lobster claw, both sharp and angular but regal in their own unique way.

"That's it!" Stan slapped his palm against the table. "The Daisy Hop is coming up soon, isn't it?"

"I guess so. I'd forgotten all about it."

Okay, so that wasn't entirely true. The Daisy Hop had always been one of his and Eliza's favorite traditions. Millie Rogers, an eccentric salon owner and musical theater enthusiast, founded Poppy Creek's first dance studio specializing in both ballroom and swing. Each year, the Dancing Daisies hosted an elaborate shindig and invited the entire town to join in the waltz and jitterbug. The Daisy Hop was the last time he and Eliza had danced together, save for the night in the bakery. And most notably, it was the one and only time they'd successfully executed the Charleston Flip.

"Are you and Mom going?"

"I doubt it. Your mother finds the dances in this town depressing. She says they can't compare to the events she used to attend in New York." Stan lifted his shoulders in a small resigned shrug before adding, "But you should go."

"I might…." Grant trailed off, although he already knew he wouldn't. Not without Eliza. And getting her to agree to a date with him seemed about as likely as getting his mother to attend.

Stan studied the painting again, his eyebrows pinched in thought. "How does the tradition go? When you want to ask a girl to the dance."

Grant smiled, recalling the first time he'd invited Eliza their freshman year of high school. "You give her a daisy chain."

"That's right. I seem to remember you making a necklace for Eliza. I wonder if people still do that?" Stan rose from the wrought iron chair, set the painting on Grant's keyboard, and strode to a nearby planter box.

"Probably. Traditions in Poppy Creek rarely die out. If anything, they get more extreme."

"True." Stan dipped his head in agreement, plucking a single white daisy from among its sage and lavender companions. "And you know what? Maybe I will ask your mother if she'd like to go. After all, stranger things have happened."

"Maybe. But I think the daisy's optimism might be rubbing off on you."

Stan chuckled. "Well, I won't know if I don't ask, right?"

On that note, Stan tossed the daisy onto the table before grabbing his cooler and heading toward the house.

Grazing the soft petals with his fingertip, Grant stared at his father's retreating back, watching him disappear through the screen door.

Had his dad just encouraged him to ask out Eliza?

⁂

The moment Cassie descended the sweeping staircase and stepped into the cottage's cozy living room, Eliza forgot all about her disastrous evening with Grant. Her friend looked breathtaking in ivory lace that melded to her curves as effortlessly as buttercream frosting on a white chiffon cake. And the sight of five women who loved and adored her, all standing in her new home, seemed to leave Cassie speechless.

Eliza stole a glance at Maggie, who fought back tears at the resplendent vision of Cassie clothed in her hand-me-down gown.

"You look stunning," Maggie murmured, dabbing her eyes with a leftover swatch of cappuccino-colored charmeuse.

"It's the dress." A modest blush dusted Cassie's cheeks as she ran her palm along the delicate fabric.

"Luke doesn't stand a chance," Penny grinned. "He's going to fall apart the second you walk down the aisle."

"He's just like his father," Maggie mused with a soft, dreamy smile. "Leonard cried the first time he saw me in that dress. Then several more times throughout the ceremony."

Eliza nearly cried herself as Maggie and Cassie embraced, knowing with complete certainty that her friend couldn't have hoped for a more loving, accepting mother-in-law.

"The style has held up well," Dolores pointed out, admiring the high lace collar and tight-fitting bodice.

"Vintage is the way to go," Penny agreed. "Except when you need matching dresses. Then you can't beat handmade." She stretched her arms out to the side while Beverly measured her waist.

"And I couldn't be blessed with a better team of seamstresses." Cassie gazed at the group of women, her green eyes shimmering with gratitude as they resumed the alterations.

While Dolores fussed with the hem of her gown, and the chatter turned to other wedding preparations, Eliza's thoughts wandered once again to her evening with Grant. The night had never quite recovered after he'd asked her about Ben's father. And they'd packed up a few minutes later, riding most of the way home without uttering a word. But the drive wasn't anything like the comfortable silence they'd shared on the way to the lake. Instead, the air felt heavy, clouded with secrets and regret.

Tiptoeing into Ben's room, she'd kissed her sleeping son good night, a ritual she'd never missed in all of his seven years. Retiring to her own room down the hall, Eliza had drifted in and out of sleep, fragments of her recurring dream scattered throughout her mind like disjointed puzzle pieces. The teetering tree swing. Ben's laughter echoing through the branches. The soft, shaggy fur of the family dog. And Grant's smile... an image much hazier than the rest.

An abrupt rap on the cottage's front door startled Eliza from her reverie.

The women tittered and squealed, hiding Cassie in case the visitor happened to be Luke.

As they created a human barricade, Penny waved at Eliza to answer the door. "Tell him he can't come in."

Shaking her head, Eliza laughed. "We don't even know it's Luke."

Gripping the doorknob, she turned it with a slow, deliberate twist of her wrist, prolonging the suspense with dramatic flair.

"Just open it," Penny hissed, while the other women giggled, reveling in the excitement.

Flinging open the door, Eliza blinked in surprise.

There wasn't a single soul in sight.

Poking her head outside, she peered around.

"Well, who is it, dear?" Maggie asked.

"No one." Baffled, Eliza stepped onto the porch, pausing when her bare foot rested on something cold.

Glancing down, she saw a daisy chain necklace and a plain white envelope resting on the welcome mat. Her brow scrunched in confusion, she brought both of them inside.

"Ooh, what is it?" Penny's eyes widened when they landed on the unexpected items.

"I'm not sure." Eliza shrugged, handing them to Cassie.

Maggie smiled. "I think Luke's inviting you to the Daisy Hop."

"That's odd. He invited me yesterday. He made me a crown of daisies and everything. It was quite sweet, actually." Cassie slid the note from the envelope, her lips curling as she unfolded the crisp white paper.

"What does it say?" Dolores and Beverly asked in unison, peering over Cassie's shoulder.

Grinning broadly, Cassie handed the note to Eliza. "It's for you."

"What do you mean it's for me?"

"It's addressed to *you*."

"But who knew I'd be here?"

"As I quickly learned, people have a way of finding things out in Poppy Creek." Cassie chuckled.

Her pulse fluttering, Eliza scanned the familiar penmanship. Then, unable to believe it, she read it again.

"We're dying, Liza. Who invited you to the dance?" Penny pressed both hands over her heart as though it might burst with curiosity any second.

Eliza turned her bewildered gaze toward her friend. "Grant."

"Are you going to say yes?"

"I'm… not sure."

Smiling, Cassie slipped the daisy chain around Eliza's neck. "What do you have to lose?"

Eliza buried her face in the sweet-smelling blooms, unable to meet Cassie's eye.

What did she have to lose?

Only everything.

CHAPTER 18

*C*limbing out of Grant's car, Eliza smoothed down the full skirt of her pink polka dot ensemble. She'd wondered if the retro-inspired dress was excessive, but the enamored look on Grant's face when he'd picked her up told her she'd made the right decision.

Now, if she could only be certain she'd made the right decision agreeing to come tonight.

The click-clack of her heels matched the rhythm of her heartbeat as Eliza ambled beside Grant up the stone pathway toward the picturesque setting at the top of the hill. Mitch Sanders had the classic red barn renovated several years ago, along with extensive landscaping, and ever since then, Poppy Creek held most of the town events at his idyllic farm.

With rows of evergreen trees on one side and a sprawling apple orchard on the other, there couldn't be a prettier backdrop for the Daisy Hop. And the cool evening breeze carried a bouquet of sweet floral notes from Reed's nursery next door, lending the atmosphere an added dose of charm.

As soon as they stepped foot in the barn, friends swarmed around them, pulling them into the flurry and bustle of the dance, already in full swing. While the men instantly wandered to the dessert bar, filling their plates with daisy-shaped sugar cookies and chocolate-dipped flower petals, Cassie and Penny gushed over Eliza's outfit.

"You look stunning." Penny dazzled in her own vintage gown, though more roaring twenties than sock hop, with its elaborately beaded bodice and silvery fringe.

"And I'm so glad you came with Grant." Cassie looped her arm through Eliza's, gazing fondly at the men as they wolfed down more than their fair share of desserts.

"It seems like Colt survived your rejection pretty well." Penny crossed her arms, frowning as Colt chatted up two women at once.

Eliza followed her gaze, her lips twitching as she hid a smile. "You know, Pen… you give Colt a lot of grief. Are *you* sure you don't have a crush on him?"

Penny gasped, her dewy complexion mimicking the rouge tint of her lipstick. "I can't believe you just said that."

Cassie giggled. "She has a point…."

"Because I love you both, I'm going to pretend this conversation never happened."

"Is he a tad arrogant? Sure. A little irresponsible? Definitely. But he's not so bad." Eliza muffled a laugh as Penny's nose twitched.

"Actually, I think he's incredibly sweet," Cassie added earnestly. "He dotes on Maggie. She practically can't lift a finger when he's around. And he's been a big help with the wedding preparations. He spent two hours with Luke and me last night gluing coffee beans to the place cards."

"Colt? Doing a craft project?" This time, Eliza couldn't contain her laughter. Her eyes danced as she stole another glance, surprised to find him conversing with Grant.

Both men were animated, Colt gripping Grant's shoulder as he grinned, making sweeping gestures with his free hand.

Grant caught Eliza's eye and winked, sending a warm flush up her neck and across her cheeks.

Throughout the evening, she found her gaze continually drifted in Grant's direction, her pulse skittering at every stolen glance and secret smile.

If Eliza didn't know any better, she'd assume there was something between them. But despite the plethora of signs, it seemed foolish to hope.

When Dean Martin's playful rendition of "Mambo Italiano" reverberated around the room, Grant plucked a daisy from the floral arrangement on the refreshment table and strode to her side. Placing it between his teeth, he offered her his hand as he waggled his eyebrows.

"Isn't that supposed to be a rose?" she teased.

"Fewer thorns," he mumbled before spitting it out in his hand. "Bleh! But roses might taste better."

Laughing, Eliza snatched the daisy and snapped off the stem, tucking the bloom behind her ear.

"Much better." Grant flashed her an approving smile.

A harrumph drew their attention to the table behind them.

Frank rose and held out his hand to Beverly. "While you two are playing with flowers, we'll show you how to mambo."

Frank led Beverly onto the dance floor and twirled her in his arms, executing each step with a surprising amount of hip action for someone close to needing a hip replacement.

Eliza's mouth dropped open, a giggle escaping. "Why, Frank! I didn't know you had it in you."

"See if you two can keep up." His gray eyes glinted with humor as he spun Beverly around the room.

"I think they might steal our title of Daisy Hop king and queen." Grant sounded both incredulous and impressed.

"They will if you just stand there." Eliza gave his shoulder a good-natured jab.

"You're right." Grant reached for her hand, drawing her into his arms.

For the duration of the song, they followed Frank and Beverly around the dance floor, barely able to keep up. At the conclusion, breathless from dancing and laughing so hard, Grant and Eliza bowed humbly to their rivals, acknowledging defeat.

"You win, good sir." Grant shook Frank's hand, tipping an imaginary hat in respect. "I concede the crown."

"I had no idea you two could dance like that." Eliza swept flyaway tendrils from her glistening forehead, glancing from Frank to Beverly with admiration.

"Never underestimate a navy man," Frank told her with a gratified grin.

When the lively trumpet notes of Frank Sinatra's "Come Fly with Me" piped through the speakers, Grant asked, "Rematch?"

Frank snorted. "Kids these days. And their tomfoolery…" He shook his head for Beverly's benefit.

Chuckling softly, she tucked her arm through his, patting the back of his hand. "Let's get you some punch." She turned to Grant and Eliza, her eyes shimmering with a knowing smile. "You two have fun."

Eliza suppressed another giggle as Frank hobbled off the dance floor. While he might not be a spring chicken, the man had moves and moxie. She'd give him that.

"What do you say?" Grant stretched out his hand. "One more dance?"

"Or as long as it takes…." Eliza trailed off with a mischievous smirk.

"For what?"

"The Charleston Flip."

"*W*e did it! I can't believe it! " Eliza threw her arms around Grant's neck, planting a kiss on his cheek in her excitement. "The flip was perfect!"

When she pulled back, her hands lingered around his neck, her dark eyes glittering as they gazed into his.

Grant took in her flushed cheeks and her full, rosy lips stretched into an inviting smile. His breath came in short, ragged bursts, either from the exertion of dancing or because he desperately wanted to kiss her.

Casting a furtive glance over his shoulder, Grant noticed a few curious onlookers. But no sign of his parents. Not that he was surprised. Or particularly disappointed, under the circumstances. He could only imagine the grief his mother would give him for dancing with Eliza all evening.

Suddenly, her cryptic words flew into his mind unbidden.

There are things about her you don't know....

Grant gritted his teeth, willing the unwelcome thought to disappear. He wouldn't let her get inside his head. Especially tonight. "Why don't we get some fresh air?"

"I'd love to."

Almost as a reflex, Eliza slid her hand in his as he led her outside. His heart sputtering at her touch, Grant curled his fingers even tighter, never wanting to let go.

They stepped into the calm of night, the darkness dispersed by a sky full of silvery stars and strands of golden, twinkling lights stretching from the eaves of the barn across the expansive field of Kentucky bluegrass. The music followed them, providing a mellifluous soundtrack as they strolled to the edge of the lawn overlooking the apple orchard.

"Remember when we used to play tag between the rows of trees?" Eliza kept her hold on Grant's hand. Her soft, tender grip made it difficult for him to concentrate.

"I sure do. You were quick back then."

"I still am," Eliza laughed.

Grant's breath hitched in his throat at the sight of her captivating smile framed in the moonlight. Did she have any idea how beautiful she was? Or how he longed to be the one to keep that vivid sparkle in her eyes?

The dulcet notes of "It Had to Be You" carried across the lawn, prickling the back of Grant's neck with goose bumps. They used to joke that this was their song. Although, they'd loved so many, they found it hard to choose. Years later, when Grant really wanted to torture himself, he would play it when he was alone in his apartment and let the lyrics mock him. Now, as the words washed over him, an uncomfortable tightness seized his throat, and he coughed to clear it.

"Care to dance?" he asked, ignoring the huskiness in his tone.

"Here?" Eliza bit her bottom lip, her wary glance darting back toward the barn.

They were completely alone, save for a lone owl hooting in the distance. Grant liked to think the sage creature was imparting its wisdom, encouraging them to go for it.

Eliza seemed to agree as she stepped into his arms, her lips tipped into a playful smile. "I suppose here is all right."

Grant chuckled softly, pulling her against him. "Glad you approve."

As they swayed to the familiar melody, Eliza rested her head against Grant's chest, and he closed his eyes, breathing in her sweet scent. The scent he'd tried to hold on to for as long as possible. Even refusing to wash the hoodie she'd habitually borrowed in high school. The soft cotton fabric provided a passport back in time whenever he became fearful of forgetting.

Grant splayed his fingers across her lower back, relishing the feel of her body nestled against his. For so many years, he'd physically ached to hold her in his arms again. And now, here they were. His most fervent dream encapsulated in a single moment in time, and Grant never wanted to wake up.

But what if he told her how he felt? Would the protective curtain surrounding them come crashing down? Or did he have a chance to turn this—whatever *this* was—into something more?

"Lizzy..." Grant started, soft and tentative, as though tiptoeing upon his confession. "There's something I want to tell you. But I'm not sure if I should...."

"What is it?" Eliza murmured, nuzzling against him, her voice distant and dreamy.

Grant inhaled, noting the way her head rose and fell with each breath he took. It was now or never. He'd have to take the leap or learn to live with his regrets.

And the latter seemed impossible.

"The truth is... I've never stopped thinking about you, wondering if I gave up on us too easily." His chest constricted at the memory of all those years ago, when he'd let her walk away.

Grant allowed himself a fragment of time to revel in the blissful sensation of their entwined fingers, the pulse of their heartbeats thrumming as one, in case his next words broke the spell. "If there's any hope of a future together, I will fight for you with everything I have. But if you love someone else... if there's a chance that you, Ben, and his father can be a family... I won't come between that. But if I have a shot... even if it's a long shot, I have to know. If not, don't sugarcoat it. I can handle the truth."

Finished with his proclamation, Grant held his breath, wondering if she could hear his desperate heart pummeling his rib cage.

Eliza gazed up at him, her dark eyes shimmering like the twinkle lights draped above them.

A small hesitant smile graced her lips as she asked, "What are you doing tomorrow night?"

CHAPTER 19

*D*rawing in a purposeful breath, Eliza attempted to steady her trembling fingers as she applied a final coat of Hot Pink Sunset. The vibrant fuchsia lipstick would act as her armor, a defense against kissing Grant on their date tonight. Because she couldn't kiss him. Not yet. First, she had to untangle herself from the mess she'd made.

The truth was her only hope.

And her greatest obstacle.

The doorbell chimed, and Eliza heard Ben shout, "I'll get it!" as he clomped across the house to answer the door.

Setting down her lipstick, she scrutinized her appearance one last time before heading downstairs. Despite wearing more makeup than usual, she left her hair loose, tumbling in soft, casual waves around her shoulders. Since she wasn't sure what Grant had in mind for their date, she'd paired white capris with simple wedges and a floral off-the-shoulder blouse.

When she reached the bottom of the staircase, Grant glanced up from his conversation with Ben, his words faltering mid-sentence. Eliza hid a smile at the dazed look on his face. Guess she'd chosen the right outfit.

"You look... incredible," Grant breathed.

"Thank you." She did her best to sound breezy despite the butterflies having a hoedown in her stomach.

"Ben was just telling me all about his guys' night in with his grandpa tonight."

"Which, knowing Dad, probably consists of watching back-to-back John Wayne movies," Eliza said with a laugh.

"That doesn't sound so bad. If it were my dad, it'd be war documentaries."

"What are you guys gonna do?" Ben gazed up at Grant, his head tilted in curiosity.

"It's a surprise."

Ben scrunched up his face. "Mom doesn't like surprises."

"Is that so?" Grant's eyes twinkled as he met Eliza's gaze, scattering goose bumps across her bare arms.

"Well, don't you two look nice." Sylvia sailed into the room wearing a Regency-style gown, complete with elbow-length gloves.

"You, too, Mom," Eliza giggled. "I thought tonight was book club?"

"It is, dear. Tonight is a theme night. We're reading *Pride and Prejudice*. Don't I look the part?"

"Prettier than all the Bennet sisters," Grant said, bowing at the waist.

Sylvia beamed. "Liza, I like this one."

"Flattery will get you everywhere," Eliza told Grant with a grin.

"You kids have fun." Sylvia winked at Grant as she wrapped an embroidered cloak around her shoulders. Then, turning to Eliza, she added, "I assume the cupcakes for the school bake sale are still at the bakery since I didn't see them in the kitchen."

"The bake sale!" Eliza gasped, covering her face with her palm. "I completely forgot."

Sylvia shot her a reproachful glance, and Eliza winced.

Trying to juggle all of her responsibilities, Eliza lived in a constant state of guilt mixed with exhaustion, plus a dash of memory loss. And the icing on her overburdened cake was a thick layer of anxiety sprinkled generously with fear of failure. "Can't I bring something I've already made? I have dozens of desserts lying around."

"You know Daphne was extremely specific. She wants three dozen ladybug cupcakes."

"What's a ladybug cupcake?" Grant asked.

"Regular cupcakes, but Daphne wants the frosting to look like ladybugs. I guess she's doing a garden theme for the bake sale this year." Eliza did her best to suppress an eye roll, but Grant picked up on her annoyance and flashed a sympathetic smile.

"Grandpa and I can make them," Ben volunteered.

"Bless your heart, child." Sylvia patted the top of Ben's head, mussing his blond hair. "Your grandfather can't follow a recipe to save his life. Want me to stay?" Sylvia asked Eliza.

Eliza twirled her silver cuff bracelet around her wrist, toying with the idea. The offer was tempting. But the bake sale was her responsibility. "No, that's okay," she sighed, sliding the cuff farther up her arm like Wonder Woman's Bracelets of Submission. Turning to Grant, she summoned her most apologetic smile. "I'm so sorry. Can we postpone for another time?"

"Why don't I stay and help?"

"Yeah!" Ben cheered, hopping up and down at the suggestion.

"Oh, um…" Eliza chewed her bottom lip, smudging her strategically applied lipstick. Sure, she wanted to spend more time with Grant. But all three of them together? That seemed like a recipe for disaster, no pun intended.

"What a lovely idea! It's settled." With a flourish, Sylvia plopped a bonnet on her head and reached for the door. "Enjoy your cozy date night in."

"Thanks." Eliza cringed at the anxious croak in her voice,

subconsciously running her tongue along her front teeth in case she'd transferred any Hot Pink Sunset where it didn't belong.

"Ta-ta!" With a regal wave, Sylvia left in a flurry of ruffles and lace.

When the door finally swung shut, Grant released a pent-up breath. "Your mom takes book club pretty seriously."

"Any excuse to wear a costume." Eliza attempted a laugh, but it barely made it past the lump in her throat. Spending time with Grant and Ben together *wasn't* the plan. She needed to lay groundwork first. This was all happening much too quickly. And she could only hope the evening wouldn't blow up in her face like the time she'd made pie filling in the blender and forgot to replace the lid.

Plastering a smile on her face, she turned to Ben. "Who's ready to make some cupcakes?"

"Me! Me!" Ben whooped, skipping toward the kitchen.

Eliza and Grant fell in step behind him.

"Thank you for being flexible. I hope you didn't have anything too elaborate planned." Eliza tried to hide the disappointment in her voice.

"Only a carriage ride, a string quartet, and our very own fireworks display."

"Oh, no! Remind me to make sure the apple we give Daphne at the end of the school year has a worm in it."

Grant snorted with laughter. "I take it you're not her biggest fan."

"She's not so bad, I guess. I think I'm just overly sensitive because she's threatened to hold Ben back a grade."

"What? Ben's a bright kid. What possible reason could she have for holding him back?"

Eliza shrugged. "His grades on his homework are great. But she doesn't think he's developed the skills he needs in the classroom. She's worried he won't be able to keep up with the other kids in third grade. And she says it's easier to hold him back now than later on."

"I'm sorry, Lizzy. How does Ben feel about it?"

"I... haven't told him yet." Eliza grimaced. "I know that sounds awful. But I keep hoping we'll figure out the problem and get a handle on it before the end of the year. Which is only a few weeks away." She sighed, a heaviness settling around her heart. "But I'm probably kidding myself."

"Hey." Grant reached for her hand and gave it a squeeze. "You're a great mom. And Ben's a great kid. You don't have to solve everything tonight."

"You're right," she murmured, gazing at their entwined fingers. "We just have to bake three dozen cupcakes that look like ladybugs."

"Think she'll notice if we throw a few dung beetles in there?" Grant asked with mock seriousness.

Laughter spilling from her lips, Eliza jabbed his shoulder. "Don't you dare."

When they reached the kitchen, Grant released Eliza's hand, and she instantly missed the feel of him—the comfort a simple touch provided in a difficult situation.

For a moment, it felt like she'd had a teammate to help carry the burden.

And Eliza would do almost anything to get that feeling back.

S queezed into the small kitchen, Grant reveled in fond memories of baking with Eliza. Although, strangely, he found it even more enjoyable with Ben around. His quirky antics and childlike curiosity added a certain richness to the experience that Grant hadn't expected.

Plus, it wasn't a bad idea to have someone provide a buffer between him and Eliza. Every time he thought her allure couldn't become any more intense, she did something even more adorable.

Like turn on music and dance barefoot across the slick hardwood floor with her son while they assembled the necessary ingredients.

To Grant's surprise and delight, they included him in all of their goofy games, flicking flour at each other and seeing who could keep a straight face after licking a spoonful of salt. For the first time, Grant understood what it felt like to be part of a normal, loving family. A thought that instantly filled him with guilt.

He loved his parents and adored his sister. But they didn't know how to interact with one another. Or, at least, not like this —lighthearted and free from years of tension and resentment.

Before Eliza and Ben, Grant had resigned himself to never knowing the fullness of having his own family. Now, he glimpsed a glimmer of hope on the horizon. And it appeared to be a lot closer than he'd originally thought.

"Here." Eliza held out the pair of whisks from the electric mixer, each one dripping with chocolate cake batter. "You two can share."

"This is my favorite part," Ben told Grant. "Except for making frosting."

"I couldn't agree more." As Grant accepted the whisk from Eliza, their fingers grazed, shooting a jolt of awareness up his arm. He jumped, flinging the whisk into the air, spraying globs of batter across the countertop. His face coloring, Grant snatched a kitchen towel to mop up the mess. "I'm so sorry."

"It's fine." Eliza waved away his concern with a smile. "Don't worry about it." Dampening a washcloth in the sink, she helped him clean up the splatter.

"Do I have to share mine now?" Ben asked, his tone willing, albeit disappointed.

Grant chuckled. "No, that one's all yours. But I'll have to be more careful when it's time for the frosting." He stole a glance at Eliza and caught her watching him. Had she felt the same spark he had?

Eliza returned her gaze to the speckled countertop, her cheeks noticeably rosier. "Speaking of frosting, you guys go ahead and get started while I finish cleaning up."

"You got it." Grant straightened and surveyed the ingredients spread around the kitchen. "Frosting... frosting..."

Eliza raised one eyebrow and paired it with a smirk. "Did you forget how to make it?"

"Not exactly. I remember that it involves copious amounts of sugar. And... lard? Lard's a thing, right?"

Shaking her head, Eliza laughed. "There's a recipe in the cookbook."

"We need butter. Right, Mom?"

"Yep. Lots of butter."

"Okay, that settles it." Grant gave a definitive nod. "Ben, you're in charge of assembling the ingredients. I'll start mashing the butter. With this, right?" He plucked a meat mallet from the utensil holder and waved it around for comic effect.

Eliza slapped her forehead, but Ben bubbled over with laughter.

"He's worse at baking than Aunt Cassie!"

"I'll take that as a compliment." Grant winked.

As Grant and Ben worked together on the frosting, Eliza moved to the stack of dishes in the sink. But Grant noticed her sneak glances at the two of them together, and he couldn't tell if her expression was pleased or... pensive.

"All right." Grant directed his attention back to Ben. "After I add the vanilla, what's next?"

"Um..." Ben leaned over the cookbook, his forehead scrunched as he squinted in concentration. "The milk."

"How much?"

The tip of his tongue sticking out the corner of his mouth, Ben traced a finger across the page. "Two tablespoons."

"Great. Thanks." As Grant measured the milk, he cast a sideways glance at Ben, a thought niggling at the back of his mind.

No... it was probably nothing.

CHAPTER 20

*T*hings with Grant were going well. Almost *too* well.

Eliza had spent the entire morning at the bake sale reminiscing about the night before. Although they'd been crammed into a small kitchen, they'd fit together perfectly. Like a three layer cake.

On the car ride home from school, Ben couldn't stop babbling excitedly about Grant, wondering when they could hang out and paint again.

As though he knew they were talking about him, a text from Grant pinged Eliza's cell phone the moment they pulled into the driveway.

I found some of my old art supplies from high school and thought I'd pass them along to Ben. Mind if I bring them by this afternoon?

Her stomach flipped as she reread the text. Grant was becoming increasingly more enmeshed in their lives. And if Eliza allowed it to continue, she would have to tell him everything. But at what cost?

Then again… what would be the cost if she *didn't* tell him?

Eliza vacillated between the two options almost as regularly as the passing of each hour in the day, torn between her desire to tell the truth and her dread of the consequences.

"Ben…" Eliza turned to face her son in the back seat. "What do you think about sharing our special family tradition with Grant?"

"Yay!" He unclipped his seat belt with gusto. "Today?"

"Yep. We need to spend a little time on homework first. Then we'll set everything up in the backyard."

With a huge grin stretched across his face, Ben scrambled out of the car and raced inside, hopping up the porch steps two at a time.

Chuckling, Eliza followed. She'd never seen him in a bigger hurry to do his homework.

As Ben settled at the dining room table with a glass of apple juice and his first assignment, Eliza pulled out her phone. Her fingers hovered over the keys.

Once she sent the text, there would be no going back. They'd never invited anyone into their quirky tradition before. Not her parents, not Luke and Cassie. No one. Maybe they weren't ready for this step?

"Do you think Grant'll like it?" Ben set down his pencil and took a big gulp of apple juice. His dark eyes held hers, so full of hope and earnestness.

Eliza melted. "Of course he will, Bug. He'll love it."

After sending Grant the text, telling him when and where to meet them, Eliza said a silent prayer she was right. Because the only thing worse than having her heart broken…

Was breaking her son's.

*A*s Grant rounded the corner of the Carters' home toward the backyard, his heart thudded louder than boot stompers in a dance hall.

Eliza's text couldn't have been more ambiguous.

That'd be great. Meet us in the backyard in one hour. Wear grungy clothes and flip-flops.

That was it. No explanation. Not even a hint as to what he could expect.

So, here he was... toting an easel and bag of art supplies with no clue why Eliza wanted him to meet them in the backyard. With a strange dress code, no less.

Shifting the tote bag to his other shoulder, Grant eased open the side gate. A familiar high-pitched squeak emanated from the rusty hinges. But that's where the similarities to his youthful memories ended.

Grant noticed the huge play set first, with its spiral slide and double swings. A new addition for Ben's sake, no doubt. A portable soccer net occupied one corner of the expansive lawn next to a tetherball set. More toys Grant didn't remember.

Then his gaze fell on Eliza. More specifically, on her tanned, toned legs clad in white denim cutoff shorts.

When he realized his mouth had fallen open, Grant snapped it shut, tearing his gaze from her legs to her bare arms, finally registering the bright pink water balloon clutched in her hand. By her side, clothed in a faded T-shirt and swim trunks, Ben gripped a green balloon, a goofy grin splashed across his face.

"What's going on?" Setting his belongings in the grass, Grant took a step closer, squinting at the huge canvas tarp beneath their bare feet.

"Well... Since you've been so generous sharing your love of

art with Ben, we decided to let you in on one of our favorite art projects." Eliza turned to her son. "Right, Ben?"

"Right," Ben snickered, barely able to contain his giggle.

"Art project?" Grant cast a curious glance at three five-gallon paint buckets filled with water balloons.

"Should we show him?" Eliza asked Ben, her dark eyes glinting mischievously.

Ben nodded, his grin widening as he wound his right arm, the water balloon poised and ready.

Grant instinctively took a step back.

But not far enough.

Eliza and Ben lobbed their water balloons in his direction, one smacking Grant in the shoulder, the other hitting his left calf. Pink and green paint dripped down his body, sprinkling the grass.

Giggling, Ben ran to one of the buckets. "Now you have to stay on the tarp!" He grabbed a green balloon and chucked it at Eliza, who squealed and tried to duck out of the way. It hit her square in the stomach, much to Ben's delight.

In a split second, Grant had recovered from his shock, kicked off his flip-flops, and sprinted toward the bucket filled with blue water balloons. Snatching one in each hand, he rapid-fire released them, nailing Ben in the leg and decorating Eliza's backside.

Peals of laughter filled the air as they splattered paint all over the tarp—and each other—slipping and sliding in the puddles of pink, blue, and green. Although Grant suspected the paint was washable, he didn't care. He was having the time of his life! Saddened only to find his supply of ammunition had dwindled.

Down to his last balloon, Grant knew he needed to make it count. He zeroed in on Eliza and made a beeline straight for her.

Disregarding the rules to remain on the tarp, Eliza shrieked with laughter and took off across the lawn.

Grant followed in close pursuit, keeping an eye on the pink water balloon gripped in her hand.

Rounding the tool shed, Grant closed the gap, grasping her forearm.

Eliza squealed, trying to fight him off between fits of breathless laughter.

Unable to wiggle free, she flung the balloon at his head, but Grant dove out of the way, dragging them both to the ground in a tangle of slippery limbs.

His body braced over hers, Grant held up his balloon, grinning devilishly. "For your sake, I hope this is washable paint."

"It is," she gasped, her dark eyes locked on his, her breath ragged.

For a moment, all Grant could think about was lowering his mouth to hers, finally drinking her in. Every muscle in his body tensed, and he was certain she could hear the pounding of his heartbeat, mere inches away from her own.

Eliza's pupils dilated, signaling to Grant that she was thinking the same exact thing.

Tossing the water balloon aside, Grant cupped the back of her head, bringing her closer as she parted her lips, her eyelids fluttering closed.

This was it.

The moment he'd dreamt about nonstop. The one that would reveal the barely contained emotions he'd been too cowardly to share. The one moment that would change everything....

Smack!

A short, sharp pain pricked the back of Grant's neck and green paint slowly dripped down his collarbone, trickling onto Eliza's throat.

"Got you!" Ben hopped up and down, wiggling his arms in some sort of victory dance.

Eliza shifted beneath him, but not before Grant caught the

look in her eyes—a mixture of disappointment, longing, and… fear?

But fear of what?

Of things not working out?

Or was Eliza more afraid of what would happen if things *did* work out?

Whatever the reason, Grant would make it his mission to eliminate any ounce of apprehension. For both of them.

Because somehow, when he'd least expected it, these two oddballs had become his family. And he'd give up everything— even his biggest account—in order to keep them.

CHAPTER 21

*W*hile Grant worked with Ben at one of the bakery's bistro tables—Grant on the website, Ben on his homework—Grant stole glances in Eliza's direction. Occasionally, he'd catch her staring at him out of the corner of her eye while she polished the antique cash register.

It felt as though they were performing a dance, sidestepping around their feelings, never quite admitting the truth.

And the truth was, Grant loved Eliza with every fiber of his being.

In fact, he'd never *stopped* loving her. And the next time they were alone, Grant planned to say exactly that.

"Ben, would you mind reading off the latte flavors for me?" Grant poised his fingers over the keyboard, ready to add them to the website.

"Um... okay." Gazing at the board, Ben squinted, scooting toward the edge of his chair. "Vanilla?"

Based on his scrunched features and uncertain tone, Grant wondered if Ben had made a lucky guess. "And?"

"Chocolate?"

Peering over his shoulder, Grant surveyed the list. No vanilla or chocolate. Cassie had come up more creative names for her concoctions. Swiveling back to Ben, he studied his tense features, the dip in his eyebrows, the pucker of his lower lip.

On a hunch, Grant handed him his glasses. "Here. Try these on for a second."

His dark eyes wide and curious, Ben slipped the wire frames over his nose. Too big for his face, they hung slightly crooked.

"Now try reading the board again." Grant gave him an encouraging nod.

Tentatively, Ben studied the menu. "H-Honey Lavender. Cinnamon Twist. Li-Li—"

"Licorice. That's a tough one. But well done! I think we've solved the mystery behind your trouble in school." Grant glanced at Eliza, surprised by her blanched features and misty eyes. Why didn't she look happy? She'd been stressed for months over Ben's problems in school, blaming herself. She should be glad it's something as solvable as getting Ben a pair of glasses. Shouldn't she?

"Here you go!" Cassie sailed in from the kitchen carrying a tray with two slices of cheesecake. As she set the plates on the table, she noticed Ben's glasses. "Well, don't you look adorable." She ruffled the top of his head before smiling at Grant. "Playing dress up?"

"Actually, we just figured out Ben's nearsighted." Grant could have kicked himself for not noticing sooner, especially when Ben read the frosting recipe a few nights ago. His intense level of concentration should have been a dead giveaway.

"Nearsighted?" Cassie glanced at Ben, who wolfed down his slice of cheesecake, oblivious to the world.

"Yeah. Which explains why he always did great with his homework, but has trouble in class. He probably can't see the whiteboard. Or anything else that's not directly in front of him."

"Oh, my goodness! Why didn't he say anything?"

"Kids don't always know what's going on. I didn't. I was ten when I got my first pair of glasses. But probably needed them sooner." Turning to Ben, Grant asked, "So, what are we having?"

Ben mumbled an unintelligible response, scattering crumbs across the tabletop.

Cassie laughed. "It's Eliza's tiramisu cheesecake. We plan on serving it as our free teaser dessert during the grand opening. What do you think?"

Swallowing, Ben gave her an exaggerated thumbs-up, chocolate sauce smeared across his face. "Tiramisu is my favorite."

"No kidding! Mine, too. Even when I was your age. Which my mom always thought was weird since most kids don't like the coffee flavor." Grinning at their newfound connection, Grant lifted his fork, eager to try his first bite.

Cassie inhaled a sharp breath, and when Grant looked up, she'd turned the same pale shade as Eliza.

What had gotten into them? It was as though they'd both seen a ghost or something.

***

*E*liza winced as Cassie pulled her into the kitchen. The shelves, countertops, oven... everything blurred together.

"What's going on?" Cassie's eyes were wide with shock. "Please tell me Grant isn't... he can't be..." Cassie couldn't finish her thought.

Feeling light-headed, Eliza stumbled toward the sink, bracing herself against the cool metal basin.

Breathe... just breathe...

She stared at the streaks of greasy butter and dried clumps of batter baked onto the cookie sheet, suddenly compelled to scrub away every single stain.

Without thinking, she flipped on the faucet.

Coming closer, Cassie lowered her voice. "Liza, please talk to me."

Squirting soap onto the sponge, Eliza scrubbed with all her strength, oblivious to the scalding temperature of the water as it turned her hands bright red. Why wouldn't the scorch marks come off? Suddenly, nothing else mattered except getting the baking sheet sparkling clean.

Cassie switched off the faucet and grabbed her elbow, steering her out the back door onto the patio.

Only once she was outside, with the cool breeze caressing her skin, did Eliza realize hot tears stained her cheeks.

Leading her to a quiet bench tucked beneath a wisteria-covered arbor, Cassie pulled Eliza down beside her.

They sat in silence for several minutes, Eliza watching the soap suds drip from her hands onto the smooth cobblestone where they burst and disappeared through the sinewy cracks.

"How long have you known?" Cassie asked softly.

"Since always," Eliza croaked, the words burning the back of her throat. "There's never been anyone else." Swiping at her tears, she flinched as the soap stung her eyes.

Cassie waited without saying a word, rubbing a soothing hand along her back.

"The night of graduation, Grant gave me a promise ring," Eliza continued, her voice distant as though it came from across the courtyard. "A delicate rose gold band. He'd even had the inside engraved." She gazed at her ring finger, now barren, save for a few lingering soap suds. "It never should have happened. No one knows that better than me. But Ben..." Her voice broke, and Cassie wrapped her arm around her shoulders.

"Ben is my greatest earthly treasure. I—"

"I know," Cassie murmured, stroking her arm.

"I wanted to tell Grant about Ben as soon as I found out. I—I went to his house right after I took the test. But..." Eliza squeezed her eyes shut, not wanting to relive the memory.

"But what?" Cassie pressed gently.

"As soon as Harriet saw me, she knew something was wrong. She... she made me tell her." The tears fell unrestrained as a painful sob rose in her chest. "She told me Grant had a promising future and she wouldn't let... someone like me ruin her son's life."

"She didn't!" Cassie gasped, her fingers clenching Eliza's arm.

"I told her Grant had a right to know. And to make his own decision. But..." Eliza's gaze dropped to her hands. The bubbles had disappeared, leaving her exposed skin dry and raw.

"But what?"

The fervent compassion in Cassie's voice broke Eliza's resolve. She couldn't keep the secret any longer. "Grant's father is my parents' accountant. According to Harriet, my dad never paid taxes on any of the handyman work he did around town." Eliza's cheeks burned with shame and she kept her gaze locked on her hands. "Harriet said if Stan turned him in to the IRS, my parents would lose everything. And my dad could go to jail."

Cassie's hand flew to her mouth, her eyes shimmering with sympathy. "Oh, Liza. I'm so, so sorry. I... I don't know what to say."

"I didn't, either. I was so... terrified." The word came out in a whisper, and Eliza shivered despite the warm afternoon sun. All the fear and loneliness of that moment came rushing back, pulling another sob from her lips.

Her own tears spilling down her cheeks, Cassie squeezed tighter.

"Harriet's threat kept me quiet for years. But on Ben's third birthday, when Luke gave him his first baseball mitt... I broke down. Grant should've been there. I knew it wasn't right that I'd been sacrificing my son's relationship with his father so I could protect my parents. And I'd resolved to tell him everything. But that's when the article came out."

"What article?"

As the clouds shifted, Eliza hugged herself, running her hands up and down her forearms to banish the sudden chill. "Grant's company got a write-up in a magazine. Everyone in town was talking about it. The headline was 'Superstar Startup.' I'll never forget the quote they pulled from the interview and turned into a giant graphic. 'The secret to my success? Zero distractions. No ballet recitals or Little League. One hundred percent focus, one hundred percent of the time.'"

The ache in her chest suddenly too intense to ignore, Eliza hunched forward, burying her face in her hands.

"I'm sure he didn't mean—"

"That's not all...." Taking a deep breath, Eliza forced herself to sit up and meet Cassie's gaze. "He also said, 'I've always known a family wasn't in my future. And it's allowed me to take certain risks. And those risks have paid off.'" Eliza recited Grant's interview with uncanny accuracy, having read and reread the article a thousand times until every single word was scorched into her memory. "That's when I realized Harriet had been right all along. Or... at least, I *thought* she was. But now... I don't know what to do, Cass. Please, tell me what to do." Crumbling inward, Eliza allowed the sob to escape, racking her entire body.

Cassie didn't stir, holding her until the trembling in her shoulders subsided.

Finally, when Eliza lifted her tear-streaked face, she noticed a soft, wistfulness in Cassie's features.

"What are you thinking?" Sniffling, Eliza wiped her damp cheeks with the back of her hand.

Cassie tilted her chin toward a planter box filled with sunny daffodils. "Beautiful, aren't they?"

"Sure, I guess." Eliza stared at her friend in bewilderment. Why were they talking about flowers?

"Did you know they're symbolic of rebirth and new beginnings?" Cassie continued, a small smile lighting her eyes. "Every spring, they get another chance. It's the same bulb; it can't change where it's been planted. And yet, it's technically a brand-new bloom. Pretty neat, huh?"

As Cassie's words took root, Eliza's lips twitched. "Are you sure you didn't grow up in Poppy Creek? Because you sure know how to speak the language."

Cassie grinned before her features softened, her gaze earnest. "No matter what happens, we're all here for you. You know that, right?"

Her heart full, Eliza nodded.

While she had no idea how things would turn out, she was certain of one thing.

The truth was long overdue.

CHAPTER 22

*O**h, no!** What was he doing here?*

Tossing her journal aside, Eliza leapt from the window seat, sweeping back the floral curtains for a better look.

She wasn't ready to see Grant. After spending hours scribbling down all her thoughts, Eliza still hadn't figured out how to tell him the truth.

Yet, there he was... strolling up their walkway as casual as could be. Meanwhile, her heart felt like egg whites being whipped for meringue.

Eliza raced down the staircase and rushed to the front door, flinging it open before Grant had a chance to knock.

"Hi." He stepped back in surprise as Eliza yanked the door shut behind her.

"What are you doing here?" She grabbed his forearm and dragged him down the steps and away from the house.

"I thought I'd volunteer to go with you and Ben to the eye doctor. You know, since I have experience being vision impaired." Grant flashed her a grin, but it quickly disappeared. "What's the matter?"

"You can't come with us." Eliza paced the driveway, the accusatory crunch of the gravel heightening her agitation.

"Why not?"

"Because." Wringing her hands, she drew in a shaky breath, trying to gather courage from who knew where.

"What's going on? You're acting... strange. Is Ben all right?"

"Ben is..."

Crunch, crunch, crunch...

Why was the gravel so infernally loud?

"Ben is..." Eliza repeated then paused, the air around them suddenly still and silent.

Too silent.

Not even a hush of wind through the trees.

"Lizzy?" Grant prompted, his voice strained with worry.

Drawing her gaze to meet his, Eliza forced her lips to part, willing the words to slip past her fear. "Ben is... your son."

The truth dispersed on a whisper, lighter than a fallen leaf fluttering to the ground. Eliza held her breath, waiting for her words to land with the force of the entire universe.

"Very funny." Grant's laugh sounded more like a bark, short and tense, as though he wasn't quite sure what to make of her joke.

"Grant..." Painfully, Eliza stepped toward him, although every self-preserving instinct told her to flee. From the guilt. The shame. The repercussions.

But she couldn't. Especially when the flicker of realization blazed across Grant's face. His features settled into a heart-wrenching mix of anguish, shock, and fear, leaving her winded like a blow to the stomach.

Oh, what she wouldn't give to erase his pain—the pain *she* had caused.

Her legs trembling, Eliza took another step.

Grant stumbled backward, both hands raised. "Don't."

"Please, let me explain." Tears blurred her vision as she tried to move toward him. Let her explain? As if that would somehow fix what she'd done. Her throat constricted, making breathing nearly impossible, let alone words.

"You know," Grant murmured, his throat raspy. "When I first found out you were pregnant, I thought that maybe the child was mine. But then I heard you'd told everyone in town that the father was a tourist and I knew you'd never lie about something like that. But I guess I was wrong."

Hot tears streamed down her face as he spoke, each one searing her skin. She opened her mouth to speak, but no words came out.

Not that it mattered.

Grant had turned his back to her, crossing the driveway with long, rapid strides. He might as well be running away from her.

And Eliza couldn't blame him.

She'd spent years protecting the ones she loved from the fallout of the truth. But now that she'd unleashed it, she feared the destruction would be even worse than she'd imagined.

*B*y the time Grant pried his fingers from around the steering wheel, they shook uncontrollably.

Clenching his eyes shut, he leaned against the headrest, drawing in a desperate breath. But no matter how deeply he inhaled, his lungs wouldn't fill.

His entire world had tipped on its axis; every emotion converged together, leaving him devoid of energy and the ability to think straight.

Or more accurately, the ability to think at all.

Hauling himself up the porch steps, Grant barely noticed his father reading on the wicker love seat.

"What's the matter? Are you sick?" Setting his book on the side table, Stan uncrossed his legs, leaning forward in concern.

"Something like that." Grant pressed the back of his hand to his forehead, noting it did feel warm.

"Have a seat." Stan scooted over, patting the space beside him.

"Not right now, Dad. I—" In the middle of his protest, Grant's limbs weakened, and he sank onto the plush cushion, hanging his head in his hands. He winced as a sharp pain pierced his left temple.

"Here, have some water." Ice cubes clinked together as Stan handed him the tall glass.

Grant threw his head back, downing huge gulps, slightly invigorated by the hint of lemon and mint. After he'd chugged the last drop, he handed the glass back to his dad.

Stan smiled as he eyed the remaining chunks of ice and lemon wedge. "Feel better?"

"A little, thanks."

"Why don't you tell me what's on your mind?"

"You're not going to believe it."

"Try me." Stan shifted in his seat to face his son.

Grant raked his fingers through his hair, wondering how he'd break the news. News he still hadn't digested himself. After a deep, ragged breath, he decided on the blunt approach. "I just found out that Ben is my son." As the words left his lips, they sounded distant and removed, as though someone else had spoken them.

When Stan didn't respond, Grant snuck a sideways glance, fearing the worst. Would he be angry? Would he lecture him? Because that was the last thing Grant needed.

Ever since the night after graduation, Grant had lived with remorse. Even though they'd both been complicit, he'd apologized to Eliza for his lack of self-control, reaffirming his desire to wait until their marriage vows. But after that moment, their relationship had changed. And Grant had always wondered if it was the reason Eliza broke up with him. Which made it all the more painful when he'd learned she'd been with someone else. Of course, now he knew that was a lie.

It was all a lie.

But the worst part... the truth that had wrenched Grant's heart right out of his chest... was that Eliza didn't want him to be the father of her child. To the point that she'd kept their connection a secret. Grant didn't think he'd ever get over that.

"Congratulations."

When Stan finally spoke, Grant flinched, certain he'd imagined it. "What?"

"Congratulations," Stan repeated, his voice warm and even. "Being a father is a wonderful gift."

"Ha!" Grant grunted. "Even if it's a gift that's given begrudgingly?" He shook his head, the sharp pain now dull and throbbing. "She didn't tell me, Dad. I've missed the first seven years of my son's life."

"I'm sure she had her reasons."

"Yeah," Grant snarled, bitterness rising in his throat like bile. "She knows I'll make a lousy father and didn't want me messing up her son."

"I'm sure that's not it."

"How do you know? No offense, but I don't come from the most functional family."

Stan's gaze flickered to the ground. "No, you don't. And I bear a lot of responsibility for that."

Grant shrugged, guilt overpowering his grief. "It wasn't all bad. We had some good times together. Especially before we moved." *Before you and mom stopped speaking to each other,* he mused, deciding to keep that particular observation to himself.

A shadow of sadness passed over Stan's features, and he looked away.

Something in his father's expression pricked Grant's curiosity. "Why *did* we move?"

Stan remained silent, staring off into the distance, so Grant pressed again. "Dad? I think I deserve to know."

"I never intended to tell you or your sister," Stan murmured, twisting his watchband around his wrist. "But I always wondered if she suspected."

"Why would Olivia know anything about it?"

"Because Olivia was the one being bullied in school."

Grant's eyes widened in shock. "What?"

While his sister was three years younger, and they'd never had the same circle of friends, Grant wanted to believe he'd know if she'd been bullied.

"Private schools can be wonderful. But they also have a dark side. Intense pressure and an unhealthy need for approval. Your sister... didn't fit the mold."

"Why? Because she was a tomboy? So what?" Grant's chest heaved with anger. "Who bullied her?"

"All the other girls in her class. They were vicious, too. Stuff I couldn't believe any child would think of."

"How come I didn't know?" Grant whispered, his heart shattering.

Stan's features softened as he placed a hand on Grant's shoulder. "You went to different schools, had different friends. And you know Olivia, she doesn't open up easily. Your mother and I suspect it had been going on for a long time before we found out."

"What did Mom have to say about it?" Knowing his mother's vindictive streak, Grant had to assume her reaction wasn't pretty.

"She thought we could work things out with the parents. But I could tell the apples didn't fall far from the trees. Those kids came from the type of parents who would do anything to get ahead, even if it meant tearing others down. Those children were merely modeling what they were taught at home."

Grant felt sick, his fingers clenching. He'd punch a brick wall, if it would do any good.

"Moving was drastic," Stan admitted. "One of my clients vacationed in California and stumbled upon Poppy Creek on their trip. At the time, it sounded like the sort of town we needed. Of course, that's the hard part about being a parent. Not every decision you make will be the right one."

They sat in silence a moment. A lone bird warbled in the distance, its melancholy timbre sending shivers up Grant's arms.

"For what it's worth," he said softly, turning to face his dad, "I think you made the right decision."

Stan held his gaze and a healing glance passed between them.

Over the last several days, one thing had become undeniably clear to Grant. Things weren't always simple and straightforward. Life was messy and complicated. And any worthwhile relationship required digging deep, occasionally venturing into dark and difficult places. But you often came out better for it.

"Want to finish our chess game?" Stan asked.

"That sounds great." Rising from the love seat, Grant felt as though he'd left a crippling weight behind him.

And regardless of what Eliza thought—or anyone, for that matter—Grant would do whatever it took to be the best father possible...

For his son.

CHAPTER 23

The latch clicked, and Eliza leaned against the door, her heart still pounding, rebelling inside her chest as though it couldn't stand to be near her, either.

"You told him, didn't you?" Straightening from half-moon pose, Sylvia readjusted the tie-dyed sweatband around her glistening forehead.

"Wh-who?" Eliza stammered, wincing at the self-conscious catch in her voice. Between the fact that she'd steered Grant away from the house, and the loud flute music emanating from her mother's yoga video, there was no way Sylvia could have overheard them.

"Grant, of course. I assume the shell-shocked expression on your face is because you finally told him he's Ben's father."

Her knees weakening, Eliza slid a few inches down the door frame, like buttercream frosting melting in the sun. "You knew?"

"Sweetheart, I'm an actress. I know how to read people. Besides, you're my daughter. You came to me with some cocka-mamie story about a tourist boy you barely knew. Please. It's way too out of character." Grabbing the remote off the coffee table, Sylvia hit pause.

"Who else knows?"

"Your father. Maybe Maggie. But we've never discussed it. I only assume because she knows you almost as well as I do."

Eliza stumbled the few steps from the threshold into the living room and collapsed onto the couch, wishing she could bury herself in the oversize cushions and never come out. "Why didn't you ever say anything?"

Sylvia shrugged, the wide collar of her neon workout top slipping off her thin shoulder. "I figured you'd tell me about it when you were ready."

"So, let me get this straight." Eliza hugged one of the plump throw pillows, seeking comfort in the soft folds of the fabric. "You grill me like a secret service agent whenever you get even a whiff that I might be dating someone. But you never once mention this? I have to say, Mom. That doesn't seem like the best parenting decision."

"Well, you would know." Sylvia smirked, the twinkle in her eyes adding levity.

Despite herself, Eliza laughed at the somber irony, deep and cleansing, until tears spilled down her cheeks. Then, coming to her senses, she hurriedly muzzled her face with the pillow. "This isn't funny. It's horrible. Grant is really upset. And he has every right to be. I desperately want to fix things, but I don't know how."

"Well..." Sylvia perched on the edge of the coffee table, stretching the thin spandex of her yoga pants as she crossed her legs. "We Carters might be a lot of things, but we certainly aren't cowards. Whatever it takes to make things right, I'm confident you'll find a way."

Her mother's words did little to reassure her. The hole she'd dug was too deep, and insurmountably wide. And she hadn't even told her the worst part.

Peeking above the frilly lace trim, Eliza met her mother's gaze. "There's something else you should know."

"What's that?"

"The reason I never told Grant about Ben. Or, at least, one of the reasons I never told him."

Sylvia leaned forward, revealing a hint of her leopard print sports bra. "I'm your captive audience."

Fidgeting with the large decorative button on the throw pillow, Eliza kept her gaze lowered. "Harriet knows that Grant's Ben's father. And… she knows about Dad not paying taxes on the handyman jobs around town. Stan must have told her…."

The color drained from Sylvia's face and she didn't move or speak. Or seem to be breathing at all, for that matter. The high-pitched warble of a pan flute emanating from the CD player lent an eerie tone to the atmosphere. And all the lavender-scented incense in the world couldn't cut through the cloud of tension hanging over their heads.

"I'm so sorry, Mom," Eliza whispered. "Harriet said if I kept quiet about Ben, Stan wouldn't report you. But now, I'm afraid—"

"That soulless viper!" Sylvia leapt from the table, cracking her knuckles as she paced across the shaggy carpet. "When I get my hands on her…"

Eliza's eyes widened as she watched her mother transform into one of the gang members from *West Side Story*. "Mom?"

Sylvia whipped around, her dark eyes blazing. "That woman lied to you. Your father *wasn't* going to report the money he made from odd jobs. But after we had a long talk about it, he brought all the receipts to Stan and had him amend the tax paperwork."

"What?" Eliza's heart lurched to a stop, pain shooting through her chest. "No… that can't be right. She said all the paperwork was in Stan's office, and she'd show me proof…." Squeezing her eyes shut, Eliza pressed her fingertips against her throbbing temples, trying to quiet the condemning voices jeering inside her head. How could she have been so naive? Doubling over, Eliza covered her mouth, suddenly feeling ill.

Sliding onto the couch beside her, Sylvia wrapped her arms

around her daughter. "Don't be too hard on yourself, honey. You were still a child back then."

"It's been over seven years, Mom. And I never once suspected it was a lie." Tears of shame tumbled down Eliza's cheeks, and she didn't bother wiping them away. She should have known better. She should have been smarter.... Once the thought process started, the *should haves* spun through her mind like a hand mixer switched on high speed, making her dizzy.

"And why should you have suspected it was a lie?" Sylvia's eyes flashed with indignation. "That kind of evil is unconscionable. What possible reason could she have had for keeping Grant away from his son, anyway?"

"She said having a child would ruin his life."

"Hogwash," Sylvia snorted. "They'll ruin your body, but Grant hardly had to worry about that."

"Is it hogwash, though?" Holding her mother's gaze, Eliza willed herself to get everything out in the open, once and for all. "Having me so young meant you had to give up on your dream of becoming the next Audrey Hepburn."

"I'm really more of a Katharine, don't you think? She seems much feistier."

Eliza groaned. "So not the point, Mom."

"I know, I know." Sylvia slipped her arm from around Eliza's shoulders and grabbed her hand, holding it between both of hers. "I want you to listen to me closely. Are you listening?"

"Yes." Eliza's lower lip trembled, her tears falling anew.

"You didn't ruin my dream. I *chose* to give up acting. Do I occasionally miss the bright lights and grand costumes? Sure. But being your mother is the greatest role I've ever been given. And it was brilliant casting on God's part, if I do say so myself."

"Gee. And so humble, too." Eliza sniffled, cracking a small smile.

"Want to take a guess at my greatest performance of all time?"

"When you were Sandy in *Grease*?"

"Not even close." A soft, wistful smile lit Sylvia's dark eyes. "I believe you were Ben's age the first time you used your Easy-Bake Oven. You had the biggest grin on your face when you handed me this gooey glob of shortening, raw egg, and a lethal amount of salt. I thought for sure you'd poisoned me. But I ate that weird, oddly cold blob of goo as if it were the queen's secret supply of chocolate."

"I actually remember that! The way you raved about it made me want to become a baker someday."

"Lucky for us, you've improved slightly." Sylvia winked, giving her hand a squeeze. "I couldn't be prouder of you, sweetheart. And I know you'll find a way to mend things with Grant. Just give it time."

Eliza leaned in to her mother's embrace, hoping with all her heart that she was right

*A*fter their game of chess, Stan left Grant alone in the office to work, and a funny thing happened.

Grant used to think being single allowed him endless creative freedom. But now, spurred by his newfound parental responsibility, Grant's mind flooded with inspiration. Not only did he want to provide the best life possible for his son, but he wanted to make him proud.

In just over five hours, Grant had completed the preliminary design for Landon's website and sent him the link for his approval.

As their video call connected, Landon's magnetic smile filled the screen. "Hey, man. The design is awesome!"

"I'm glad you like it." Grant hadn't been worried, confident it was his best work to date.

"Like it? I love it. We'll need to make a few minor layout

changes and update some of the text, but the design is perfect. Well done."

"Thanks. Once I got the idea, it all came together pretty quickly."

"I knew you'd pull through. Although..." Landon grinned. "For a couple of days there, I thought you'd gone AWOL."

"I'm really sorry about that. I've been... going through some stuff. But I should have been in more frequent communication."

"No worries, man." Landon shrugged, exuding a complete lack of concern. "The job got done. And it turned out even better than I expected. Besides, out of curiosity, I did some googling on your hometown. Seems like a cool place. I can see why you went back. I may even visit one of these days. There's this café there that looks amazing. They have a whole line of desserts infused with coffee. Right up my alley. Hmm..." Landon tapped his fingers against his desktop. "Now that I think about it... I wonder if they'll ship to the city? I'd be willing to pay any price."

"I'll bring something back for you," Grant offered, hiding a smile. He'd pushed publish on the website yesterday, as a surprise for Eliza's grand opening tomorrow night. He hadn't expected anyone to find it so soon, let alone Landon Morris.

"So, you're coming back to the city, then?"

"Yeah." The innocuous one-syllable word lodged in Grant's throat. He hated to think about leaving. Especially now.

After the men conversed for a few more minutes and exchanged goodbyes, Grant closed his laptop with a somber hand. His entire life existed in San Francisco. But now he had a child who belonged in Poppy Creek.

When he'd woken up that morning, Grant wouldn't have thought twice about moving back home to be with Eliza and Ben. But after what she'd done, Grant didn't know how he could look her in the eye again, let alone live in the same town.

Sharp heels clattered against the hardwood floor, growing louder as they neared the office.

"Are you all right? What did she say?" Harriet burst into the room, her eyes wild and frantic.

"I'm fine, Mom." Grant forced a smile. How could he end this conversation quickly? He really couldn't handle his mother's current state of panic. He'd barely come to grips with his own.

"I came as soon as I got your father's voice mail. What exactly did she say to you?"

Grant's gaze fell to her hands, which nervously fidgeted with the leather handle of her purse. Drawing his gaze upward, he noticed stray tendrils of her overly processed hair plastered to her damp forehead. "Are *you* all right?"

"What did she say?" Harriet hissed, about to come unraveled.

"She said Ben is my son. But I imagine Dad told you that already."

"Is that *all* she said?"

"I didn't give her much of an opportunity to say anything else. The whole 'Ben is your son' thing came as a shock." Why did relief flicker across her face? Grant expected her to explode. "You don't seem particularly surprised."

"Of course I am!" she snapped before her features softened. "I'm sorry. This is all quite distressing. I suspect you'll be heading home now."

"I haven't decided, Mom." Grant twisted the laptop cord around his finger, trying to work out why his mother's reaction bothered him so much. She had a grandson. Why didn't she seem to care? "I'm not sure what the future holds for me, except that I have a son. And from now on, he comes first."

Harriet blanched, her mouth coming unhinged. "You can't seriously mean..." Her eyes widened as Grant stood, collecting his things. "You're actually thinking of staying, aren't you?"

"Possibly."

"But what about your career? You've worked so hard to—"

"I can build websites from anywhere."

"What about networking? Client lunches and wooing new

accounts?" Looking visibly ill, Harriet clutched the opal pendant at her throat. "You know it takes more than good work to get ahead in this world. It takes sacrifices. Like—"

"Your family?" Grant stared at his mother with startling clarity, harsh reality gripping his heart with cold, cruel hands. All this time, he'd resented his father's blind ambition to climb the ladder of success no matter the cost, never once realizing he had someone dragging him up the rungs by his collar. Why hadn't he seen it sooner?

Harriet didn't respond, but her pale, impassive expression said it all.

Before today, the realization would have solidified Grant's fear of parenthood, reaffirming he was damaged goods and had no business being a father.

But as Ben's face flickered through his mind, conviction crowded out his fear.

He loved his son.

With an unexplainable, deep-in-his-core kind of love.

And Grant knew he'd only scratched the surface.

Harriet's lips parted before snapping shut. Without another word, she spun on her heel and stormed out of the room.

As the haze of outrage settled in her wake, Grant sat down at the desk, flipping open his laptop again. His stomach churned as the idea formed in his mind.

The next step would change everything.

And he could only hope it was the right decision.

CHAPTER 24

The grand opening should have been one of the best nights of Eliza's life.

The renovations for The Calendar Café showcased beautifully beneath shimmering twinkle lights framing the windows and door, while candles flickered on every tabletop, softly illuminating the faces of friends and family members gathered to share in the celebration.

The buzz of laughter and chatter mingled with the pleasant hum of the frothing wand as Cassie manned the espresso machine, creating unique and individualized latte combinations that filled the room with the heady scent of freshly ground coffee and spices. She looked radiant in a silvery cocktail dress, partially obstructed by an apron gifted to her by Dolores with the café's name embroidered across the front in exquisite red lettering.

"Are you having a good time?" Penny appeared by Eliza's side, balancing a tray of mini tiramisu cheesecakes.

Eliza had spent all afternoon drizzling each one with her special coffee sauce, followed by a generous dusting of cocoa powder and a single plump raspberry. "Yes, everything is perfect," she lied, forcing a smile. Her thoughts had remained on Grant all evening, no matter how many people had offered congratulatory hugs and well wishes.

"Are you sure? You seem a little… distracted."

"I think I'm just feeling overwhelmed. It's been months of work culminating in one evening. But thanks for checking on me. And for helping out." Eliza gestured toward the cheesecakes. "Do people seem to be enjoying them?"

"Are you kidding?" Penny laughed, shifting the tray to her other hand. "Jack's had three already. And Luke isn't too far behind. By the way, Grant hasn't shown up yet. And none of the guys have heard from him. Did he mention anything to you about arriving late?"

"No." Eliza glanced at her wrist, twisting the chunky beaded bracelet Ben made for her with Sylvia's help. He'd been so excited to give it to her earlier that evening as a gift to celebrate the grand opening.

Thinking of Ben caused an unbearable ache in her chest. What would happen now? Would Grant want custody?

Suddenly, Eliza's throat felt tight and tears swelled in her eyes.

Mistaking her rush of emotions, Penny rubbed her arm. "Hey, don't worry. I'm sure he'll show up soon."

Sniffling, Eliza nodded. "I'm sorry. I don't know why I'm so emotional tonight."

"Like you said, there's been a lot of build up to this event. It's completely understandable."

"Thanks, Pen. Maybe I need a little fresh air."

"Want me to come with you?"

"No, I'll only be a minute. Besides, I think Jack is still hungry." Eliza nodded toward the other side of the room where Jack waved his arm over his head, mouthing the words, *More cheesecake.*

"Seriously? Where does the man put it?" Shaking her head with an incredulous smile, Penny leaned over and planted a kiss on Eliza's cheek. "We're all really proud of you, Liza. Especially Maggie. I heard her tell Frank and Beverly that you and Cassie have surpassed her wildest dreams for this place."

Tearing up again, Eliza wrapped her arms around Penny, careful not to tip the tray of desserts. "Thank you," she whispered, grateful for the support of good friends. She had a feeling she'd need them now more than ever.

Pushing through the front door, Eliza stepped onto the cobbled sidewalk, relishing the crisp, cool breeze that rustled her loose curls against her bare shoulders. Closing her eyes, she leaned against the cold brick wall, finding solace in the shadows as she drew in a deep, cleansing breath.

She'd almost cleared her troubled thoughts when distant chanting caused her eyes to flutter open.

"Coffee and cake, a big mistake!"

Startled, it took Eliza a moment to register the dark silhouettes marching down the street toward her, waving handmade signs.

As they drew closer, the leader of the group materialized beneath the glow of the lampposts, stealing a gasp from Eliza's throat.

It was Harriet Parker.

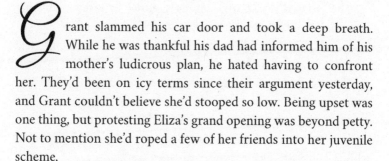

*G*rant slammed his car door and took a deep breath. While he was thankful his dad had informed him of his mother's ludicrous plan, he hated having to confront her. They'd been on icy terms since their argument yesterday, and Grant couldn't believe she'd stooped so low. Being upset was one thing, but protesting Eliza's grand opening was beyond petty. Not to mention she'd roped a few of her friends into her juvenile scheme.

As he strode toward the small group of women, he could hear

them chanting, "The Calendar Café should go away!" while they waved their hand-painted signs in the air like pitchforks. To add to the menacing effect, the light from the street lamps cast an eerie glow across the glitter paint letters.

"Mom, what are you doing?" Grant took in Harriet's sign, which read Caffeine Kills. "Really? Don't you think that's a bit extreme?"

Harriet lifted her chin. "Did you come here to stop me?"

"Of course I did. You're behaving like a crazy person."

"I'm doing this for you."

"Are you sure about that?" Grant crossed his arms, one eyebrow raised. "What exactly do you hope to accomplish, anyway?"

Overhearing him, Clara Grossman, one of Harriet's knitting club friends, chimed in. "Harriet says they're trying to get our kids addicted to caffeine by sneaking coffee into their milk and chocolate chip cookies."

Grant flashed his mother a disapproving glare before directing his attention back to Clara, trying to calm his fury. "You've known Eliza her entire life. Do you really think that's what's going on here? Do any of you?" He let his gaze rest on each woman individually as they guiltily lowered their signs. "I'm sorry, but you've allowed yourself to get roped into a personal vendetta that, I assure you, has nothing to do with coffee."

The women murmured among themselves a few moments, appearing rightfully embarrassed.

Finally, Clara said meekly, "I heard they're serving free cheesecake…."

"And Cassie's making everyone a personalized latte," another woman added.

After a quick affirmative glance, the women stuffed their signs in the nearest trash can and headed for The Calendar Café while Grant marveled at how easily they were swayed.

"Traitors," Harriet mumbled, watching them desert her cause with a venomous scowl.

"Not as dedicated as your New York friends?" Grant asked, recalling an occasion where his mother and her cohorts protested a dry cleaner for twenty-four hours straight because they'd left a stain on her one-of-a-kind Valentino gown.

"I know you're mocking me. But what that girl did to you was unforgivable."

Grant winced at the harsh, dispassionate use of *that girl*. No matter what Eliza had done, she deserved to be treated with more respect. "Mom, can we please not argue about this here?"

"Then where?" Harriet gave a desperate sweep of her hands. "You won't talk to me at home. Can't you see I'm trying to help you?"

"I'm sure you believe that... in your own strange way. But I'm asking you to stop *helping*." Grant could barely resist putting air quotes around the word. "I need time to think and figure things out on my own."

Harriet wavered a moment before retrieving her car keys from inside her purse. Clutching the cold metal in her hand, she met Grant's gaze, her eyes shimmering with unexpected emotion. "I do love you, you know."

Grant opened his mouth to respond, but Harriet clicked the sensor on her key fob, the BMW's distinct beep cutting him off. As she retreated down the sidewalk, she cast one last glance over her shoulder before climbing inside the driver's seat.

Grant stood on the curb, watching his mother back out of her parking spot before pivoting slowly, heading to his own car.

A few days ago, he'd looked forward to this evening more than anything, eagerly awaiting the moment he'd unveil the website to Eliza. He'd also planned to tell her how much he loved her. And confess his intentions to stay in Poppy Creek.

But now...

He'd do almost anything to avoid catching even a glimpse of her.

"Grant, wait!" Emerging from the shadows, Eliza hurried toward him, extending her hand as if reaching for him.

But as he turned, unable to hide his anguish at hearing her voice, Eliza froze, dropping her arms at her sides.

"Thank you," she whispered, staring at the ground.

Grant stood motionless, wanting to look away, but unable to take his eyes off of her. The glittering, rose gold cocktail dress highlighted the subtle blush of her cheeks and made her dark, bewitching eyes stand out even more in contrast.

Then his gaze fell on the beaded bracelet adorning her wrist, and his thoughts instantly flew to Ben. His own pain pushed aside any previous desire to rush to her side, gathering her up in his arms, shielding her from his mother's spiteful attack.

"There's something I need to say." Grant struggled to keep his voice steady.

Glancing up, relief flickered across Eliza's features. "I'm so glad. I've been dying to talk. I've kept calling but…" She shook her head, biting her lip. "Never mind. I'm sorry. You talk first."

"I…" Grant hesitated, finding the words harder to say than he'd thought. He lifted his chin, determined to get through this without caving. "I… want to take Ben back to San Francisco with me when school is out. I'll bring him back for the wedding, but I'd like to keep him for the summer. I've already looked up a summer art program I think he'll love."

Stricken, Eliza took a step back. "Grant, I—"

"It's my turn, Eliza. Please don't make me fight for it."

His throat burning, Grant forced himself to meet her gaze. The utter devastation in her eyes made him shiver.

And for a moment, Grant wondered if he was doing the right thing.

CHAPTER 25

*T*he lamppost flickered, followed by a crackle, then darkness.

Although every other lamp burned warm and bright, competing with the vibrant shop windows to light Main Street, everything around Eliza appeared inky black, mirroring her mood. Standing alone on the sidewalk, she fought the urge to slink back into the shadows and disappear from sight.

She couldn't go back inside and face everyone. Not when Grant's words compressed around her chest, squeezing all the air from her lungs like a rolling pin flattening dough. Take Ben? He wanted to take Ben away from her? This couldn't be happening.

Hot tears spilled down her cheeks, ruining her carefully applied mascara. How could she let Grant leave with her son? Ben was her entire world. For over seven years, it had been the two of them together. She'd be lost without him.

Sobs ripped through her body, forcing Eliza to double over, clutching her chest.

A door hinge creaked.

"Eliza? Are you ready to give the toasts?" Cassie's question preceded a loud gasp.

Rushing to her side, Cassie threw her arms around her shoulders, propping up Eliza's crumpled body as she continued to sob. "What happened?" Panic seeped from Cassie's voice as she held her, smoothing back her hair.

"Grant wants to take Ben. He's going to take him away, Cass." Her words muffled as she covered her face with her hands.

"Shh… it's going to be okay. Just breathe." Cassie rubbed Eliza's back, murmuring soft reassurances. "Let's get you home, okay?"

"What about the party?" Eliza hiccupped.

"I'll text Luke. He'll tell everyone you weren't feeling well and I took you home."

"No one will believe that."

"Maybe not. But it's the best I've got right now." Cassie slid her arm around Eliza's waist. "Come on. We'll take my car."

"No, you stay." Eliza swiped at her tears, smearing the mascara tracks across her face. "I'll call Mom to pick me up. She and Dad took Ben home an hour ago to put him to bed."

"Don't be silly. I'm here. I'll take you." Ignoring Eliza's protests, Cassie half carried her toward her car parked in front of Sadie's Sweet Shop. Drawing her eyebrows together, Cassie gave her a pointed stare as she opened the passenger door. "Sit down and don't make me buckle you in myself."

A small smile broke through Eliza's tears. "I think my bossiness is rubbing off on you."

"I prefer to call it your perseverance." Cassie grinned, shutting the car door before hurrying around to the driver's side.

When they pulled up to the farmhouse, Cassie cut the engine. "Want me to come inside with you?"

Eliza gazed at the imitation Tiffany lamp glowing in the front window. "No, that's okay. Thank you, though." Her words sounded dull and hollow.

Cassie reached for her hand and gave it a squeeze. "Hey, I

know everything seems hopeless right now. But I promise you, it's not."

"Thanks." Her palms clammy, Eliza gripped the door handle and shoved it open.

"I'll come by tomorrow. Try to get some sleep." Cassie's car purred back to life.

"Good night." Eliza winced as the car door slammed shut with a thud of finality.

Once inside, she slipped out of her heels and crept down the dark hallway toward the sliver of light peeking beneath Ben's bedroom door. Cracking it open, she caught sight of her son sound asleep, his Marvel night-light casting shadows across his peaceful features. Her heart wrenched, and Eliza quickly covered her mouth, stifling another sob.

She tiptoed across the plush carpet and knelt beside his bed, tucking her bare feet beneath her. Holding her breath, she took in every infinitesimal detail. The tiny flutter of his eyelids. The delicate wisps of blond hair splayed across his forehead. The way his lower lip stuck out farther than the other, giving him an adorable pout.

Everything about him was perfection. And even though he changed all the time, growing and maturing faster than an egg timer, he remained perfect in her eyes. Her little Bug. Her glorious light in the midst of darkness.

She couldn't let him go. She *wouldn't* let him go.

As she reached for the switch to the night-light, a splash of color on the nightstand caught her attention. Gently, Eliza lifted a crinkled sheet of paper, the watercolors still damp on the surface.

Her hand flew to her throat.

Ben's latest work of art depicted two figures rendered with bright, bold smears of paint and confident, unrestrained brush-strokes.

Two figures who clearly represented Grant and Ben.

Father and son.

Together.

Large, unbridled tears cascaded down her cheeks, rolling off her chin and onto the page, dispersing the colors like ripples in a lake. Frantic, Eliza dabbed at the splotches, merely spreading the damage.

"No, no, no..." she murmured under her breath, grabbing a tissue from the nightstand to mop up the mess while tears continued to ping across the page—tiny, cleansing raindrops washing away the painful image.

Yet when Eliza gazed at the marred painting, Grant's features nothing more than a smudge, she came face-to-face with her past.

She'd wiped Ben's father from his life before.

Did she really want to repeat the same mistake?

---

licking on the switch, Grant winced as harsh light flooded the room. *His* room. Four walls that once held his odd assortment of Star Wars posters and reproduction prints of Van Gogh's *Starry Night* and *Water Lilies* by Monet. The ceiling he used to stare at every night in high school, daydreaming about Eliza.

Now, the walls were painted a muted mint green, adorned with select pieces of original artwork, none of which were Grant's. His frayed navy-blue bedspread since replaced by a pastel floral quilt. Nothing of his former years survived, save for the back corner of the closet where a few belongings he'd left behind had been swiftly banished.

Grant shoved aside the cedar hangers laden with expensive designer gowns his mother no longer had use for, his gaze resting on a stack of dusty shoeboxes. The one on top housed his beloved

Chuck Taylor All Stars. The one beneath contained his barely worn Air Jordans. But the bottom box...

Well, that one was special.

Reverently, he slid it from underneath the stack and sat cross-legged on the floor.

His heart thudded against his rib cage as he carefully removed the lid, coughing as dust particles flitted into the air.

A leather sketchbook filled with drawings of Eliza caught his attention first, followed by the note she'd tucked inside the first tin of cookies she'd ever baked him.

Grant smiled wistfully as his fingers grazed a bundle of love letters they'd passed back and forth in Ms. Lassen's English class, which eventually resulted in the one and only time he was ever sent to Principal Whittaker's office.

As Grant sifted through the trinkets and photographs, tears blurred his vision. He removed his glasses and wiped his eyes with the back of his hand before slipping them back on.

One item remained to be found. A small velvet box.

After removing each item individually, revealing nothing save for a few dust mites and flecks of lint stuck to the bottom of the cardboard, Grant's pulse slowed to a standstill.

Where was the promise ring?

Grant was certain Eliza had given it back to him. The cold metal had singed his palm when she'd shoved it into his hand. Where could it be? He acutely remembered placing it back inside the ring box before stashing it beneath the rest of the memorabilia.

He knew it was foolish to save it. But keeping it gave Grant a tiny glimmer of hope.

A glimmer that had recently been snuffed out.

His phone buzzed on the nightstand. As he reached for it, his breath cut short.

Eliza's name flashed across the screen.

Grant briefly adjusted his glasses, not trusting the words before his eyes.

You can take Ben for the summer. I'm glad you want to get to know him. And I don't want to get in the way of that. I'm so terribly sorry I hurt you. I pray that someday you can forgive me. Love, Lizzy

Grant pressed a hand to his chest, attempting to keep the intense ache from spreading. His eyes, throat, skin... everything burned.

Why did it have to be like this? He wanted to forgive her. Deep in his core, he didn't believe Eliza had meant to cause him pain. Every muscle in his body tensed, itching to run to her, to put everything in their tangled past firmly behind them.

His love for her had never been in question.

But could he trust her?

CHAPTER 26

*E*liza scanned the town square, searching for Grant amid
the billowy white tents and shoulder-to-shoulder
throng of parents and children converged for the Summer Kick-
Off Carnival put on by the school.

Ben had run off with a few friends to try their hand at the
homemade carnival games, and Eliza crossed her fingers he
didn't come back with a live goldfish. Although she supposed
keeping it alive would be Grant's responsibility now. Her
stomach twisted, and she immediately banished the thought.
They were supposed to be celebrating. And they had extra reason
to revel this year. After they'd explained Ben's vision issues to
Daphne, she'd agreed to pass him to the next grade with the
condition he got corrective lenses. A task Grant offered to handle
himself.

"So, you're telling Ben today?" Cassie kept her voice low, her
hand clasped firmly in Luke's as they strolled past the silent
auction raising funds for next year's events.

"That's the plan. We thought it would be easier in the midst of
the fun and excitement." Eliza's stomach flip-flopped again, and

she tried to focus on the festivities rather than their difficult talk with Ben later that afternoon.

They passed a booth of contestants wearing blindfolds, trying to guess various pie flavors. Jack wore a red gingham bandana over his eyes, and he smacked his lips loudly. "Maple bacon apple pie?"

Beverly, the score keeper, wrote down his answer on a clipboard, while Frank mumbled, "Should we tighten his blindfold?"

Cassie snickered. "I think Jack has an advantage when it comes to anything with bacon in it."

"You've got that right." Luke grinned as they wandered toward the edge of the lawn, pausing near the ominous dunk tank that sat ready for the special event later in the day. Reaching his hand over the side, Luke tested the water and grimaced. "It's freezing."

"Did you sign up to be dunked this year?" Eliza asked.

"The guys are all placing bets on who will dunk him first. Even I might have a go at it." Cassie's eyes danced with mischief.

"Wait until we cut our wedding cake. I may get my revenge with a little frosting on the tip of your nose."

"You wouldn't dare!" Cassie laughed.

"Wouldn't I?" Luke dipped his hand in the tank again, flinging water droplets at Cassie who shrieked, then giggled as she tried to duck out of the way.

A pang of envy tore through Eliza's heart as she watched them tease each other. She'd been so close to having that with Grant. Then her lie had ripped it away. And deservedly so. It was foolish to think he'd ever forgive her.

As if sensing her train of thought, Cassie's features softened, and she leaned against Luke, seeking comfort. "Liza, have you explained to Grant why you didn't tell him about Ben?"

"No." Her gaze flickered to Luke's face, noticing the way his hazel eyes clouded with compassion. "Did Cassie tell you?"

He briefly glanced at his soon-to-be bride, then nodded slowly.

"I'm so sorry." A blush swept across Cassie's cheeks. "It sort of… slipped out. But he's the only one I told. Cross my heart."

Eliza smiled as Cassie drew a giant X in the air. "It's fine. Really. You two are almost newlyweds. I don't expect you to keep secrets from each other."

Luke's warm expression conveyed his gratitude as he slid his arm around Cassie's waist, drawing her closer. "Can I ask why you haven't told him?"

Eliza dropped her gaze to the ground, studying the contrast of her pink nail polish against her teal wedge sandals. The truth was, she'd thought about telling Grant countless times. For her sake, she *wanted* to tell him. But whenever she'd come close, she couldn't bring herself to say the words out loud, knowing they would only cause him more pain. "Grant's always had a difficult relationship with his dad. How would he feel if he knew his mom had blackmailed me into keeping silent about his son?" Eliza shook her head. "No, I couldn't tell him. I don't want to come between the one parent he feels remotely close to. I've hurt him enough."

A loud crash drew their attention to Colt dancing around a tipped bucket, small, yellow balls spilling around his feet.

His head down, Colt scrambled to scoop them back inside.

Eliza's breath hitched.

How much had he overheard?

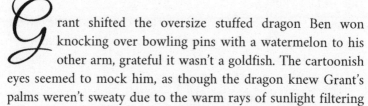

*G*rant shifted the oversize stuffed dragon Ben won knocking over bowling pins with a watermelon to his other arm, grateful it wasn't a goldfish. The cartoonish eyes seemed to mock him, as though the dragon knew Grant's palms weren't sweaty due to the warm rays of sunlight filtering through the wispy clouds. But rather, because he and Eliza were walking across the town square on their way to spill the big news to Ben. "What are you going to call him?"

"Claude." Ben didn't even pause to think. Or tear his attention from his giant cone of cotton candy.

"Claude the Dragon, huh?" Grant cocked his head, studying the goofy expression of the floppy-eared creature. "I guess that works. But why Claude?"

"Because I like his paintings best," Ben said simply.

Grant scrunched his features in thought before his eyes widened. "Claude Monet?" His gaze flitted to Eliza, who stared straight ahead as they wove through the crowd, her cheeks tinged pink.

Ben nodded. "Mom's been teaching me about famous people who like to paint, just like me. Do you know Claude? His paintings are really pretty."

"I've heard of him." Grant hid a smile, stealing another glance at Eliza. His heartbeat sputtered strangely at the thought of Eliza sitting down with Ben, pointing out paintings by one of his favorite artists.

It wasn't fair that every time he decided it would never work between them, she did something to weaken his resolve.

When they reached the courthouse, they climbed to the top step and sat down with Ben in the middle. Nervous tension sizzled between Grant and Eliza, but Ben seemed oblivious to everything except his sugary treat.

"Ben..." Eliza began softly. "Grant and I have something important to tell you."

Grant considered placing the plush toy on the step below, but couldn't bring himself to set it down, grateful for something to occupy his fidgety hands. He also couldn't stop swallowing profusely. Why was his mouth so dry?

Ben gazed up at his mother, a sticky ring of pink sugar around his mouth.

"You like Grant a lot, don't you?" Eliza asked without looking in Grant's direction.

"Yeah." Ben plucked another clump of cotton candy, stuffing it in his mouth.

"I'm glad because..." Eliza hesitated, and Grant noticed a slight twitch in her jaw. For a moment, compassion washed over him. While his own heart felt permanently lodged in his throat, he could only imagine how difficult this was for her.

"Because... Grant is your dad."

They both drew in a collective breath, waiting for Ben's reaction.

He tilted his head toward Grant, his dark eyes glinting with curiosity. "You are?"

Grant swallowed again, clutching Claude for moral support. "Yes."

Yes? *Yes?* Is that all he had to say? *Say something else, you dolt.*

While Grant mentally berated himself, Ben's eyes remained locked on his face, his expression unreadable.

After five seconds that felt like forever, Ben said, "Okay," and gathered another wad of cotton candy.

"Bug, do you understand what we're telling you?" Eliza's gaze briefly met Grant's, exchanging a flicker of uncertainty, before returning to her son.

"Grant's my dad," Ben said matter-of-factly.

"And do you understand what that means?" Eliza pressed.

"I have a mom *and* a dad."

A chuckle rose from somewhere inside Grant, and he coughed to keep it from escaping. Leave it to a seven-year-old to uncomplicate the matter.

"Are you going to come live with us now?"

Grant nearly choked. *Scratch that.* Ben had just made things a million times *more* complicated. "Um..." He looked to Eliza for help.

A shadow of sadness darkened her features before she forced a smile that didn't quite reach her eyes. "No, he's not coming to live with us. Grant would like you to visit him in San Francisco for the summer. You two can hang out and get to know each other better. Grant even found an art camp that I know you'll love."

"Art camp?" Ben sounded intrigued.

"Yeah, you go for a few hours every day and they have really cool art projects for you to make. The city also has a ton of parks, museums, and a zoo." Grant hated to feel like he was selling himself, but in a way… he was.

Ben perked up at the mention of the zoo. "Do they have lions?"

"Yep. And tigers and bears." Grant caught himself before adding *oh my!* He glanced at Eliza, almost certain a microscopic smile tugged at the corner of her mouth. For an instant, a thin thread tied them together, and Grant wanted to hold on to it for as long as possible.

"Do you have any questions for us?" Eliza asked Ben, catching Grant off guard.

Questions? What kind of questions? And what if he didn't have the answer?

Ben glanced between them, then shook his head.

"Well, when you do, you can ask us anything, okay?" Eliza reached out and gently brushed Ben's bangs aside, and the tender gesture stirred the dull ache in Grant's chest again, the one that made it hard to breathe.

A bell chimed, signaling the start of the dunk tank event, and Ben cheered. Jumping up, he raced down the steps shouting, "I'm going to dunk Uncle Luke!"

Eliza cast a sideways glance in Grant's direction, as though she wanted to say something but immediately thought better of it. Pushing off the cool, stone step, she brushed the loose dirt from her hands, then took off after her son.

Grant watched her graceful form skip down the steps, then

disappear into the crowd, realizing his heart went with her. He supposed it always would, leaving a hollow feeling in his gut.

Glancing at Claude, he flashed a wry smile. "What do you think? Am I a hopeless case?"

Grant tipped the dragon, and its floppy head fell forward.

"Yeah... that's what I thought."

CHAPTER 27

*E*liza huddled in her circle of friends, thankful the hoopla surrounding the dunk tank drowned out her deafening heartbeat. But as soon as Colt ascended the ladder, her heart stilled, dread constricting her throat as their eyes locked.

He knew. She could feel it.

She didn't really care that he knew about Grant and Ben. The whole town would probably know in a matter of days. But the truth about Harriet…

That needed to remain a secret. For Grant's sake, at least.

Raking in a calming breath, Eliza felt her anxiety abate. What did she have to worry about? Colt and Grant weren't exactly close. It wasn't as if the conversation would come up naturally.

Eliza's pulse steadied as Penny stepped up to the throwing line, tossing a small yellow ball high in the air, catching it with ease.

"Perfect. I've never felt safer." Colt grinned, exposing his endearing dimple.

"You shouldn't. I've been practicing nearly every day since you came back into town."

Colt laughed, but as Penny raised her eyebrows, his laughter floundered. "You're serious?"

She smirked, pulling her arm back into a pitcher's pose. "Hope you're ready for a nice, refreshing dip in the tank."

Luke, Jack, and Reed hooted and hollered in support.

A flicker of doubt darted across Colt's face, but his features quickly set in a cool, confident smile. "I am feeling a little *hot.*"

He waggled his eyebrows, and Penny blushed before setting her jaw in a determined scowl.

In one deft motion, the ball sailed from her fingertips, spinning with a velocity that belied her slender arms.

The ball smacked the target with a definitive thud, plunging Colt into the icy water.

When he broke through the surface, he looked directly at Penny, a blaze of awareness in his searing blue eyes.

Eliza wasn't sure if the glint was respect or admiration. Or perhaps a hint of something more….

The guys held up their hands for a high five, which Penny gladly doled out.

Colt hopped out of the tank, his sopping wet T-shirt clinging to his not-so-subtly-defined abs.

Eliza suppressed a laugh as she caught Penny steal a peek.

"Nice job, Pen." Grant appeared by Penny's side, offering her a congratulatory fist bump. "I hate to say it, but I kind of hoped you'd miss. I'm next in line to throw."

"Sorry to disappoint," Colt teased as he dried himself off. "Who's next in the tank?"

In her peripheral view, Eliza saw Luke grip the ladder, and before she could stop herself, her hand shot up. "I am!"

All eyes turned on her, including Bill Tucker, who manned the tank. He shifted his glance to Luke, his brow furrowed.

Eliza's eyes pleaded with Luke to let her go first, and he graciously stepped aside. "Yep, Eliza is next. I must have gotten the order mixed up."

She flashed him an appreciative smile, her knees wobbly as she moved toward the ladder. What had come over her? She'd never signed up for the dunk tank before. But in a moment of madness, it seemed like a good idea.

Gathering her resolve, she unbuckled her wedge sandals, kicked them into the grass, and mounted the ladder in her pink sundress.

"Are you sure about this?" Luke whispered as he helped her up.

"Not even a little bit." She grinned, her teeth chattering in anticipation of her impending ice bath.

As she seated herself on the ledge, she glanced at the water below, observing the ripples from Colt's recent plunge.

When she looked up, her eyes locked on Grant's. He gripped the ball in both hands, appearing decidedly uncomfortable with the prospect of sending her for a swim. Truthfully, she wasn't looking forward to it any more than he was.

But it needed to be done.

A small, albeit strange, step toward making amends.

❀

*A*s Grant stood at the throwing line, he racked his brain for an excuse to pass the ball off to someone else. A hand cramp, maybe?

A bee buzzed in front of his face, and he seriously contemplated provoking it.

"Come on, Parker. We don't have all day," Jack ribbed with a good-natured drawl.

Swallowing hard, Grant directed his gaze at Eliza.

She'd tucked her dress around her legs, clutching the fabric to her thighs in anticipation of her impending swim. Apprehension creased her forehead, but her expression remained resolute.

Grant guessed she hadn't actually been in line for the dunk

tank. And only jumped ahead of Luke at the last minute. He wasn't sure *why*, exactly, but he had a sneaking suspicion.

His gaze drifted to the bright red target. Somehow, he'd have to miss without making it appear intentional. Which shouldn't be too hard, considering his athletic abilities were practically nonexistent.

Winding back his arm, he focused on a few inches to the right of the target.

Nice and easy....

As the ball flew from his fingertips, Grant's heart stopped.

It took eons for the small round sphere to span the short distance.

Then a single shriek preceded a loud splash.

*A*s Grant spotted Eliza duck behind the pie tent, he surreptitiously followed.

Rounding the corner, he caught sight of her shivering as she dried herself off with a striped beach towel. Beads of water poured off her sopping-wet sundress, and her blond hair hung in damp, bedraggled strands.

But she looked beautiful nonetheless.

And for a moment, all he could do was take her in.

Grant still couldn't believe she'd climbed up there and perched on the ledge like a peace offering.

He also couldn't believe he'd accidentally hit the target. Turns out, he'd been doing it wrong all these years. And the key to hitting your mark was aiming *away* from it. Go figure.

"You didn't have to do that."

Eliza jumped, relaxing when she realized who'd startled her. "What do you mean?"

"You volunteered as some sort of restitution."

"I did no—" Her protest died on her lips, as she seemed to think better of telling another lie.

Even if only a white one.

Grant took a step closer, noticing the goose bumps scattered across her arms. "It was sweet, but not necessary. I'm not mad at you. I'm..." He paused. What was he? Confused? Hurt? His feelings melded together, a jumbled mess he wasn't yet able to untangle.

A strand of wet hair clung to her forehead, grazing just above her right eye. Grant moved toward her, instinctively brushing it aside, sweeping it behind her ear.

Eliza's breath faltered, and her eyes flew to his, water droplets still clinging to her long dark lashes.

What was he doing? He needed to walk away and put a safe distance between them. But he couldn't move. He didn't *want* to move.

His mind wandered back to the night she'd called things off between them. No explanation. No conversation. Simply a tearful, *It will never work*, followed by a cataclysmal kiss goodbye.

Her lips had tasted bittersweet, like forbidden fruit dipped in pink Himalayan salt. And the all-consuming craving lingered long after she'd walked away.

Grant closed his eyes, longing to remember.

At first, he thought he was dreaming as the feather-soft kiss grazed his lips. But as it deepened, awareness ripped through him.

Grant's hand instinctively found Eliza's waist, pulling her against his body. She fit so perfectly, as though they were never meant to be apart. The moisture from her damp dress seeped through his clothing, but he didn't care. He barely even noticed as he concentrated on the feel of her soft skin, her sweet, intoxicating taste.

Their kiss grew urgent, almost desperate, as though they both knew this would be their last.

His lips, fingers, toes... everything tingled. Grant felt at once acutely aware of every imperceptible sensation and yet oblivious to anything beyond the confines of their kiss.

He sensed himself slipping away, too willing to get lost in the moment, regardless of the consequences.

But he needed to think. This was too much. Too fast.

He couldn't sort out one emotion from the next.

Pulling away, Grant pressed his forehead to hers, breathing in her honey-scented shampoo. "I'm sorry. I... need some time."

"I understand," she whispered, dropping her hands to her side.

As soon as she did, Grant missed her touch.

But getting some space in order to think more clearly would be a good thing.

Healthy. Responsible. Rational.

And maybe if he repeated the words often enough, he'd actually believe them.

CHAPTER 28

The crunch of Ben's suitcase across the gravel drive pounded in Eliza's ears like ominous thunder. Yet there wasn't a single cloud in the brilliant blue sky. The bright, cheery sun and twittering sparrows were oblivious to the unfortunate event unfolding before them.

Eliza glowered, raising a hand to shield her eyes from the offending sunlight.

This couldn't be happening so soon; she needed more time to prepare.

After their kiss, brief as it was, Eliza had dared to hope Grant had forgiven her. Perhaps even been willing to give her another chance.

But here they were….

Worlds apart, though only on opposite ends of the driveway.

Grant leaned against the side of his car, his hands stuffed inside his pockets, shoulders slumped. When he heard them approach, he straightened, yanking his hands free, raking them through his hair instead.

As they drew closer, it became harder for Eliza to lift her feet. Halfway down the drive, they stopped working all together.

Falling to her knees, she gathered Ben into her arms, burying her face in his soft, unruly hair.

"Mom?" he murmured, small and uncertain.

Drawing strength from the deepest part of herself, Eliza pulled back, offering a reassuring smile. "What is it, Bug?"

"Can you come with me?"

"Oh, honey. I can't. Not this time." She swallowed the shakiness in her voice, keeping the smile firmly in place. "But you two will have a lot of fun together, I promise."

Ben shot a sideways glance at Grant, appearing unconvinced. "When will you come get me?"

"Grant—your *dad*," Eliza corrected, still stumbling over the word, "is bringing you back for Luke and Cassie's wedding. You have a very important job, remember?"

A brief glimmer of pride illuminated Ben's eyes. "I'm in charge of the rings."

"Exactly. Which means they can't get married without you."

His gaze flickering to Grant again, Ben asked, "Do you think I'll like it there?"

"You're going to love it." She swept aside his feathery bangs, wishing her heartache could be as easily tamed. "You'll see all sorts of new and fun things. Like the ocean. You've always wanted to see the ocean, right?"

Ben nodded, gradually warming up to the idea, though they'd been over it all before.

"See, it'll be great." Eliza surprised herself with how cheerful she sounded.

Wrapping her arms around him one last time, she inhaled his little boy scent as she held him against her heart. After planting a kiss on his forehead, she stood, nudging him forward. "Have fun." *Good grief.* How many times would she say that word? It wasn't as if it had magical powers, and the more frequently she said it, the less her heart would break.

"And call me anytime, for any reason. Even if it's simply to say hi or hear my voice," she added, feeling a sob rise in her raw, swollen throat.

Chewing her pinky nail, she watched Ben continue down the driveway on his own, wheeling his small suitcase with Claude secured on top. The plush, floppy-eared head bobbed back and forth each time the wheels hit a rough patch of gravel, as if the dragon were nodding his farewell.

When Ben reached the car, Grant placed a hand on his shoulder, directing him toward the back seat.

Instinctively, Eliza cupped both hands over her mouth, uncertain how much longer she could suppress the swelling sob.

Ben glanced over his shoulder, and the second their eyes locked, he dropped his suitcase and bolted down the driveway.

Tears spilling down her cheeks, Eliza scooped him into her arms, cradling him against her, though he'd long since outgrown being held.

"I don't want to go," he cried into her hair. "I want to stay with you."

Cooing softly, Eliza caressed his back, swaying back and forth. "Shh… it'll be okay."

"He can stay." Now standing only a few feet away, Grant met her gaze. His eyes glistened, and he was unable to hide the raspy pain in his voice.

Grant set Ben's suitcase beside her, a selfless act that wasn't lost on Eliza.

As she studied Grant's face, each subtle crease in his brow speaking volumes, his internal conflict was clear. They both wanted to do what was best for their son.

Their son…

Whether united or apart, they were in this together now.

Gently setting Ben down, Eliza knelt and wiped the tears from his eyes. "Bug, I know this seems scary because it's new and different. But you and your dad will have a great time. I promise.

I wouldn't let you go if I didn't believe that with all my heart. You know that, right?"

"Yeah," he sniffled.

"Okay, then." Straightening, Eliza offered Ben her hand. "Ready?"

He nodded, then glanced up at Grant.

Reaching out his other hand, he slipped his fingers through Grant's, linking the three of them together.

Grant met her gaze over the top of Ben's head, and for a moment, Eliza couldn't breathe.

Her eyes pleaded with him not to go, but her feet started moving forward.

Side by side, they walked toward the car.

Her heart wrenching a little more with each step they took.

*A*s they pulled out of the driveway, Grant stared straight ahead.

Don't do it... Don't look back....

Unable to stop himself, Grant glanced in the rearview mirror.

Eliza's figure slowly grew smaller as they drove away. As he watched her disappear before his eyes, the tightness in Grant's chest rose to his throat. He tried to swallow, tilting his head back as unwanted tears threatened to spill out.

He couldn't cry. He had to keep it together. For Ben.

Grant stole another glance in the mirror, this time at his son in the back seat.

Ben fidgeted with the air vent.

"Are you hot? Cold?" Grant poised his finger over the climate control, ready to make any adjustment Ben wanted. Heck, he'd buy him the moon, if he wanted it. Anything to make the transition smoother.

"These don't work in our car," Ben told him. "Only the ones by our feet. I like them. The air kind of tickles."

"I can turn it up higher, if you want." Grant touched the keypad and the screen illuminated.

Ben's eyes widened. "You have a computer in your car?"

Grant grinned. It had never occurred to him that Ben wasn't exposed to many late model cars, let alone one as tech-advanced as his Tesla. It was endearing how excited Ben got about features Grant barely noticed anymore. "Cool, huh? This is a pretty smart car. It can even drive itself."

"You mean like a robot?"

"Yeah, kind of like a robot. When we get out of the windy mountain roads, I'll show you how it works."

"Your car smells different, too," Ben pointed out, sniffing the air. "Ours smells like vanilla. Mom dropped some under the seat and can't get it out. The bean. Not the other stuff. Vanilla bean looks funny. Like a stick. Or a dead caterpillar. Mom says not to tell people that because then they won't eat her cupcakes and stuff. But I think people would still eat them, even if I said vanilla bean looks like a dead caterpillar. Do you think they would?"

"Uh-huh." Grant nodded, doing his best to keep up with Ben's rambling. He'd never talked this much before. Maybe he was nervous? Grant could certainly understand that.

He lifted his clammy palm from the steering wheel, shaking off the moisture before returning his grip. He'd already thought of a million different ways he could screw up, from ordering the wrong pizza toppings to failing to safety proof the house properly. Most of the information he'd read online pertained to infants or toddlers. But he'd ordered locks for the medicine cabinet and cleaning supplies, just in case.

"Wanna order pizza and watch a movie tonight?" Grant asked, then flinched realizing his mistake. How would he know what a seven-year-old could watch? Maybe he should call Eliza….

Grant drew in a breath, ready to activate his car's Bluetooth, then firmly clamped his mouth shut. He couldn't call her fifteen minutes after they'd left.

It was time to man up.

For the rest of the summer, he'd be on his own.

A thought that left his heart numb, for more reasons than one.

*T*he vacant black screen refused to illuminate no matter how hard Eliza stared at her cell phone.

"Hello?" She tapped the hard plastic cover to no avail, whimpering as she buried herself deeper into Ben's Spider-Man sheets.

Was it weird she'd crawled into his bed waiting for his good night phone call? Maybe. But she didn't care. She wanted to breathe in his scent and be surrounded by things that reminded her of his adorable smiling face.

Plus, it was forty-five minutes past Ben's standard bedtime and she could barely keep it together. Either Grant allowed him to stay up late or Ben hadn't wanted to call to say good night.

Eliza prayed it wasn't the latter.

All day long she'd been preparing herself for their first night apart. And for two whole seconds, she'd thought she could handle it. *Ha!* What a joke.

Nestling into the pillows, Eliza fixed her gaze on the ceiling, distracting herself with the strange shadows cast by his nightlight.

How would she survive an entire summer without him? It didn't seem possible.

Her mother had actually told her to try to enjoy it. *Take some time for yourself,* she'd said. *Get a hobby,* she'd said.

Eliza covered her face with the pillow, muffling an exasperated scream.

Maybe she should call? Maybe something was wrong.…

Jolting upright in bed, Eliza snatched the phone off the nightstand, her heart hammering inside her throat.

Her fingertip hovered over the screen while she chewed her bottom lip raw. Was she being paranoid? Too needy? Too *mothery*? Was that even a word?

The trill of her cell phone reverberated around the room, and in her surprise, Eliza chucked it into the air. Scrambling to catch it, she tumbled from the bed in a tangle of cotton sheets.

"Hello? Ben? Hello?" Breathless, she squashed the phone against her ear, not waiting for a response. "Are you there?"

"Eliza? It's Grant. Are you okay?"

Wincing, she glanced at her scraped elbow. She must have banged it against the nightstand in her haste to answer the phone. "Yes, I'm fine. Is Ben there? It's an hour past his bedtime." She winced again. This time, due to her reproachful tone.

"Sorry. We started the movie later than I thought."

Eliza sighed, sitting cross-legged on the floor. "No, I'm sorry. I shouldn't have said that. I… it's…"

"It's hard being apart?" Grant asked softly.

For a moment, Eliza wasn't sure if he meant from Ben… or him.

"Harder than I thought," she admitted, although that wasn't entirely true. She'd anticipated it would be like ripping her heart from her chest cavity with her bare hands. And she'd been pretty spot-on.

"So," she said quickly, banishing the emotion from her voice with a cough. "How's it going?"

"Good. I showed him around the neighborhood. Then we ordered pizza and watched a movie. He's brushing his teeth now."

To her horror, Eliza felt tears prick the backs of her eyes. She held the phone away from her face as she sniffled.

"Eliza?"

"Yeah, I'm here." Distracting herself, she yanked the bundle of sheets across her lap, smoothing out the creases.

"Thank you." Grant's words floated through the speakers barely above a whisper. And yet she had to stop herself from reading into his tender inflection.

She bit her lip, blinking back tears even though he couldn't see her face. "You're welcome," she said at last, her tone convincingly steady.

She heard him clear his throat before saying, "Ben wouldn't go to sleep without saying good night to you first. I thought about a video call, but it's late and…"

He trailed off, and there was so much Eliza could infer in what he *didn't* say. But rather than ask, she said, "A video call would be great."

"Okay. Then I'll have Ben call you back."

"Thanks." Eliza held her breath as they sat in silence, not speaking for several seconds.

"Lizzy?"

Her pulse skipped. "Yes?"

"Good night."

"Good night."

Call Ended flashed across the screen as tears slid down Eliza's cheeks.

Gathering a breath, she quickly rubbed away any sign of sadness as she accepted the incoming video call from her son.

"Hey, Bug."

At the cheerful lilt in her voice, no one would ever know that her heart was slowly crumbling.

CHAPTER 29

*F*rom his position at the dining room table, Grant shifted his gaze from the art camp registration form to the small balcony beyond the sliding glass door.

Ben perched on a barstool, adjusting his brand-new glasses while he studied the sheet of watercolor paper clipped to the tall easel. Ben had picked out the lime-green frames all by himself and seemed to love them so far. Minus the slight discomfort that stemmed from having a foreign object attached to your face at all times. But he would get used to it eventually.

After dipping his paintbrush into the palette, Ben dabbed it against the canvas, mimicking the bright petals of the potted bougainvillea Grant had purchased last summer at his mother's insistence.

It wasn't lost on Grant that Ben had chosen to paint the only plant he owned, rather than the flashy, modern apartment building across the street or the towering high-rises in the distance. It also hadn't slipped past Grant that the vibrant petals happened to be Eliza's favorite color.

The sliding door remained open, the frenetic sounds of the

city emanating beneath them—car horns, dogs barking, and the occasional shouting match on the street corner.

Grant never minded the cacophony before. But after the peacefulness of Poppy Creek, each siren wail seemed louder somehow. Almost intrusive.

At first, he'd wondered if the plethora of unfamiliar noises would make it difficult for Ben to sleep in his new surroundings. But Ben had quickly developed a habit of calling Eliza after Grant tucked him into bed. Several minutes later, Grant would tiptoe into his room and find Ben sound asleep, the phone limp in his tiny hand.

Grant would carefully slide the phone from his grasp and spend the next half hour filling Eliza in on the details of their day. He'd grown to cherish these moments, eagerly awaiting the pleasant lilt of her voice. Her vivacious laugh. The way she'd sigh deeply whenever he'd share one of Ben's adorable mannerisms or silly expressions.

Sometimes, he'd imagine what it would be like if they were raising Ben together... cuddled up on the couch, munching on warm fresh-from-the-oven snickerdoodles while Ben and some pudgy, floppy-eared pup wrestled on the carpet. He'd have his arm draped around her shoulders, while she nuzzled against him, teasing him for getting crumbs in her hair. They'd share a laugh. And he'd kiss her softly... just because.

Getting lost in the daydream again, Grant shook his head sharply, steering his attention back to the registration form. Pushing all thoughts of Eliza from his mind, he focused on the next question.

Child's full name.

Grant filled in the spaces for Ben's first and last name before shouting, "Hey, what's your middle name?"

He poised the ballpoint pen over the empty box, waiting for Ben's response.

"Thomas!"

The pen clattered to the tabletop.

"Thomas?" Grant repeated, though not loud enough for Ben to hear him over the wail of a passing ambulance.

Shock pinned Grant to his seat.

Eliza had given Ben *his* middle name.

But why? What did it mean? It was as if she'd intentionally kept a link between them.

Grant stood, pacing the floor as he tried to untangle his conflicting emotions.

Over the last few days, he hadn't been able to stop thinking about her. And each time her face materialized in his mind's eye his heart physically ached to hold her.

They belonged together. All three of them.

And he'd never been more confident of that truth until this precise moment.

A knock at the door yanked Grant from his thoughts. It couldn't be her... could it?

Grant crossed the room in quick, purposeful strides and threw open the door.

Shock, disappointment, and confusion rippled through him in rapid succession. "Colt? What are you doing here?"

"Why, yes. I'd love to come in. Thanks." Grinning, Colt breezed past him as though Grant had anticipated his arrival.

"I'll repeat..." Grant said slowly, swinging the door shut. "What are you doing here?"

The loud slam drew Ben's attention, and as soon as he caught sight of Colt, he slipped off the barstool and ran in from the balcony. "Hi! Is Mom here, too?"

"Sorry, kiddo. Just me today. But I brought you something." Colt held out a small pink box emblazoned with The Calendar Café's logo—the one Grant had designed.

Ben's eyes brightened as he flipped open the lid, revealing a mini tiramisu cheesecake. Glancing at his dad, he asked, "Can I?"

"Sure." Grant smiled. "But eat it out on the balcony while Colt and I talk, okay?"

Racing into the kitchen for a fork, Ben hummed happily to himself as he skipped outside with his treat.

"He seems to be doing well." Colt's gaze followed Ben a moment before flickering back to Grant.

"He is. All things considered." Grant crossed his arms, not really in the mood for chitchat. "How did you find me?"

Colt snorted. "You make me sound like a hit man. I asked your dad. He didn't seem to think it was a matter of national security, Mr. President."

Grant cracked a smile and lowered his arms. "Sorry. I suppose I've been wound pretty tight the last few days. It's tough being a single parent."

"That's why I'm here." Crossing into the living room, Colt plopped onto the leather bucket chair, kicking one foot onto his knee.

"You want to co-parent with me?" Grant teased, sinking onto the couch. He shifted a few times, the slick leather squeaking as he tried to get comfortable. No easy feat given the bout of nervous energy triggered by Colt's visit.

Colt pulled a face. "No, thanks. Much as I love Ben." Uncrossing his legs, he leaned forward, an uncharacteristically earnest expression straining his features. "I'm here because I think you made a mistake leaving Poppy Creek. And Eliza," he added with a meaningful glance.

Grant stared, blinking a few times to see if Colt would evaporate into thin air. The whole situation was too surreal.

"Look, this isn't exactly easy for me to say." Colt sprang from the armchair and strode toward the gas fireplace, leaning against the mantel. "You and I haven't always gotten along, so you may not care what I have to say. But there's something you should know…" Colt paused, hesitation sparking in his turquoise-blue eyes before adding, "About your mom."

"What about my mom?" Grant tensed, a muscle in his jaw twitching.

"Well…" Colt ran a hand through his dark blond hair, struggling with what to say next. "Jeez. Eliza will kill me for telling you, but if it were me, I'd want to know."

"Know what?" Grant gritted his teeth, ready to shake the words right out of Colt's mouth.

"Okay, here it goes.…" Colt exhaled, turning to face him. "Your mom blackmailed Eliza into keeping quiet about Ben. I don't know how or why, but that's the truth. I overheard her talking to Luke and Cassie about it the day of the carnival."

"What?" Dazed, Grant shook his head. "That can't be true. Why wouldn't Eliza tell me?"

"Because she's trying to protect you, man." Colt sounded exasperated, as though annoyed he had to spell it out for him. "She knew you'd be crushed, so she didn't tell you. Sacrificing her own chance at happiness to protect your relationship with your mom. Arguably, a pretty dumb decision, but there you have it. The woman's crazy about you. I mean, even all *this* didn't tempt her." Colt grinned, humorously flexing his biceps.

Grant threw his head back, laughing until he had to fight for breath.

"Jeez. It wasn't *that* funny," Colt drawled with mock offense.

Grant swiped a stray tear of laughter from the corner of his eye. "Thank you. Seriously. Thanks."

"Does that mean my magical powers of persuasion worked?"

Glancing at Ben gobbling up his mini cheesecake on the balcony, Grant smiled. "Believe it or not, I think I'd already made my decision before you arrived."

Colt arched one eyebrow as Grant stood and held out his hand. "But I'm really grateful you stopped by. Honestly. And… I think I might have misjudged you."

"Don't sweat it." Accepting Grant's hand, Colt pulled him into a side hug, slapping his shoulder. "I think we're all guilty of misreading things every now and then. Which is why I've become a big proponent of 'say what you mean and mean what you say.'"

Briefly wondering if Colt had alluded to something personal with his pronouncement, Grant nodded in complete agreement.

He had a whole slew of things he needed to say.

To one person in particular.

None of which would take place over the phone.

◈

*a*s Eliza stuffed small personalized packets of coffee into white ceramic mugs, she tried not to think about Ben. But Cassie's cottage held so many memories of her son. All the evenings they'd spent playing board games and putting together elaborate puzzles with Edith. Or helping with chores around the house after her husband passed away.

Then there were all the new memories with Cassie, like decorating the tree and opening gifts in front of the cozy, crackling fire on Christmas morning.

The cottage felt like home.

But what good was a home without Ben?

He'd only been gone a few days. Yet her heart ached as though she hadn't seen him in months.

"Thanks for helping with the wedding favors." Cassie tied a gold ribbon to the handle of the mug before setting it on the table and grabbing another one. "I'm glad Maggie recounted. Otherwise, we'd be short fifty of them."

"Anytime," Eliza murmured, barely listening. Gazing at the delicate mug in her hand, Eliza took in the beautifully stenciled lettering. *Love Always Hopes.* She believed the words to be true. But they proved to be stubbornly elusive in the present moment.

"Is it helping to take your mind off Ben being gone?"

"A little," Eliza croaked, tears welling in her eyes.

"Funny, but I don't believe you," Cassie teased, rising from the couch. "Why don't I make us some coffee?"

"That would be nice, thanks." Eliza sniffled.

Halfway to the kitchen, Cassie paused, startled by a knock at the door.

Eliza's heart skipped into her throat. He'd come back!

Grant had come back for her!

Raising both eyebrows, Cassie shot her a look confirming she'd had the same thought.

As Cassie ambled toward the foyer, Eliza quickly dried her eyes and smoothed back a few flyaways from her forehead.

Casting a hopeful grin over her shoulder, Cassie threw open the front door. But her greeting died on her lips as all the color drained from her face.

"Mom?"

"M-may I come in?" Donna Hayward shifted her feet, tucking a strand of glossy, dark hair behind her ear.

Dazed, Cassie stepped to the side, letting Donna enter before closing the door.

The two women stood near the threshold, unsure how to greet one another, deciding on a stiff nod, rather than the typical hug one might expect between a mother and daughter.

From her perch on the couch, Eliza marveled at how physically alike they were, with the same ripples of mahogany curls and striking green eyes. Although, Cassie appeared more girl-next-door, with her understated makeup and sweet demeanor. While Donna could be Cassie's older, more vivacious sister, with her heavy black eyeliner and low-cut blouse.

Eliza tensed as Donna's gaze drifted in her direction.

"Mom, this is my dear friend Eliza. Eliza, this is my mother, Donna." Cassie led the way into the living room, taking a seat beside Eliza on the couch.

"Nice to meet you," Eliza said weakly, wondering if she should leave and give them privacy. As far as she knew, Cassie hadn't spoken to her mother since Donna skipped out on rehab right before Christmas.

Donna offered a tentative smile before alternating her gaze between two armchairs. Finally, she chose the one closest to the fireplace, not that it mattered, since it hadn't been lit in months. She crossed and uncrossed her long legs, wearing her discomfort as blatantly as her costume jewelry.

"Why don't I go start the coffee?" Eliza whispered, ready to excuse herself when Cassie reached for her hand.

Her furtive squeeze and clammy palm communicated all Eliza needed to know. Squeezing back, she remained firmly in her seat.

"I've been trying to contact you for months. I thought something horrible might have happened to you." Cassie's voice cracked, and Eliza tightened her grip on her hand.

"I know. And I'm sorry." Donna stared at her fingers laced in her lap. "I've been... unavailable."

Unavailable? She had to be kidding. Her only child was getting married in two days. And she hadn't sent a single text, phone call, letter... nothing. She hadn't even bothered to decline Cassie's wedding invitation. And Eliza knew for a fact that her friend had kept a seat open in the front row, just in case.

Eliza wanted to scream. Instead, she focused on taking slow, intentional breaths. She needed to be a pillar of support for Cassie, not fly off the handle in indignation. No matter how deserved it may be.

"What happened?" Cassie whispered, her fingers trembling in Eliza's grasp.

"I... couldn't do it." Shame flickered in Donna's eyes and, for a moment, Eliza softened. It was a feeling she knew well.

"I wanted to. I wanted to be strong. So very badly." An inky-black streak followed the tear trailing down Donna's cheek. "That first night in rehab, I knew I'd never make it. And I kept thinking about everything you'd sacrificed to get me there." A second tear followed the first, stalling on her chin. Donna brushed it aside roughly, as though she blamed the tear for every-thing wrong in her life. "So, I left during the trial period. When you could still get your money back."

Except for the $1,000 deposit.... Eliza winced, dismissing the unkind thought as soon as it entered her mind. She knew Cassie didn't care about the money.

Sniffling, Donna reached into her purse and pulled out a thick white envelope. Leaning forward, she set it on the coffee table. "I know it's a little late, but that's your deposit. Plus a little extra for all the times I borrowed money and never paid you back."

"I don't want the money, Mom." Cassie wiped at her damp cheeks, tears tumbling freely. "I just want you to be okay."

A tender, unexpected smile lit Donna's eyes. "I know. You've always been more than I ever deserved."

At the catch in Donna's voice, it took all of Eliza's self-control not to become a sobbing mess.

"When I left rehab, I... relapsed." Donna dropped her gaze back to her lap. "A week-long binge. If I hadn't run into my friend Gretchen when I did, I-I..." Anguish contorted her features, and Eliza heard Cassie inhale sharply. Her hand went limp, and Eliza traced soothing circles against her skin with her thumb, willing herself to remain strong for Cassie's sake. But even the thought of her dear friend losing her mother in such a horrific way sent shivers down Eliza's spine.

"Gretchen and her AA sponsor helped me get sober. I wanted to get in touch with you sooner, but... I didn't want to get your hopes up in case I failed." Reaching back into her purse, Donna retrieved a shimmering green token. She placed it on top of the envelope. "I just got my three month chip. The next one is blue, for six months. I..." Donna paused, glancing toward the empty fireplace as color swept across her cheeks. "I'd like it to be your wedding present. That is, if I'm still invited."

Slipping her hand from Eliza's, Cassie leapt off the couch.

Donna rose to meet her daughter, and the two women

embraced in the center of the living room, their tears falling unrestrained.

Eliza watched the scene unfold, her heart breaking and mending all at once.

Suddenly, her phone buzzed on the coffee table, Ben's face flashing across the screen for their good night call. Not wanting to disrupt Cassie and her mom, Eliza snatched her cell and ducked outside.

"Hey, Bug."

"Mom!" Her heart swelled as his cheerful chatter filled the speaker, Grant's voice muffled in the background.

Oh, how she longed to all be together again.

But for now, she would cherish the little things.

Like good night phone calls.

And above all…

She would hope.

CHAPTER 30

*R*aucous country music pumped through the speakers of Jack's diner, spilling onto the patio where the rehearsal dinner was already in full swing.

Eliza stared at the condensation trickling down the side of her water goblet like sympathetic tears.

Grant had promised her that they'd be there. And yet the rehearsal came and went without so much as a text or phone call.

Throughout the evening, Eliza's parents kept checking in on her. As did Cassie and Luke, in between introducing Donna to everyone she didn't already know, as well as filling her in on everything she'd missed.

Donna still seemed skittish. And Eliza recognized the strained look of a mother trying to put aside her own discomfort for the sake of her child. But she was there, nonetheless. Which was more than Eliza could say for Grant.

To add to her befuddlement, Jack frequently shot glances in her direction, as though he knew something she didn't. And Penny stuck to her like fondant to a petit four.

"Here. Eat something." Penny slid a plate of tri-tip and coleslaw in front of her, but Eliza pushed it aside.

"No, thank you."

"Two bites. You'll feel better," Penny insisted.

A small, wistful smile tugged at the corner of Eliza's mouth. Everyone mothering her couldn't have been sweeter, yet it merely served as a reminder of her own child's absence, making the emptiness more pronounced.

"Vinny! Stop!"

Eliza's pulse fluttered at the familiar voice shouting above the music.

"Yeah, wait for me!" Ben's higher-pitched cry sent her heart soaring.

"They're here!" Leaping from the table, Eliza nearly knocked over her glass of water. Rushing to the edge of the patio, she froze as a scruffy gray blur shot across the lawn, a bright blue leash trailing behind him.

"Slow down!" Ben giggled, racing past her. "Hi, Mom!" He waved but didn't slow down.

Eliza gaped as Grant followed close behind, coming to a halt a few feet away. Panting, he doubled over, both hands on his knees. "That little stinker took off as soon as I opened the car door."

Eliza blinked, glancing from Grant to the lawn, where Ben and a little ball of wiry fur pranced about in a lively game of tag. Ben's laughter mingled with the scraggly dog's excited bark.

"Sorry we're late. We had to stop in Primrose Valley to adopt Vinny."

"Vinny?"

"Short for Vincent van Gogh," Grant laughed. "Ben named him. But I have to say, it fits. They both have a beard and mustache."

Eliza shook her head, all the scrambled pieces slowly coming together. "Wait, did you say *adopt*?"

"Yeah." Grant wore a sheepish grin. "He's ours. But before you say no, Jack already said I could keep him with me in the chicken coop."

"Wait, hold on." Eliza pressed her fingertips to her temple. She hadn't heard anything past *ours*. "You're not making any sense. What's all this about Jack? And a chicken coop?"

"It's simple. I'm moving back to Poppy Creek." Grant beamed, holding her gaze. "Jack said I can stay in his guest house, which he calls the chicken coop because it used to be one way back in the day, before he fixed it up. But that's another story." He chuckled. "It's only until I find my own place, of course. And he doesn't mind the dog."

Swaying slightly, Eliza thought she might faint. "You said he was ours?"

"Right. Yours, mine, and Ben's. I figured it was time we had a family dog. That's why we're late. We picked him out at the shelter on our way here."

Tears of joy stung the backs of her eyes as she stared at him, mouth agape. "You got us a family dog?"

"You'll love him. He's feisty. Just like you."

Eliza blushed at the tender glint in Grant's eyes. "What about..." She paused, hating to mention anything that could ruin the breathtakingly perfect moment.

"We all have our share of regrets," he said softly. "My biggest one is letting you walk away."

"Forgive and forget?" she asked hopefully, her voice trembling.

"No. Never."

Eliza flinched, taken aback by his response.

Grant took a step toward her. "Forgive? With all my heart. But never forget. Because every time I remember losing you, I'll cherish each second we're together like it's our last. That is... if you'll have me."

Her heart bursting with love for this sweet, forgiving man, Eliza ran to him, flinging her arms around his neck.

Engulfing her in his embrace, Grant lowered his mouth to hers. And all the secret tears, silent prayers, and sacrificed moments were eclipsed by their kiss, leaving them breathless. Eliza wanted to weep with joy, but couldn't stand the thought of their lips ever parting.

Regretfully, she pulled away when a rough, slimy tongue slobbered on her leg.

Two adorable gray-blue eyes stared up at her beneath thick, bushy eyebrows.

"Hey, there." She reached down for the pup to sniff then lick her hand.

His shaggy tail wagged in approval, and Eliza laughed.

"Do you like him, Mom? Do you like him?" Ben gripped Vinny's leash, his dark eyes hopeful.

"I..." Eliza turned to Grant, and her heart swelled at the magnitude of love communicated in a single glance. For a moment, she took in every extraordinary detail he'd passed on to their son... the thick, unruly hair. The dark, expressive eyebrows. The smattering of freckles across the bridge of his nose. And now, his adorable glasses. Ben was no longer her Mini-Me. But a beautiful blend, the best of both of them put together. And she couldn't wait to discover more ways he'd be exactly like his father.

Gazing back at her son, she smiled. "I think he's a perfect addition to the family."

And at that, Vinny barked in complete agreement.

The mattress creaked as Grant shifted his weight. Slowly sitting upright, he did his best not to disturb Vinny curled into a ball by his feet. Stifling a yawn, he stretched his arms overhead, squinting against streaks of bright sunlight that infiltrated the heavy, plaid drapes.

Nearly every inch of the chicken coop was covered in plaid, from the curtains to the bedspread to the upholstery of the portly armchair. Although not enormous by any means, it resembled a small studio apartment and was larger than Grant expected. The original structure must have housed hundreds of chickens, and Jack had clearly added a decent chunk of square footage when he'd installed the plumbing for the bathroom. All in all, it wasn't a bad place to call home.

Or a temporary home, at least.

Grant slung his feet over the side of the bed, rubbing a kink in the back of his neck. He'd have to do something about the pillow, though. Too lumpy. He made a mental note to replace it without bothering Jack, along with the scratchy towels.

Grant was beyond grateful to his friend for giving him a place to stay. After learning what his mother had done to Eliza, he could hardly stomach staying in the same town with her, let alone the same house.

Gathering a deep breath, he padded barefoot across the pine slat floor. Opening the rustic armoire, Grant unzipped the garment bag housing his suit. The rich, dark chocolate wool gleamed in the sunlight, stirring a hankering for a strong cup of freshly brewed coffee.

As he dressed, Grant's mind wandered to last night, when he'd told Eliza about Colt's visit and asked her to fill in the missing pieces of the story. At his request, she'd tearfully told him everything, and he'd never felt so sick to his stomach. How could his mother do something like that? How could *anyone*, for that matter?

A knock on the door drew Grant from his thoughts, momentarily disturbing Vinny.

The pup raised his small, scruffy head, shooting a lazy glance toward the offending sound before burrowing back into the bedspread.

Chuckling, Grant eased open the door to find Jack standing on the stoop, deep creases of frustration etched into his forehead.

"The darn tie won't tie," he grumbled, stomping inside.

"Don't you hate it when they won't tie themselves?" Grant's lips twitched as he made room for Jack's hulking frame. At six four, Jack could barely stand up straight without his head grazing the ceiling.

"It's too early for jokes, Parker." Irritable, Jack scratched his jawline while Grant tried to undo the havoc wreaked on the silk tie.

Suppressing another chuckle, Grant noticed his friend's burly beard had been trimmed down to one step above clean shaven, accentuating his strong features. "You should trim your beard more often. You look like a normal member of society rather than a madman who lives in the woods eating moss and bark beetles."

Jack narrowed his eyes. "What did I say about making wise-cracks at the crack of dawn?"

"It's hardly the crack of dawn, sunshine. Now hold still." Grinning, Grant draped the tie around Jack's neck.

"Remind·me again why we have to be ready at nine in the morning for a five-o'clock wedding?" Jack tugged on the cuffs of his crisp button-down shirt, clearly uncomfortable in the formal wear.

"It was written in the wedding rule book many moons ago by nefarious wedding planners. Along with their conspiracy with photographers for family photos to take six hours longer than necessary."

A hearty chuckle rose from Jack's chest. "Ain't that the truth." As his laughter subsided, Jack's features softened. "I'm glad you and Eliza worked things out. You guys always made a great team. And it's a shame for issues to go unresolved on a day like today."

"What do you mean?" Grant kept his gaze glued on the Windsor knot, his fingers stalling only a moment.

Jack shrugged. "I don't know. I guess weddings are about bringing two people together, for better or worse. Seems sad to think about division or animosity on an occasion celebrating unity, don't you think?"

Grant lifted his gaze to meet Jack's, his stomach twisting like the knot he'd just tied. "Yeah, I suppose."

Jack turned toward the tiny token mirror hanging on the wall, studying his reflection in the aged patina. "Nice work. As long as it doesn't strangle me to death before the actual ceremony."

Pivoting on the heel of his fancy oxfords, Jack slapped Grant on the shoulder. "Well, I'll leave you to it. I'm sure you still have things to do."

With a knowing smile, Jack headed for the door.

Leaving Grant to dwell on his parting words.

CHAPTER 31

Cassie's cottage hummed with excitement as the bride and her entourage wrapped up the few last-minute details.

Maggie, Beverly, and Dolores remained on hand for wardrobe emergencies, like the unexpected loose strap on Penny's dress. And surprisingly, Donna lent her talent for wielding a mascara wand and contour brush.

As the time for the ceremony drew closer, the women bid Cassie emotional goodbyes before heading to the town square.

Donna and Eliza were the last to leave, Donna lingering in the doorway of Cassie's bedroom as her daughter counted off the final checklist.

"Something old… check." Cassie wiggled her fingers, the sunlight catching on the antique diamond of her engagement ring. "Something new." She caressed the stunning silver barrette Luke had custom made by an artisan designer he'd met a few weeks ago. He'd traveled all the way to San Francisco to pick it up from the specialty shop, and the delicate red enamel poppies looked stunning against Cassie's dark, glossy hair.

Tears glistened in her eyes as Eliza thought about how

fervently Luke loved this woman standing before her, radiant both inside and out. Though only a few years older, the couple had become her role models, displaying a kind of love that defied the odds.

"Something borrowed," Cassie continued, running her hand along the delicate lace of Maggie's wedding dress. "And..." Her eyes widened. "I don't have anything blue!"

Eliza frowned, her pulse stuttering. Why hadn't they gone over this list before? Personally, she'd never even thought about the antiquated tradition. And it seemed a little late to worry about it now.

Glancing around the room, Eliza racked her brain for an idea. Maybe they could tuck a blue flower in her hair? There was probably some lupine growing in the backyard. Or was that considered purple?

"Yes, you do." Smiling softly, Donna stepped forward, fidgeting with something clasped in her palm.

"I do?" Cassie peered curiously at her mother.

Donna bit her lower lip, disturbing her perfectly applied lipstick. "When your grandmother passed away and left you this house, you asked if she'd left me anything in her will. I told you she gave me a letter."

Cassie nodded slowly. "Yes, I remember."

"Well..." Donna's gaze darted to the floor, then back to her daughter. "She also left me this." Pinched between her fingers, Donna displayed an exquisite sapphire ring. The oval gem glittered in a regal, art deco–style setting of soft yellow gold.

"What is it?" Cassie asked in a reverent whisper.

"Your grandmother's engagement ring. The one my dad... your grandfather gave her." Donna's voice quivered. "I wish you could have met him. He would have loved you so very much."

Dabbing her eyes, Eliza watched Donna slip the ring on Cassie's right hand, her heart bursting with gratefulness. Ben had gone seven years without knowing his father, and she couldn't imagine him experiencing another day without Grant in his life. Poor Donna had lost her father as a teenager, before Cassie was born. What an ache that must have left in her heart.

"Are you sure?" Cassie asked, gazing at the intricate facets of the intense blue stone. "Don't you want to keep it?"

"I want you to have it. In a way, this is your blue chip."

"What do you mean?"

A tender smile illuminated Donna's face, brightening her glistening green eyes. "You've overcome a lot to be standing here today. I know that more than anyone. And I'm…" Donna's lips trembled as she fought back tears. "I'm proud of you, Cassandra."

Eliza drew in a breath, startled to hear Cassie's full name for the first time. It sounded strange to her ears, yet oddly fitting coming from Donna's lips, as though it held special meaning between mother and daughter. And Eliza marveled at how the inverse of a nickname could feel so intimate.

As the women embraced, Eliza thought she heard Donna whisper *I love you*, but couldn't be certain.

Tracing her fingertips along the rims of her eyes, removing any remnants of smeared eyeliner, Donna bid them goodbye before slipping out of the room, leaving Cassie and her maid of honor alone.

Cassie sniffled, turning toward the mirror above the dresser to inspect her makeup.

"Are you okay?" Eliza handed Cassie a tissue, thankful they'd chosen waterproof mascara.

"I still can't believe she's here." Cassie dabbed an imaginary smudge. "My heart feels so… full."

Eliza smiled, her own heart overflowing. "Since you decided to move in with Luke, do you think you'll offer the cottage to your mom?"

"No." Cassie shook her head, setting the tissue on the dresser. "I don't think Mom will ever move back. I mean, you've seen her over the last few days. She's trying to hide it, but she still hates it here for some reason I can't fathom."

Eliza's features softened in understanding, amazed at Cassie for being so perceptive despite all the distractions.

"But since we're on the subject…" Cassie pulled open the top drawer of the dresser and removed a small wooden box engraved with tiny daffodils.

Immediately, Eliza recognized Luke's craftsmanship as she accepted what she assumed to be her bridesmaid's gift. "It's beautiful."

"Open it." Cassie's eyes glittered expectantly as Eliza popped open the lid.

Her brow furrowed, Eliza lifted a simple silver key, unclear what it represented.

"It's a key to the cottage." Cassie beamed, bouncing on her tiptoes in her excitement. "I'd like you and Ben to live here, rent free, for as long as you'd like."

Shaking her head, Eliza stuffed the key back inside the box and closed the lid. "Cass, I can't accept this. It's too generous." She held the box out to Cassie, but her friend crossed her arms, a smirk playing about her lips.

"I'm sorry, but it's against the rules to defy the bride on her special day. Besides," she added, "Grandma Edie would want you to live here. If you won't accept it for yourself, then take it for Ben. And that adorable new dog of yours."

A flood of emotion overwhelmed Eliza, and she choked back a sob. "I… don't know what to say."

"Say you won't be upset when I tell you that Luke and Colt spent the morning hanging a swing on the maple tree while we were getting ready." Cassie's eyes danced with glee, as though she could hardly contain her happiness.

"What? But how did they…" As awareness dawned, Eliza's eyes widened. "That's why you turned up the music when we were doing our makeup…."

"I thought for sure you'd catch on," Cassie laughed. "Instead, you must have thought I really, *really* like 'Pretty Woman' by Roy Orbison."

"It's a good song," Eliza giggled, reaching for a tissue to blot her damp cheeks. "What made you think of the swing?"

"It was Colt's idea, actually. He said every little boy needs a tree swing. And I happen to agree."

Flinging her arms around Cassie's neck, Eliza hugged her friend, not caring if they crumpled both of their dresses.

The deep rumble of an engine pulled them apart.

Taking a step back, Eliza regarded Cassie one last time before she became Mrs. Luke Davis.

Moved beyond words by her beauty, which emanated from within, Eliza whispered, "I think your ride is here."

*G*rant fiddled with his gold cuff links as he stood facing the back door, the solid oak separating him from the unpleasant conversation awaiting him on the other side.

He shouldn't be here.

The wedding would start any minute. But Jack's words about resolving conflict followed him like a stubborn shadow, niggling at the back of his mind.

With a deep breath, he stepped onto the porch, flinching as the door slammed shut behind him.

His mother turned from her kneeling position at the edge of the garden, and as Grant approached, he observed her red, puffy features.

At first, it looked like she'd spent several hours crying. Then he noticed the rash covering her neck and arms.

"You got poison oak?" he asked, though he could hardly believe it. While the poisonous plant was pervasive, his mother meticulously kept anything remotely resembling the leafy pest from attacking her pristine flower beds. She must have been particularly distracted to have come in contact with her bare skin.

Surprise flickered in her pinched eyes. "What are you doing here? Shouldn't you be at the wedding?" As she spoke, the inflamed flesh around her mouth cracked.

Grant cringed. Each word must be torture.

"I wanted to talk, but I can see you're in a lot of pain. I'll come back later, when you're feeling better." He turned to go.

"Wait." Harriet winced as she carefully rose to her feet, causing Grant to suspect the rash had spread to her legs as well. "I have something for you."

As she crept toward the house, Grant could hardly stand to see the discomfort evident in every step she took.

"Mom, whatever it is, don't worry about it right now."

She waved her hand in dismissal before disappearing inside.

While he waited, Grant glanced around the backyard, searching for a shrub with the telltale clusters of three leaves, usually bright green this time of year. For the life of him, he couldn't understand how she'd become infected. His mother was always methodical; carelessness wasn't in her nature. He wondered if their quarrel had somehow contributed to her inattentiveness.

Grant shifted his weight, conflicted between his concern over her present condition and his anger at what she'd done. Anger that felt completely justified.

But deserved or not, he couldn't live with the bitterness. Not only had it slowly deteriorated his relationship with his father, but it had eaten away at his soul for years. In some ways, his unforgiving spirit had been more infectious—and damaging—than his mother's poison oak. He needed to confront the issue. But he wasn't sure how….

When she returned, she held something clasped in her hands,

now clad in thick oven mitts. "I put these on first, just in case..." Her gaze dropped to her raw, itchy skin.

"Thanks. I appreciate that." Dragging his teeth across his bottom lip, Grant drew in a breath. His chest tightened, making it difficult to exhale. "Listen, Mom. This may not be the best time, but we need to talk." He resisted the urge to back down, meeting her swollen, bloodshot eyes. "I know what you did to Eliza. To me. To your own grandson, for that matter. And it's—"

"Wait. Please." Her tone earnest, Harriet splayed her hands, revealing the mysterious object.

Grant inhaled sharply, his gaze darting to her face.

His mother's dry, cracked lips trembled. "I'm so sorry, son. And I know this doesn't... I don't deserve..." Her voice broke as a small sob escaped. "This belongs to... Eliza."

Startled, Grant blinked. She'd said Eliza's name. No sneer. No grimace, as though the letters arranged in that particular order provoked an involuntary gag reflex. She hadn't even called her *that girl.*

Grant's features softened as he drew his attention back to the item in her hand.

Wrapping his fingers around the smooth velvet, he knew exactly what it was.

And what it meant.

"Thank you," he whispered, his voice hoarse.

While mending their relationship would take time, Grant held out hope.

That maybe... just maybe...

They could *all* be a family one day.

CHAPTER 32

*E*liza had promised herself she wouldn't cry.

But as she took in the ethereal beauty of the town square, transformed for Luke and Cassie's wedding, she couldn't help it.

A tear slid down her cheek as she caught sight of Maggie sitting in the front row, gazing at her son who stood beneath the arch he'd built with his own hands, her eyes shimmering with unspeakable love and joy.

Eliza's breath hitched. That would be her someday, when it came time for Ben to get married.

Another tear escaped, gently following the trail of the first.

Strong, warm fingers slipped through hers, and Grant gave a comforting squeeze, reaching over to wipe the tear from her cheek.

"You look beautiful," he whispered, his gentle breath ruffling the wispy curls framing her face.

Too emotional for words, she squeezed back, grateful Luke and Cassie had gone with an unconventional wedding party— Jack, Penny, and Reed on one side, Colt, herself, and Grant on the other. Ben squirmed by Grant's side, looking far more eager to sit with Vinny, who lounged dutifully by Donna's feet in the front row.

As the processional music shifted, the dulcet melody of the "Christmas Waltz" floated across the lawn, the guitar and violin lending a magical quality to the familiar notes.

Eliza's lips curled into a smile. Only Luke and Cassie could pick a Christmas song in summer and have it fit with utter perfection.

A low rumble drew everyone's attention to Main Street, where a glimmering 1951 Chevy convertible parked at the end of the square. Sunlight gleamed off the deep-purple paint, highlighting its elegant curves as the sun dipped behind the trees.

Frank Barrie emerged from the driver's seat, gallantly clothed in a tailored suit the color of rich French roast. He confidently strode around the car and opened the passenger door, offering Cassie his arm.

At the look of intense pride on his face, Eliza nearly broke down completely, recalling the warmth in Cassie's voice when she'd recounted asking Frank to walk her down the aisle. They'd been sipping coffee on the front porch, and according to Cassie, Frank had cried. Although in true Frank fashion, he'd insisted the moisture in his eyes stemmed from the steam radiating off the freshly brewed coffee. But Cassie hadn't been fooled for a second.

A collective gasp stirred the crowd as she emerged from the vehicle, a breathtaking vision in vintage ivory lace, her dark curls cascading down her back in silky tendrils.

While everyone stood, turning their attention to Frank and Cassie as they glided down the aisle, Eliza stole a glance at Luke.

He stood perfectly still, barely even breathing as his gaze locked on his bride, tears pooling in his warm, hazel eyes.

As Cassie drew closer, Eliza caught Luke's lips move almost imperceptibly, forming the words *I love you*.

Her gaze flitted to Cassie, and she observed her mouth the same words back to Luke.

As the music swelled, Frank handed Cassie off to her groom. But not before planting a gentle kiss on her cheek. Leaning in to Luke, he shook his hand while whispering something in his ear.

Luke's eyes crinkled in an affectionate smile as he gripped the old man's hand, shaking on whatever promise he'd just made.

Everyone sat as Pastor Bellman began the ceremony with a few jokes, followed by a brief message on love and the significance of marriage.

Then came Eliza's favorite part: the wedding vows.

Her heart fluttering in anticipation, she handed Cassie the leather-bound notebook containing her handwritten vows, trading it for her bouquet. As she clasped the arrangement of white roses dotted with bright red berries, Eliza smiled, remembering how Cassie had wept the first time she'd laid eyes on Reed's special addition.

Per Luke's request, Reed had spent nearly six months cultivating the coffee shrub in his green house, babying the tropical plant until the blossoms transformed into vibrant cherries. All the care and effort wasn't lost on Cassie, who'd gushed over the surprise for hours, touched by the thoughtfulness.

Tearing her gaze from the perfect arrangement, Eliza focused on Cassie, moved by the look of complete and utter adoration on her friend's features.

"The first time I saw you..." Cassie began, her voice shaky. "You were wearing a Frosty the Snowman sweater. And I confess to thinking you were a little bit crazy."

Luke chuckled, wiping a tear from the corner of his eye as Cassie beamed at him.

"But it didn't take long to realize you were more than crazy about Christmas. You were also the most generous man I'd ever met. Generous with your time. And with your love." Her voice broke, all attention to her journal forgotten, her gaze fixed on Luke. "You showed me what unconditional, unfailing love looks like. You taught me to hope. And that hope blossomed into assurance." Passing the vows back to Eliza, Cassie reached for Luke's hands, her trembling fingers steadying as they laced through his. "I, Cassandra Marie Hayward, vow to never give up hope. To persevere through whatever trials come our way. And to love you more than I love myself. And yes, even more than I love coffee."

Laughter and sniffling rippled across the sea of guests as Luke kept his grip on Cassie's hands, ignoring the booklet Colt offered containing his vows.

With his gaze anchored on his bride, Luke cleared his throat. "The first moment I saw you... spitting the coffee I'd made back into your thermos, I fell for you. *Literally.*"

Luke grinned as Cassie smiled through her tears. "And the more I got to know you, the more I realized your beauty ran far deeper than I'd ever imagined. Your caring heart is visible in the way you love others, from your family to those you barely know. I admire your courage and kindness. And loving you makes me strive to be a better man. I, Luke Ryan Davis, vow to pursue you no matter what. To fight with you and for you. And to joyfully accept the bad with the good. And that especially goes for the cuckoo clock."

Sharing the laughter of their private joke, they squeezed each other's hands, earnest desire to seal their vows with a kiss evident across both of their faces.

Eliza sucked in a breath, struggling to keep the tears of joy at bay.

Grant squeezed her hand again, and she stole a glance in his direction, flushing as he winked before returning his gaze to the bride and groom.

Oh, what she wouldn't give to know exactly what he was thinking in that moment.

"Now, for the exchanging of the rings." Pastor Bellman gestured to Ben whose bored expression lit up in excitement.

Proudly handing Colt the rings, he beamed at Eliza, and she whispered, "Good job," as he skipped back to Grant's side.

Holding out the diamond-encrusted band, Luke slid it on Cassie's finger. "Ru, do you take me to be your lawfully wedded husband?"

"I do," Cassie said empathically, a slight catch in her throat. Accepting the solid, tungsten ring from Colt's grasp, she held it out to Luke. "Sprinkles, do you take me to be your lawfully wedded wife?"

His lips twitched. "I do."

"You may now kiss your bride." Pastor Bellman took a step backward as Luke eagerly swooped Cassie into his arms, kissing her for so long, the pastor had to clear his throat.

After he pronounced them husband and wife, Luke led Cassie down the aisle to the boisterous cheers of their friends and family, his arm looped around her waist as though he had no intention of ever letting go.

"Shall we?" Grant held out his arm.

Eliza hooked her hand through the crook of his elbow, gazing fondly after the newlyweds.

Someday, she hoped it would be their turn.

And she could hardly wait.

◈

*H*er pulse skittering, Eliza observed Grant lean over Tommy Jensen, a high schooler and volunteer DJ, and whisper something in his ear.

Flashing a toothy grin, Tommy gave him a thumbs-up.

As Grant strode toward her, the sultry notes of "It Had to Be You" spilled across the dance floor. He offered her his hand, his tender gaze stealing the breath from her lungs.

She floated into his arms, thankful Tommy had chosen the slow, silky rendition crooned by Frank Sinatra, the Sultan of Swoon.

Resting her head against Grant's chest, Eliza relished the way he nuzzled her hair, whispering the lyrics, low and husky, sending shivers tiptoeing across her bare shoulders. She drank in his intoxicating scent, unaware of anyone else in the world.

"I have something for you," Grant murmured, pulling back to look at her.

Eliza glanced up, hoping he meant a kiss.

He tucked his hand inside his breast pocket, retrieving a small velvet box.

Eliza froze, her gaze darting from the box to Grant's face.

"Eliza Lansbury Carter... you deserve the kind of proposal that takes world-domination-level planning, with a thousand moving parts and surprises wrapped in chicanery, tied with a bow of subterfuge."

Eliza giggled. "But I hate surprises."

"I promise... when it happens, you'll love every single second."

At the look of intensity in his eyes, Eliza's breath sputtered, stalling in her throat. Heat swept across her cheeks, and every inch of her body, for that matter.

Grant cleared his throat. "Until then... I believe this is yours." He popped open the lid, revealing a delicate rose gold band. The intricate engravings shimmered in the glittering lights overhead, bringing tears to her eyes.

Grant plucked it from its resting place with one assured motion. "Lizzy, my promise to you has never changed. You are, and always will be, the one and only woman I've ever loved. And I will continue to cherish you with each and every breath I take, for as long as I have air to breathe. And delicious desserts to sample."

Laughing through her tears, she nudged him with her elbow.

Grinning, he slipped the ring on her finger, his deep-blue eyes glistening behind his glasses.

As the smooth, familiar metal grazed her skin, a tear tumbled down Eliza's cheek.

Tenderly brushing it aside, Grant grasped her newly adorned

hand, drawing her against him, swaying to the dulcet notes they'd both long since memorized.

Eliza slid her arms around his shoulders, clasping them behind his neck. "Tell me what it says," she murmured, although she knew every word by heart.

"What?"

"The inscription."

A smile teased Grant's lips as he gazed into her dark eyes, his own glinting with affection. "One life…"

"One love," she finished on a whisper. Rising onto her tiptoes, she gently brushed her lips against his, quivering as he pulled her closer, deepening their kiss.

As her eyes fluttered closed, she could still see his face, no longer a shadow engulfed in a crowd.

Steady. Constant. Devoted.

A truth she could count on.

For the rest of her life.

EPILOGUE

Standing on the outskirts of the dance floor, Colt Davis didn't notice the lively music, boisterous laughter, or swirl of colors as couples spun and twirled past him. He couldn't take his eyes off Penny Heart, an arresting vision in a coffee-colored dress that accentuated her slender figure and perfect coloring. Although he'd teased her for her red hair and copper eyes in school, he'd never seen a more remarkable combination. He only wished he'd been brave enough to tell her back then.

As he brought a bite of cheesecake to his mouth, cold metal prongs collided with his front teeth. Wincing, he glanced down at the empty fork before noticing the white smear on his silk tie, then the glob of whipped cream on the tip of his Oxford shoes.

He suppressed a groan.

"Maybe you should consider wearing a bib?" Jack teased, handing him a napkin.

"Or stop staring at Penny long enough to make sure the cheesecake makes it all the way into your mouth," Reed added with a chuckle.

"You two are hilarious." Rolling his eyes, Colt scrubbed at the stain in agitation. "Really, you should take your comedy act on the road."

"Thanks for the advice." Jack grinned. "Now, let me give *you* some. Give up now. Penny will never go out with you."

"Yeah," Reed agreed. "Especially after you asked out Eliza."

Colt grimaced. Admittedly, that had been a mistake. Selfishly, he'd hoped dating a single mom would push him toward a sense of responsibility and stability. But the decision had been impulsive. Desperate, even. And he wasn't proud of it.

But Penny... she was unlike any woman he'd ever met.

Ever since she'd unleashed that tiny yellow ball, plunging him into an unpleasant ice bath, she'd unleashed something else....

An intense desire for something real. Something like Luke and Cassie shared.

For the first time in his life, Colt had met his match.

No, scratch that.

Penny was his superior in every possible way.

And she made him want to do better. To *be* better.

Even if that meant facing how his father's death had changed him.

"Who says I want to ask out Penny?" Colt asked, attempting to gauge how obvious he'd been.

"Oh, the fact that you've been staring at her for twenty minutes straight." Jack grinned, loosening his tie. "Unless you're just trying to get some pointers on how to eat a piece of cake properly."

Reed joined in Jack's laughter.

"Ha-ha," Colt mumbled. Although, he had to admit Jack was on a roll tonight. "I was thinking I'd ask her to dance. That's all."

"You can try," Jack snorted.

Gathering his courage, Colt squared his shoulders.

The odds were definitely against him. But part of turning over a new leaf would require persistence and patience. Two skills he lacked, miserably.

Wadding up the napkin, he tossed it onto a nearby table, acutely aware his pulse had picked up tempo, matching the rhythm of the music being pumped through the speakers.

He'd never been nervous to pursue a woman before.

But this time, everything felt different.

For once, his heart was on the line.

◈

*P*enny Heart *wanted* to like weddings.

Really, she did.

Especially when everyone kept saying how *magical* they were.

But she simply couldn't see the appeal.

She tapped her fingertips against the taupe tablecloth, taking in the way the canopy of twinkle lights glittered across the amber-colored apothecary jars brimming with white roses and eucalyptus. Their sweet fragrance scented the crisp night air, complementing the equally sweet notes of laughter and music.

Okay… so she could see *some* of the appeal. But it wasn't as if the wedding itself deserved any credit for making a marriage last.

No, that happened far, far away from the revelry. In the hidden corners and crevices of a person's life, where light and beauty were hard to find. In the places where secrets were exposed and scars were made.

That's when marriages either thrived or failed.

And it was usually the latter.

Her muscles tense, Penny reached for a glass of water, the ice clinking gently as she brought the rim to her lips. Even the water tasted sweet, infused with fresh strawberries and a hint of lime. She found it hard to swallow.

Luke and Cassie were different, though. Stronger and smarter than her parents. Than most people, really. They went into marriage knowing it would be hard, choosing to hope and perse-vere anyway.

Penny allowed herself a faint smile, watching the newlyweds on the dance floor, isolated in their own bubble of marital bliss. Beside them, Grant and Eliza looked equally lost in the la-la land of love. She had no doubt they would be next to take the plunge. Or perhaps Frank and Beverly, who sashayed across the dance floor like two young lovebirds.

"Care to dance?"

Penny jumped, icy water splashing over the rim of the glass, sprinkling the tablecloth. Darting a glance at Colt, she set the glass down and dried her hands on her napkin. "No, thanks."

"Are you sure?" Colt tried again, his dimple on full display as he flashed his most irresistible grin.

Penny had no doubt it worked on countless women. Countless *other* women. "I'm sure."

"Come on, what are you afraid of?"

"Let's see. Heights, confined spaces, snakes, the dark…" Holding up her hand, Penny ticked them off one by one. "Oh, and what are those flesh-eating fish called?"

"Piranhas?"

"Yes!" Penny snapped her fingers. "Those, too."

"What about sharks?" Colt asked, his expression completely deadpan.

"Nope. Sharks don't bother me in the slightest."

"I see." He nodded, maintaining his air of seriousness. "That's quite the list. But I noticed you left off one very important item."

"I did?" Penny frowned, certain she'd mentioned everything.

"You didn't say anything about tall, blond, ridiculously handsome men."

"Well, I wouldn't know about that." Penny smirked. "I haven't come across any of those."

Colt clutched his heart, feigning shock. "You cut me to my core."

"Somehow, I think you'll survive," she teased.

Really hamming it up, Colt staggered over to where Jack and

Reed stood a few feet away, swaying as if he'd been shot. "Help. I've been mortally wounded."

Penny couldn't help but laugh at his childish antics.

Jack slung his arm around Colt's midsection, propping him up. "Why don't we take another trip around the dessert bar? We'll make sure your last meal is a good one."

As Jack dragged him away, Colt waved his arms in sweeping, melodramatic gestures. "'Good night, good night! Parting is such sweet sorrow, that I shall say good night till it be morrow.'"

Penny gaped, sensing her resolve falter. She had to hand it to him for reciting Shakespeare. "Okay, one dance," she relented, slowly rising to her feet. "But if you step on my toes, the dance is over. And I get to pick the song."

Colt bowed at the waist, accepting her conditions. "'If music be the food of love, play on.'"

Penny balked. More Shakespeare? She could have sworn he'd slept through every class in high school except the ones he ditched.

Jack laughed. "Good luck, Romeo." He slapped Colt on the shoulder before heading to the dessert bar with Reed.

"Shall we?" Grinning, Colt offered her his open palm.

Penny hesitated. This was a bad idea. She couldn't believe she'd caved because of Shakespeare. Staring at Colt's outstretched hand, she racked her brain for an excuse.

But as the wistful, dulcet notes of Nat King Cole's "Smile" swept across the dance floor, Penny found her fingers slipping through Colt's. She never could resist her favorite song; the hauntingly beautiful melody moved her to tears every time.

Hiding the emotion sprawled across her face, she leaned into Colt, letting his broad chest provide a shield against his inevitable teasing.

But much to her surprise, he seemed to be humming under his breath, so soft she could barely make it out.

"Do you know this song?" Penny pulled back, even more astonished to glimpse a faint flush color his cheeks.

Colt Davis didn't get embarrassed—by anything.

Her gaze lingered on his strong, freshly shaven jaw line, noticing a slight nick. Instinctively, she almost reached up to touch it, blushing profusely as she realized her near blunder. She quickly looked away as Colt cleared his throat.

"I like everything Nat does. But this is one of my favorites."

"Nat?" Penny raised both eyebrows, her lips twitching. "Was he a good friend of yours?"

Colt chuckled. "I like to think we would have been best friends, should our paths have ever crossed."

Penny shook her head, a small, incredulous smile lighting her coppery eyes.

"What?" Colt asked, catching her smile.

"How do you do that?"

"Do what?"

"Have so much confidence. Admittedly, sometimes it borders on downright arrogance. But I envy the confidence."

"I'm not always confident," Colt said softly.

He met her gaze, and Penny's heartbeat fluttered to a stop at the spark of sincerity.

"Actually…" Colt's voice dipped, low and gravelly. He cleared his throat again. "There's something I want to tell you…."

Penny held her breath, the bright lights and music blurring around them as though they were on a carousel spinning too fast. Her pulse raced as Colt wet his lips, then parted them slowly.

Agonizingly slow.

Penny leaned into him, subconsciously afraid to miss a single word. But why did she care? She couldn't stand Colt most of the time. In fact, she usually found him loathsome.

Then he would go and do something completely out of character, leaving her scratching her head, wondering if *maybe* she'd pegged him all wrong.

Fixing her gaze on his face, she tried to focus on what he was about to say rather than the slight bump on the bridge of his nose. Or the way his turquoise-blue eyes shimmered with flecks of gold.

He drew his teeth across his bottom lip, nervous uncertainty etched into his tan forehead.

She nodded, almost imperceptibly, as a form of encouragement.

"Pen, I—"

A sharp yelp from a few feet behind them cut Colt short.

Penny turned to see Frank slouched over, barely supported by Beverly, her eyes wide in fright.

Colt raced to Frank's side, slinging his arm around his waist, setting him back on his feet. "Are you all right?"

"Yes," Frank grunted, though he looked a little peaked. "Just lost my footing for a second is all."

"Are you sure?" Colt pressed, unwilling to loosen his grip.

Frank's gaze flitted to Luke and Cassie, who floated across the dance floor, oblivious to the world around them. His eyebrows set in a determined scowl despite his pallid features. "I'm sure." The words escaped in a strangled breath.

Colt reluctantly lowered his arm, shooting Penny a meaningful glance.

And based on his expression, he didn't believe Frank, either.

You can read **Penny's story,** and learn more about your favorite Poppy Creek characters (including what happened to Frank Barrie), in *The Secret in Sandcastles*.

ACKNOWLEDGMENTS

I am overwhelmed with gratitude for each and every person who helped this story come together. Truly, I couldn't have done it without you.

First, a special thank you to my patient and loving husband who cooked countless dinners and took the dogs on long walks while I buried myself in my writing. Not to mention the endless moral support and chocolate-caramel squares.

And for my wonderfully understanding friends and family who often went weeks without seeing my face.

While we're on the topic of family... I am blessed beyond words to have the love and support of the most incredible group of women—DaryelLee, Lynn, Cheryl, and Annalisa—you ladies deserve a world of praise. Thank you!

Without my talented cover designer, editor, proofreader, and critique partners, this story would be nothing more than a Word document on my laptop.

Never-ending thanks to:

Ana Grigoriu-Voicu with Books-design for my gorgeous cover. It's a work of art!

Beth Attwood for her impeccable editing skills, and Krista Dapkey with KD Proofreading for her incredible eye for story and detail.

Dave, Gigi, and Daria... you three took time away from your own stories to offer insights on mine. And I can't thank you enough.

Lastly, I would like to thank my readers for granting me the opportunity to share this story. Especially those of you who pre-ordered the book and emailed to say how much you were looking forward to it. You gifted me the additional encouragement I needed to keep writing... long after the coffee pot ran dry.

Thank you!

ABOUT THE AUTHOR

Rachael Bloome is a *hopeful* romantic. She loves every moment leading up to the first kiss, as well as each second after saying, "I do." Torn between her small-town roots and her passion for traveling the world, she weaves both into her stories- and her life!

Joyfully living in her very own love story, she enjoys spending time with her husband and two rescue dogs, Finley and Monkey. When she's not writing, helping to run the family coffee roasting business, or getting together with friends, she's busy planning their next big adventure!

ELIZA'S TIRAMISU CHEESECAKE

When setting about creating a unique recipe to share with you, I almost chose a classic tiramisu. With my Italian heritage and love of coffee, it seemed like the perfect choice. In the end, I decided to meld traditional tiramisu with my husband's favorite dessert. I hope you enjoy the tiramisu cheesecake combination as much as we do.

SUBSTITUTIONS

For an alcohol-free version, you can substitute the Kahlúa with strongly brewed Kahlúa-flavored coffee.

FOR GRAHAM CRACKER CRUST:

Ingredients

1 1/3 cup graham cracker crumbs

1/3 cup granulated sugar

4 Tbs melted butter

Instructions

1. Preheat oven to 350 degrees Fahrenheit.

2. Generously grease a 9 inch spring-form pan with butter.

3. Wrap the outside with aluminum foil, covering the bottom and up the sides (This will prevent any water from seeping inside the pan when immersed in a water bath).

4. Mix graham cracker crumbs, granulated sugar, and melted butter just until crumbs are moistened.

5. Pat a thin layer of the graham cracker mixture evenly along the bottom.

4. Bake at 350 for 10 minutes or until golden brown.

5. Let cool.

For Coffee Mixture:

Ingredients

2 Tbs Kahlúa or coffee liqueur

2 Tbs granulated sugar

3 Tbs espresso (or strongly brewed coffee)

3 Tbs hot water

Instructions

1. Combine all ingredients in a small saucepan.

2. Bring mixture to a boil.

3. Simmer 3 min, stirring occasionally.

4. Let mixture cool.

For Cheesecake:

Ingredients

2 Tbs espresso (cooled to room temperature)

2/3 cup heavy cream

Lady fingers (roughly 20)

3 8oz packages of cream cheese (room temperature)

1 1/3 cup granulated sugar

1/4 cup cornstarch

2 eggs

1 Tbs pure vanilla extract

Instructions

1. In a small bowl, combine espresso with the heavy cream and set aside.

2. Preheat oven to 350 degrees Fahrenheit.

3. Dip the lady fingers in coffee mixture. Coat completely but do not soak. Layer evenly on top of the cooled graham cracker crust.

4. In a large bowl or KitchenAid mixer, beat one package of cream cheese, 1/3 cup of granulated sugar, and the cornstarch on low-medium speed until smooth. Scrape sides of bowl, if needed.

5. Blend in the remaining cream cheese, one package at a time.

6. Add eggs, one at a time.

7. Add in remaining sugar and vanilla extract and beat on medium speed until light and fluffy.

8. Slowly add in coffee and cream mixture just until blended, being careful not to over whip.

9. Pour cream cheese mixture over the lady fingers and spread evenly.

10. Place pan in a large shallow dish of hot water until the water reaches about halfway up the sides of the pan.

11. Bake for 1 hour, or until the edges of the cheesecake are set, but the center is still loose.

12. Remove from oven and lift the pan from the water. Let cool on a wire wrack for 2 hours, then cover and move to the refrigerator to cool completely. Approximately 4 hours or leave overnight.

FOR THE TOPPING:

Ingredients

1 1/2 cup heavy whipping cream (still cold)

2 Tbs granulated sugar

1 Tbs pure vanilla extract

1 8oz carton of mascarpone cheese

Instructions

1. Whip the cream until it thickens and soft peaks start to form.

2. Add the granulated sugar and whip until stiff peaks form, careful not to over-mix.

3. Lightly beat in vanilla extract.

4. Gently fold in mascarpone cheese.

5. Remove chilled cheesecake from the refrigerator and spoon 2/3 of the topping over the top of the cheesecake. (The consistency will be like stiff whipped cream. For a firmer topping, place the cheesecake in the freezer for a few hours before spreading. The cold cheesecake with harden the whipped cream.)

6. Carefully remove the sides of the spring-form and spread the remaining topping evenly around the sides of the cheesecake.

FOR THE COFFEE SYRUP:

Ingredients

1 cup granulated sugar

4 ounces espresso (or strongly brewed coffee)

2 Tbs Kahlúa

1 tsp pure vanilla extract

Instructions

1. Combine all ingredients in a small saucepan

2. Bring to a boil.

3. Boil gently for 3 minutes, stirring continually. Sauce will start to thicken.

4. Let cool, then refrigerate. Sauce will continue to thicken as it cools.

To Serve:

1. Sprinkle cheesecake with cocoa powder and/or chocolate shavings.

2. Top with fresh raspberry and mint leaves.

3. Plate and drizzle each slice with a generous amount of coffee sauce.

Enjoy!

BOOK CLUB QUESTIONS

1. How did you think the title of the novel would tie into the story?

2. Who did you think was Ben's father? When did you first suspect it might be Grant?

3. Why did you initially think Eliza kept the identity of Ben's father a secret?

4. When you learned Eliza's reason for keeping the secret, how did you feel? Were you sympathetic? Upset? Frustrated?

5. Did you think Grant's reaction to the truth was realistic? Why or why not?

6. How did you feel about Grant's decision to confront his mother with the intent of reconciling? Do you think he should forgive her? Why or why not?

7. How did you feel about Donna's return to Poppy Creek? Do you think she'll make it to her six-month chip? Why or why not?

8. What do you think happened to Frank?

9. What do you think is the overall theme of the novel?

I would love to hear your answers to the book club questions! You can email your responses (or ask your own questions) at hello@ rachaelbloome.com or post them in my private Facebook group, Rachael Bloome's Secret Garden Club. I hope to see you there!